THE
SINKING
ISLAND

Don D'Ammassa

Managansett Press First Edition 2015

THE
SINKING
ISLAND

CHAPTER ONE

A sudden alteration of the pattern of the waves caught Sharon by surprise and she staggered and might have fallen if it had not been for Arthur Abbott's quick reaction. He caught hold of her elbow and steadied her for just a split second, then let his hand fall away, as though embarrassed to be caught in even such a trivial intimacy. "Mind your step, Miss Bartleby. God is stirring the ocean rather vigorously this morning."

"He certainly has been lately, Reverend. He almost tossed me out of my bed last night." She saw his fleeting expression of distaste and remembered belatedly his evident uneasiness about anything that even hinted of the indecorous. A change of topic seemed wise. "The storm seems closer, don't you think?" She put both hands securely on the railing and glanced up at the sky.

It certainly appeared that way. The heavy, gray clouds that had appeared ahead of them the previous day were larger and darker, and had spread to cloak fully one third of the horizon. The waves were noticeably taller and more frequent and there was a persistent and almost unpleasantly chill breeze. Captain Corrigan had passed word to the passengers the previous evening that he was altering course in an effort to bypass the worst of it, the announcement accompanied by reassurances that there was no actual danger and that the diversion would at most add a day to their journey.

"We're heading almost due south now, don't you think?"

Reverend Abbott had mimicked her firm grasp of the rail, although at a discrete distance. "I'm sure he is doing what he believes prudent, Miss Bartleby."

She resented his faintly censorious tone. "I only meant that it might make the trip even longer." Their troubles had started almost from the moment they embarked from Manila. The shabby conditions aboard the *Sturtevant* had not been limited to the passenger quarters, which were all too obviously a recent alteration, added to accommodate as many as two dozen passengers in lieu of cargo. Captain Corrigan was owner as well as the ship's master, and he had supported himself and his crew for years running small lots of cargo from the Philippines to the coast of China, and sometimes down into Singapore and southeast Asia. The growing tension developing between the United States and Great Britain on the one hand and the Japanese Empire on the other had added a discouraging level of complexity and danger. Some of Corrigan's former customers had been coerced into severing their relationship and others were openly hostile. There had been rumors of more serious risks as well, of Japanese gunboats stopping, boarding, and even sinking unarmed vessels.

So the *Sturtevant* was going home, crossing the Pacific for the last time, with twenty-two passengers and a nearly empty cargo hold.

"We will reach our destination whenever God means us to," Abbott said unctuously. "All events have their purpose, even if they are not always clear to us."

Sharon bit her lip, suppressing the urge to be sarcastic. Although she thought of herself as a reasonably religious minded person, the Reverend's passivity in the face of adversity rankled. This wasn't the first time she had been tempted to say something mildly outrageous, just to see if the older man could be stirred out of his placid neutrality. If he went on in this vein much longer, she doubted she'd be capable of holding her tongue.

She was spared the necessity by the sudden appearance of another passenger. "Somehow I doubt the Almighty is sitting up in Heaven contriving cryptic messages to bedevil us, Mr. Abbott." Their faces revealed starkly contrasting emotions as they turned to the newcomer. Jerry Rivers, until recently a captain in the United States Army, was not quite handsome enough to be a romantic hero, and his air of studied cynicism alternately dismayed and intrigued her. Reverend Abbott clearly disapproved of the younger man's attitude, and had flirted with actual criticism from time to time, although never when Rivers was present.

"We shouldn't presume to understand the Creator's methods," Abbott answered quietly.

"I know. He works in mysterious ways, as you've already told us. But unnecessarily complex ones, if you ask me. If He wanted us to spend an extra two weeks aboard ship, he could have arranged something a lot simpler than the plague of petty annoyances we've had to deal with." Engine trouble the first day out had nearly forced them to call for help. Then problems with the rudder on the third day, followed by a long detour to avoid Japanese naval maneuvers, another day lost when they discovered some of their fuel was contaminated, and still another after the initial makeshift rudder repairs failed.

Abbott was spared the need to devise an answer, and Sharon was spared having to listen to it, when still another passenger emerged from the stairwell. Her lips thinned and she immediately turned away, although not so far that she couldn't watch Grace Porter from the corner of her eye. Whenever she was around either Grace or her brother Nathan, Sharon felt awkward and out of place, a situation not affected by her realization that Grace deliberately sought to add to her discomfort. As usual, she was overdressed, this time in an ankle length gown that was certainly impractical on the shifting, uneven, badly maintained deck.

"Would you mind helping a lady, Captain Rivers?" She had paused on the last step and was holding one hand extended toward him.

"It's just Mr. Rivers now, Miss Porter, or Jerry actually. I've been a civilian for the past three months." His voice was neutral but he took her hand in his, steadying her as she stepped down onto the deck.

"Oh, yes, you did mention that." Her eyes moved past Sharon and Abbott as if they were invisible. "But Army officers are often called by their old titles after they retire, aren't they?"

"I'm not retired, Miss Porter. I only served for four years."

The *Sturtevant* lurched slightly, enough to be noticeable but certainly not enough to cause Grace to fall against Rivers, even if she was wearing impractical shoes. He disengaged her politely but firmly, holding her by the shoulders. "You need to be more careful, Miss Porter. You might fall overboard."

"Oh, if I did, I'm sure someone would jump in and save me."

Sharon turned away so that no one could see her face.

Further conversation was cut short when Quinn, one of the two stewards, appeared at the corner of a bulkhead and turned in their direction. "Breakfast is being served immediately, ladies and gentlemen. It would be best if you ate quickly. We're expecting some rough seas later this morning."

Without waiting for an answer, Quinn brushed past them and began to climb the stairs to the passenger cabins, presumably to roust out the others.

"My brother was up late last night playing cards with Mr. Fields and Mr. Etchison, so I'm on my own this morning." Grace glanced at Rivers with open appraisal. "Would you mind being my escort, Jerry?" She pronounced his given name with added emphasis, as though trying it out, or perhaps to flaunt a minor victory.

"I never decline an offer of pleasant company," was the noncommittal answer, but the two set off, Grace holding his left elbow possessively.

Abbott stirred himself and took a step, paused. "Aren't you coming, my dear? I would be happy to escort you."

She shook her head. "Thank you, Reverend Abbott, but I'm really not hungry just at the moment."

"Ah, yes. The ocean does tend to treat the stomach harshly. Perhaps some tea?"

"Yes, in a few minutes. Please don't wait for me." Her stomach was indeed upset, but not by the rolling waves. Why do I let her get under my skin the way she does? Sharon shook her head in bewilderment. Grace Porter and her brother had clearly been pampered all their lives, undoubtedly had been granted their every wish by their doting and extremely wealthy parents, and it was likely that neither had done a bit of honest work in their lives. Sharon knew she had nothing to be ashamed of just because her family came from a long line of country farmers. She herself was probably as widely traveled and well educated as either of the Porters. So why did she always feel somehow inferior in their presence?

She stayed by herself, watching the water rise and fall, occasionally interrupted by a line of white caps that appeared and disappeared so quickly that sometimes she wasn't sure if she had really seen them at all. Lost in her own thoughts, she might have missed breakfast altogether if she hadn't been gathered up by another of the passengers, Mrs. Winifred Galt of Baltimore, an individual who, in Sharon's opinion, possessed sufficiently personality for an entire women's club.

"Come along, dear. The ocean will still be there when you've had something to eat."

Sharon tried to beg off, suggested that the unsettled waters might make the act of eating anything a wasted effort just at the moment, but Mrs. Galt could not be fooled. "Stuff and nonsense, young lady. Some solid food is just the thing to settle you down." In the end it was easier to accede to her wishes than to resist.

Toby Walters had been a seaman all his life. He was intelligent enough to know that superstitions were nonsense, and sailor enough to believe in them implicitly. He had served aboard the *Sturtevant* for almost ten years, for most of that time as the ship's carpenter and unofficial third mate. There had been good voyages and bad ones, and he had enjoyed the former and tolerated the latter. He hadn't decided yet what he was going to do when they reached the States. Captain Corrigan was still talking about running small cargoes down around the Baja area, and maybe even doing a little low key smuggling into and out of Mexico, but after the problems they'd experienced during the past few days, even the Captain might be having second thoughts. They had a slow leak in the forward hold that forced them to run the pumps almost continuously, the engines were acting up more than usual, and the rudder assembly had just given way for the third time since they'd left Manila.

"We'll have it right in a couple of hours, Captain." That had been the Chief's opinion twice before and twice before he'd been right. But this time things were different. The rudder seemed to have frozen in place, and when they had tried to nudge it loose, they had discovered that the housing itself was bent out of shape.

"Must've been that reef we scraped," suggested Seaman Blake, but the Captain had glared at him and he'd found some urgent business that needed attending to elsewhere.

"So what's the verdict, Chief?" Lacking any other pressing duties, Walters had been ordered to help with the repairs, but so far that had meant standing out of the way while Chief Robinson scowled and muttered to himself. "Can we fix it?"

"More or less. I think I can get us back on course, but once I've forced the rudder into a new position," he paused, removed his cap with one hand and ran the other across his bald head, "I don't know if I'll be able to move her again. So the Captain better might the right choice the first time out."

Sharon sat with Mrs. Galt and the Neuland sisters, nodding when they seemed to require a response without really following the conversation. To her surprise she managed to account for a respectable amount of food, despite having to watch Grace Porter's obvious flirtation with Rivers on the opposite side of the dining room. A few of the other passengers were about, the Granbys and the Doctor Hudson among them, the latter engaged in an animated discussion with Reverend Abbott, as well as Victor Fields, who as usual sat by himself and discouraged company. Nathan Porter showed up a short while later, dressed to look dashing and managing only to appear dissolute and boorish. He and Fields exchanged greetings, but Nathan took the seat beside his sister, evidently annoying her in the process.

"Are you feeling more settled, dear?"

Sharon blinked, momentarily disoriented, then smiled at Mrs. Galt. "Yes, thank you. I guess I was hungry after all."

"One thing my husband always insists upon when we travel is a good breakfast. He would have approved of the ship's cook heartily."

"Will he be staying behind long?"

She shook her head so vigorously that Sharon feared the woman's oversized hat would come loose. "Only a few weeks. He's securing the last of the company's assets and closing down all but essential operations. It pains him to leave the bridge half finished, but there's no help for it."

"He really thinks war is coming then?"

"I'm afraid so. Harold studies history, you know, and he is convinced that economic pressures will force a confrontation within the next year or two, perhaps sooner. When we heard the news about the latest round of disagreements, he prevailed upon a close friend at the American consulate to see that I left on the next available ship." She glanced around at the unpainted wooden walls and sighed. "I wanted to wait and come home with him, but he can be very unreasonable once he has an idea firmly in his head."

Sharon laughed. "At the rate we're going, you might find him waiting for you on the dock in San Francisco."

The older woman nodded and lowered her voice. "I believe Captain Corrigan was not strictly truthful about the reliability of the *Sturtevant*. I imagine you know that we're seriously off course again."

"He's trying to avoid the storm ahead of us."

Mrs. Galt made an impatient noise. "Poppycock! I heard two of the crew talking just this morning. The rudder has seized up again. The First Mate wants to radio for help but the Captain insists that it can be repaired. The man is as stubborn as Harold, and half as intelligent."

When they emerged onto the deck a few minutes later, it was obvious that whatever the Captain's intentions might have been, they were not going to be able to avoid the storm. It had crept closer and consumed more of the horizon, so that it now seemed that they were steaming directly toward it. The sun was still visible, though obscured, and its position told Sharon that their course remained unchanged at just slightly east of south. She wondered what the weather was like in Chile at this time of year.

The conversation in the Captain's cabin was considerably less amicable. Captain Corrigan's face always turned red when he was angry and it was nearly crimson at the moment. "You're very close to insubordination, Mr. Heath! I won't have it, do you understand? Not on my ship!"

Heath had served under Corrigan for almost twenty years and was accustomed to his captain's rages. There was as always a flicker of resentment in his eyes, but his face was otherwise expressionless. "All I'm suggesting, Captain, is that we exercise a little prudence and let someone know about our situation."

"When I am satisfied that I know just what exactly our situation is, I'll take the appropriate action."

Heath sighed. He knew that he should have abandoned the argument earlier, that Corrigan would never give way once he believed that he was under pressure to change his stance. It was time to back off, let the man come to his own conclusions. The rudder was past repair, at least beyond anything they could accomplish at sea. The Chief was confident that he could accomplish one more course change through brute force and Corrigan was convinced that once they were past the storm he could plot a course that would bring them at least close to their goal. Heath was less confident. At best they'd still be caught in the fringe of the storm, but as it was moving southeast on a converging course, they were at risk of much more serious confrontation. In a high sea, their lack of maneuverability could be fatal.

"All right, Captain. But that storm bears watching."

Corrigan visibly relaxed. "Then you'd best be watching it, Tom. You've got the best pair of eyes aboard the ship."

Heath nodded and left for the bridge.

Sharon spent the rest of the morning reading in her cabin, partly because the rising wind had become actively unpleasant, partly because the Porters had followed Jerry Rivers onto the foredeck where they continued to monopolize his time. She told herself that she wasn't being petty, that she simply wanted peace and quiet, but when the steward knocked to tell her cold sandwiches and soup were available, she welcomed the excuse to quit the narrowly circumscribed quarters to which she'd exiled herself.

Her spirits lifted slightly when she reached the deck. The captain's strategy seemed to be working at last, because the nearest arm of the storm had receded appreciably. The *Sturtevant*'s bow was pointed at a spot on the horizon where the cloud ended and blue sky promised easier going. The sun was high overhead now and she couldn't be absolutely certain of their heading, but it appeared to be the same as it had been when she'd first risen this morning, which meant they were no closer to home.

She sat in one corner of the dining area near a narrow slit window, surprised that she felt little appetite even though the chicken salad was quite good. She could see the Porters, but Rivers was nowhere in sight, apparently having successfully extricated himself from Grace's clutches. That thought cheered her slightly and restored part of her appetite, and she was finishing the last of her sandwich when someone abruptly sat down across from her.

It was Nathan Porter, his face twisted into an insincere smile. "You're looking rather lonely, sitting here by yourself."

"You're mistaken, Mr. Porter. I enjoy the opportunity to be alone with my thoughts. Most people chatter on to no good purpose, don't you think?"

If Porter recognized the implied brush off, he chose to ignore it. "I suppose it's true that most people natter on about subjects they aren't qualified to discuss, or choose topics of interest to none but themselves, but you are obviously an educated, cultured woman with a mind of your own."

He dropped one forearm onto the table as though by chance, his hand extended toward her and she sat back slightly. "Culture does exist outside of Boston, you know."

He laughed humorlessly. "Well, of course, but New York is impossible, don't you think?"

Sharon forced down the last bite of her sandwich. It tasted like cardboard. She started to push back from table but Porter reached out and caught hold of her arm. "Don't rush off. We've hardly had a chance to speak."

"I doubt that I could measure up to your usual conversational partners, Mr. Porter."

"Please call me Nathan. I think we can dispense with formal introductions, under the circumstances. We're going to be stuck on this ship for even longer than we expected, apparently, and I don't suppose you find our companions any more entertaining than I do."

Sharon could see where this conversation was going. "Actually, I've had no complaints on that score, at least until now." She pushed her seat back and stood up.

His eyelids flickered but he didn't acknowledge the snub otherwise. He rose slowly and deliberately and moved to partially block her escape route. "The good weather might not last much longer. Why don't we take a walk around the deck and enjoy it while we can?"

Under other circumstances, she might have felt flattered by his attention but she had no intention of becoming Nathan Porter's shipboard romance, a fling to distract him during the long days when he would otherwise be forced to be satisfied with his own company or that of his insufferable sister.

"Thanks for the offer, but I think I'm going to take a nap. The sea was so rough last night that I had trouble sleeping."

"Let me escort you to your cabin then."

She shook her head. "Please don't bother." Suddenly she felt almost as weary as she was pretending to be. The thought of disengaging herself from Porter at her cabin door made her shiver slightly. The man was impervious to hints; he either refused to believe she wasn't interested or just didn't care. When she brushed past him, he made as if to follow, but apparently thought better of it, letting her pass with a brief nod.

"Perhaps later then."

Jerry Rivers stood at the bow, leaning forward on the rail, the cigarette in his left hand largely forgotten. It looked like Corrigan just might pull this off after all. The storm clouds had been edging to starboard imperceptibly but steadily throughout the morning. Several of the other passengers were unhappy about the course change because it would add still more time to their passage, but they were ignorant of just how violent a storm at sea could be, particularly in an elderly, faltering ship that probably should have been scrapped years before.

Nor was Rivers in any hurry to reach the mainland. His father still wanted him to join him at the firm, but he had sampled the executive lifestyle and it didn't appeal to him. Every relationship was guarded, laced with deceit, a campaign by each individual to advance his or her own interests. There seemed to be no purpose to amassing wealth beyond the act of doing so. He had joined the Army, hoping to find there what he felt was missing from his life, some sense of purpose, but he'd been disappointed. There was structure, certainly, but substitute advancement in rank for wealth and the power structure and the power games were very much the same.

The wind was still crisp and chilly enough to be uncomfortable, particularly exposed as he was, but he enjoyed the feel of it on his skin, the way it rustled his hair. It had also driven Grace Porter away, back to her cabin for warmer clothing, at the very least something to cover her breasts. Not that he minded looking at her breasts particularly, if only she'd keep her mouth shut. Her incessant chatter drove him to distraction. She was an educated woman, at least in the sense that she had memorized enough of what her teachers had presented to carry on a conversation on a wide variety of subjects. It was only when you tried to engage her, find out what she really thought rather than just what she'd been told, that you realized how wafer thin that veneer of knowledge really was.

He heard footsteps behind him, and mentally cringed, anticipating her return, but it was the first mate, absentmindedly packing tobacco into the bowl of his pipe. "Good day to you, sir."

"And the same to you as well, Mr. Heath." He nodded toward the clouded horizon. "Do you think we'll be able to stay clear?"

"The Captain thinks so." Heath was studying his pipe, as though he'd spotted something unfamiliar about it. "Wouldn't be the first time he skirted trouble. He's been at sea most of his life, has a nose for the weather. And more luck than most men." He struck a match and bent to light his pipe, shielding it from the wind with his other hand. As he did so, a third figure crossed the foredeck in their general direction. Victor Fields. The Englishman gave a peremptory nod and determinedly turned away, clearly signaling that he preferred his own company.

"Not the most sociable of men is your Mr. Fields," said Heath in a low voice. Smoke curled up from the now faintly glowing tobacco.

"Maybe he just doesn't have anything to say."

Heath grunted and drew on his pipe, let several seconds elapse before blowing the smoke out his nose. "Mr. Fields is a man with secrets, he is."

"What makes you say that?"

"Steward says he keeps his luggage locked, all the time. Always has to be there when the room is being made up."

"So what do you think he's up to?"

"Smuggling's my guess. Most of us in the crew picked up enough of the lingo back there to get by, but Mr. Fields, he speaks it like a native. Two Japanese gents saw him off when he came aboard and they were really into it. I don't think they were too happy with one another, but they clammed up every time someone came close enough to hear 'em."

"Smuggling is a crime."

Heath snorted. "There's a few things in the hold as is not on the manifest. Contraband is kind of a tradition with us."

Rivers shrugged. "Have you told the Captain?"

"It's not my place to be airing my ideas unless something endangers this ship or them as is aboard, and it don't, as far as I can see."

"So why are you telling me?"

Heath took out his pipe and tapped it against the palm of his hand. "You didn't know Mr. Fields before he came aboard, did you, sir?"

"No, and I barely know him now. Until last night's card game, I don't know that I've ever seen him talk to any of the other passengers."

"He plays it pretty close to his chest, all right. But you see, Mr. Rivers, I think he knows you from somewhere."

Rivers tightened his lips ever so slightly. "What makes you say that?"

"He watches you, sir, whenever he thinks you're not looking. I've seen him do it more than once and you're the only passenger he's interested in. And when he does, sometimes his face changes a little too." Heath stopped tapping the pipe but didn't return it to his mouth. "He's no friend of yours, Mr. Rivers. Of that I'm certain. I'd be watching out for him if I was you."

It was Rivers' turn to hesitate, but only for a second. "Thank you, Mr. Heath. I'll take what you've said under serious consideration."

Ezra Harding didn't like working in the engine room, but Nichols was in sickbay and Bonner had served watch the night before, so the duty was his. He'd felt uneasy being anywhere near the boilers since his last berth on the *Veritas*, where he'd seen two of his shipmates scalded to death when a pipe ruptured. It was a glimpse of the Hell that he was sure awaited him at the end of his life. He didn't trust the engines, was always aware of that searing, restless power barely contained and seething with the desire to burst free. It felt to him like the throbbing heart of some satanic beast, poised to strike whenever even a good Christian made a misstep or dropped his guard.

The Chief was fussing over the gauges, muttering under his breath and massaging his jaw like he always did when things weren't going the way he wanted. "Ezra, get your ass over here! I need you."

He started forward immediately, knowing it was not a good idea to get the Chief pissed. The man had a long memory and knew lots of ways to express his displeasure. Ezra feared him more than he did the Captain. He knew Ezra was afraid of the boilers and ragged him about it from time to time, but he understood the fear, felt it himself although he never acknowledged it. You were always sitting pretty close to death down here, and you were wise to remember it.

Ezra had a good memory and good hearing as well. He noticed the change immediately, and so did the Chief. Both sets of eyes snapped toward the source, but there wasn't time to react. There was a sudden sharp concussion and then the screech of metal tearing. "Down!" shouted the Chief.

Captain Corrigan looked up impatiently from the chart he'd been studying as Heath arrived on the bridge. "Well?"

Heath's expression was neutral. "Better than we had any right to expect, Captain. The Chief's got a scalded arm that'll trouble him for a while and a couple of the other men have lesser burns, but nothing serious and they can all stay on duty."

Corrigan nodded, but the injuries were of little concern to him at the moment. "What about the engines?"

Heath's eyes narrowed, but his voice remained neutral. "We're in luck there as well. Nothing we can't fix."

"How long?"

"Four hours or so. Maybe six if the split in the line extends back inside the insulation."

Corrigan shook his head and turned away, stared out toward the horizon, where the storm had already reclaimed most of the lead it had lost during the morning. "I'm not sure that we have four hours, Mr. Heath." He sighed and lowered his head. "You'd better pass word to the passengers to be expecting some rough weather. No, let's wait a bit longer. They'll insist on speaking to me when they hear the bad news and there's nothing to be gained from alarming them prematurely."

No one needed to tell the passengers that something had gone wrong. The rhythmic throb of the engines had become such a constant in their lives that they no longer consciously heard it, but when the murmuring cut off suddenly, it was the loudest silence any of them had ever experienced. Even if it hadn't been obvious that the *Sturtevant* was no longer under power, the increased activity among the crew would have told them that something was amiss.

The stewards went about calming people as best they could, but it was obvious that even they didn't know exactly what the trouble was. It was Heath who finally calmed their fears somewhat, moving from group to group, reassuring those them with his calm demeanor and forthright explanations. "We've had a problem with one of the steam lines, but we'll be underway again shortly.

Rivers was probably the only one who noticed Heath's frequent glances at the sky, which was visibly darkening. The storm front had gobbled up much of the bowl of the heavens as well as the horizon now. He waited until Heath had finished his rounds and intercepted him when he sought to return to the bridge.

"This plays hell with the Captain's storm strategy, doesn't it?"

Heath had been about to mount the stairway to the bridge, and Rivers had approached from his blind side, catching him by surprise. "We've weathered typhoons in the *Sturtevant*, Mr. Rivers."

"I'm sure you have, Mr. Heath. But how long ago? Is she up to a bad squall today?"

Heath suddenly looked much older and his voice was uneven. "She had better be, sir. For all our sakes."

CHAPTER TWO

It took less time than expected to get the *Sturtevant* underway once more, but by then it was evident even to the passengers that there was no longer any chance that they might outrun the storm. The thunderheads were visibly closer, flickering occasionally as lightning split the air, although as yet they could hear no thunder. The wind was up dramatically and all but the crew had retreated to the cabins or the small lounge. The stewards went among them, showing them how to lock the portholes, and suggesting ways to better secure baggage and other loose articles. They tried with limited success to convince the passengers that they needed to take the situation seriously without alarming them unnecessarily, but most conversations from that point forward were carried on in hushed, nervous tones.

Corrigan considered making his final course correction now, but it was obviously too late for that to make a significant difference. Even if they turned and ran directly away from the storm, it would overtake them within hours. He would play that last card when it seemed most advantageous. It required no further urging from the First Mate to convince him to visit the radio room, where he ordered the operator to broadcast their present position and course. "But no S.O.S. With luck we'll get no more than a brisk ride as the storm passes us." The bad weather was playing havoc with the radio but they finally received an acknowledgment from a Japanese destroyer. Corrigan would have preferred an American or even a British respondent, but accepted what he was given.

Restless, he took a circuitous route back to the bridge, checking the lifeboats to ensure that they were properly secured, inspecting the locks on the cargo hold, nodding to the occasional crewman he encountered. They were all experienced men, skilled at their jobs and well trained. He knew they'd do what was expected of them. He also knew that the *Sturtevant* was well past her prime and that her joints were stiff and brittle with age and that entropy was finally having its way with her. Although he'd told the crew he planned to run her along the California coast, he knew in his heart that this was probably her last voyage. Better to sell her for scrap than have her sink beneath him. He'd lived a frugal life and set aside enough to keep him well.

The only passenger he encountered was Victor Fields, who sat in the lounge with a bottle of bourbon in one hand and a cup in the other. The seas were heavy enough to roll the ship dramatically and he was pouring and drinking with exaggerated caution. "You'll be safer in your cabin, Mr. Fields. The storm's going to knock us around a bit before it lets us go."

Apparently Fields had not noticed Corrigan's arrival because he looked startled for a moment, then settled back with his usual guarded expression. "I find my cabin rather claustrophobic under the circumstances, Captain."

"We've been through worse than this. The *Sturtevant* may not be the prettiest ship but she's seaworthy."

"So was the *Titanic*." Fields turned back to his drink and Corrigan, at a lost to respond, turned and left.

Sharon clutched the edges of her bunk so hard that her fingers were starting to hurt. This wasn't the first time she had ridden out bad weather at sea, but she hadn't liked it before and had hoped for an uneventful voyage home. So far it had proven to be anything but. Despite her efforts, a few small items had broken loose and were rolling across the floor, but the rise and fall of the deck beneath her was too violent and unpredictable for her to risk retrieving them. She experienced a moment of genuine terror when the ship's lights flickered and went off, but the power was restored after only a few seconds, and her incipient panic slowly subsided. Once or twice she thought she heard someone shouting but the rain had started now, light at first but steadily growing into a torrential downpour.

Her father had not wanted her to take this trip, at least not on her own, but she had been determined to spend a year traveling the world before settling in to help manage the family business. Europe was her first choice but her father had insisted that the situation there was too unpredictable, so she had agreed to a Pacific tour, which she had cut short in Manila when word reached her of her father's illness. The *Sturtevant* had been the first ship available, but she wished now that she had waited for a more reliable vessel.

Lightning crackled nearby and her cabin was suddenly illuminated more brightly than by daylight. Her only consolation was knowing that Grace Porter would be equally uncomfortable.

Heath nodded an acknowledgment as Corrigan reached the bridge. The other two members of the bridge crew, Mercator and Miller, were too busy to notice.

"How's she handling?" asked Corrigan.

"A bit sluggish, sir. We're taking on quite a bit of water." Even as he spoke a wave slammed into the starboard side, sending spray sheeting across the deck. The rain was so heavy that the visibility had deteriorated markedly even before the last of the sunlight was gone. "Nothing to be alarmed about but it bears watching." He didn't remind the Captain that they were already pumping water from the leaking hold.

"At least we're on the weaker side. We should be able to ride her out. I've sent out our course and position, just in case."

Heath nodded in satisfaction, but if he had meant to say something in response, he never had the chance. There was a sudden bright light and he felt himself lifted into the air. Something struck the back of his head and then the light went away, along with everything else.

Jerry Rivers realized immediately that the last impact had been something other than just a wave. He had spent enough time aboard the family yacht to know something about rough seas. Waves struck from the side; this had felt as though something had been dropped onto them from above.

"Whatever that was, it isn't good." He spoke aloud, a habit he'd suppressed while serving in the Army, but which had re-emerged quickly after he resigned his commission. He slid his legs off the bunk and half rose, then settled back. Despite their sloppy appearance, the crew knew their jobs. Rivers considered himself a good judge of character, and he'd been impressed by what he'd seen. These were seasoned men who knew that spit and polish was primarily designed to boost the morale of those who were uncertain of their own abilities.

He'd do better to stay out of their way.

Ezra Harding was the only one who saw it clearly. One of the bulkhead doors had broken loose and he had just finished dealing with it. It was almost instinctive to glance up at the bridge, and he did so just as the lightning struck. The bridge exploded as though a bomb had gone off, the windows shattering, the roof erupting in flames, three of the four sides disintegrating into splinters and rubble. It was so sudden and dramatic that for the first few seconds, he thought it couldn't be real, that he had imagined the whole thing, and then the light was gone and the heavy rain drowned the fire so quickly that completely darkness was restored in a matter of seconds.

But he knew what he'd seen. The finger of God had touched the ship, and they were all in His hands now.

That's when the second blow fell.

Toby Walters was in the nearly empty hold, checking the pumps to make sure they were running smoothly. The storm was driving more water in than they could flush away, but the disparity was not alarming. As long as the pumps keep running, he reminded himself. He had felt the vibration when the lightning struck and guessed that the ship had taken a hit, although he never dreamed at how seriously they'd been hurt. The second concussion was closer and there was no disguising the magnitude of it. The lights flickered once, twice, and then went out. That wasn't the worst of it though.

The pumps stopped as well.

The darkness slowed him but not much and not for long. He knew the innards of the *Sturtevant* as well as he knew his own body, perhaps even better. By the time he reached the main passageway, he had light again, but that wasn't good news. The light came from a fire, a fire in the engine room. Not good, he told himself, and began to move faster.

Their only bit of luck was that the storm had changed course and they were already through the worst of it. The passengers remained in their cabins, most of them aware of the fact that the engines had stopped, but only Rivers and a few others were alarmed by that fact. The lights came back on after less than an hour, but they flickered constantly, powered only by the backup generator. The engines remained silent. The rain continued heavy until dawn, and tapered off quickly once the sun was up.

Rivers was the first to emerge from his cabin. He started toward the main deck and was met by Quinn, the steward, who look drawn and disheveled. Rivers asked about the ship's status but Quinn just shook his head. "We're asking the passengers to gather in the lounge, sir. I was just on my way to call everyone. Mr. Burleson will answer all your questions."

"Mr. Burleson?" Burleson was the Second Mate. Rivers had barely spoken to the man.

"Yes, sir. If you please, sir, I need to rouse the others."

Rivers was the first to reach the lounge, where Burleson and two other crewmembers sat at one table. They deferred every inquiry put to them. "Wait until everyone is assembled and we'll answer all your questions. There is no immediate danger, ladies and gentlemen." The mangled remains of the bridge had telegraphed at least part of the message they were to receive, and as the other passengers arrived, Rivers noticed that most were either artificially animated by worry, or ominously silent, as though they expected a sentence of death. Reverend Abbott and the Porters were among the former, Victor Fields and both Granbys the latter. Mrs. Galt and Sharon Bartleby behaved more like themselves, but their determined calmness betrayed their concern.

Eventually the two stewards approached Burleson, there was a whispered conversation, and the Second Mate nodded and rose to his feet. Almost immediately the crowd quieted.

"Ladies and gentlemen, as you no doubt know, we've suffered some damage in the storm. The bridge was struck by lightning. Fortunately the rain doused the fire almost immediately, so there's no danger on that score. Unfortunately there was a secondary hit toward the stern which, I'm sorry to say, destroyed our radio and killed the man on duty there."

"What about the Captain?" Abbott shouted. Several others took up the call.

Burleson raised his hands and waited for them to calm down. "I would prefer that you hold your questions until I've finished, but I regret to have to tell you that Captain Corrigan and two other crewmen died on the bridge."

"Are you in command then?" asked Doctor Hudson.

"Mr. Heath survived but is presently incapacitated. I am acting as captain until and unless he becomes fit to return to duty." There was a general murmuring following that announcement and Burleson raised his hands again.

"Please. There is more that I need to explain to you. The second strike was less obviously destructive but presents us with some problems. There was a surge which knocked out our main generator and started a fire in the engine room. The backup generator was unaffected, which is why we still have power. The engines were shut down and the fuel lines purged as a safety precaution while we dealt with the fire. It is now completely out and we are assessing the damage there. Initial reports are quite favorable and we should have the engines back in operation very soon."

Several people started to speak and Burleson waved them down again. "Let me finish, please. As you all know, we've had some trouble with the rudder. Our engineer believes that it would be possible to change course one more time. Captain Corrigan had planned to make that attempt as soon as we were clear of the storm. I have elected not to do so at this time, however." Another murmur, which subsided as he continued to speak.

"There are several reasons for my decision. For one thing, we're not absolutely certain that the rudder will respond as we hope. We might end up on a third course that would be worse than our present one. If we continue as we are once the engines are running again, we will be headed for South America, which is now the closest body of land. This will bring us into more commonly used sea lanes and increase the chances of our encountering another ship. Even without a radio, we should be able to signal for help."

"There is one further bit of bad news, I'm afraid. First let me reassure you that there is no imminent danger. That said, I regret to say that we are taking on water in the forward section of the ship. The rupture is stable and under ordinary circumstances we would be able to compensate by pumping the water back where it belongs. Unfortunately, the backup generator does not yield enough power to keep all of the pumps operating, and as a consequence, we are slowly losing ground."

"How much time do we have?" asked Rivers. His voice was level, with no hint of panic, and Burleson gave him an appreciative look.

"Perhaps as much as a week, unless another storm comes up."

"Can't we bail the extra water by hand?" Granby glanced around. "I'm sure we'd all be happy to pitch in and help."

Burleson shook his head. "This isn't a rowboat, Mr. Granby. We'd buy very little time for our effort. Given our present position, and assuming that we have full power from the engines by the end of the morning, I believe we will be able to reach the commercial sea lanes with a day or two to spare. Even then, the ship will not sink immediately, although once the engine compartment takes on sufficient water, we will be without power again. And after that, there are always the lifeboats. We lost one of them to the storm last night, but the others have all been inspected and are sound."

Nathan Porter stepped forward, his arms folded across his chest. "This is all very unsatisfactory, Mr. Burleson. We've paid rather exorbitant prices for this passage, particularly given the limited accommodations. The owners of this ship will be hearing from my lawyer when we reach home, and I'm sure many of my fellow passengers feel similarly."

Burleson suddenly looked very weary, and in fact he had not slept since the previous evening. "Since Captain Corrigan was the sole owner of the *Sturtevant*, I imagine your lawyer will have some difficulty in contacting him, but you are of course at liberty to try."

There was scattered laughter, but it was awkward and uneasy.

Burleson fielded a handful of additional questions, but no, he couldn't estimate how long it would take them to reach help, and no, he didn't know if they'd be going directly to the States or by way of South or Central America. When the questions started to become repetitive, he seemed to grow somewhat exasperated.

"I understand that you're all concerned, but that's all I can tell you at the moment. Right now, some of us need to get some rest, and some of us have work to do. For the time being, I suggest that everyone remain calm and as much as you can, refrain from calling upon the crew. Breakfast will be served shortly. We'll have more information for you later, after the engines are on line. I anticipate your patience and understanding and assure you that we are doing everything possible to ensure your safety as well as our own."

And with that they had to be content.

Inevitably, conversations were subdued for the rest of the morning. A few of the passengers congregated in small groups, speaking in hushed tones. Dr. Hudson, whose field was philosophy rather than medicine, nevertheless spoke to several of the female passengers who were willing to sit with Heath and help tend his wounds, but he died at mid-morning without ever regaining consciousness. The other injuries were minor, the most serious of which were a badly burned forearm and a broken finger.

Captain Corrigan had conducted only a single, perfunctory lifeboat drill, but Burleson ordered the stewards to take the passengers in small groups and make certain they understood how they were supposed to be lowered into the water and assigned each of them to a specific boat. "We expect to have plenty of time in the event," explained Quinn, "but it's best to be prepared for the unexpected."

Mrs. Granby alarmed them all by fainting when she heard of Heath's death, but she recovered quickly, and even Grace Porter had the sense to suspend her usual litany of complaints, although her brother more than compensated, lecturing one passenger after another about the desirability of taking punitive legal action. "The ship and its crew were obviously in a disgraceful condition, and we should have been told." Reverend Abbott nodded but didn't seem to comprehend what he was being told, having been caught up in some inner vision of imminent disaster. Most of the others listened politely but held their peace. Only Fields and Rivers responded negatively to Porter's tirades, the former turning and walking away without a word, leaving Porter caught in mid-sentence.

Rivers told him Porter that he was being foolish. "You're stirring people up unnecessarily. The only important thing right now is our safety and our chances are better if we're working together, not finding fault with one another."

Porter simply sniffed and stalked off, searching for someone more amenable to his complaints.

Shortly before noon, the rumble of the engines returned, and there was spontaneous applause from several parts of the *Sturtevant*. The sky was clear except for some wispy clouds in the distance and it was impossible not to take some cheer from the fine weather and the resumption of forward progress. Rivers felt his own spirits lift, but they dropped quickly when he noticed that none of the crew reacted with equal enthusiasm.

He wondered if there was something more that they had not been told.

As the hours passed with no further announcements of death or disaster, life aboard the *Sturtevant* returned to something like normal, at least for the passengers. Lunch was served and was as satisfying as always, but there were occasional hesitant glances toward the Captain's table, which remained unoccupied throughout the day. The weather continued clear and fair and the sea had subsided into calm, as though exhausted by its exertions the night before. Two of the crewmen made some desultory efforts to clear away the wreckage of the bridge, primarily to ensure that there were no smoldering fires and that nothing loose would fall onto the deck or passageway below.

Reverend Abbott was still visibly upset. He kept his own counsel, but requested a second glass of wine with his lunch, which he had never done before, and then a third. Mrs. Galt, who was sitting across from Sharon, gave him a disapproving look that either went unnoticed or was simply ignored. "I'll tell you something, child. I don't think much of a man who drinks to excess. Harold, my husband, says you can tell a lot about a man by the way he deals with alcohol."

Sharon was more inclined to be tolerant. "I wouldn't be too hard on him, Mrs. Galt. We've all had quite a shock. After years of quiet missionary work, all of this excitement must be very hard on him."

Mrs. Galt's eyebrows rose into peaked arches. "Quiet missionary work? Is that what he calls it?"

"I don't understand. He told me that he spent the last three years ministering to the heathen."

The older woman laughed unpleasantly. "Yes, I'm sure that's how he would describe it. A word of advice, young lady. When a man parades his virtues in public, they are usually designed to conceal his vices. The good reverend's mission was to relieve the heathen of their wealth by introducing them to the process of tithing, with the proceeds lining his own pockets."

Sharon's lower jaw dropped and her eyes widened. "Are you saying that he's a fraud?"

"Not in his own mind, perhaps," she admitted grudgingly. "It is possible that he has convinced himself that he is in fact doing God's work, and that the material rewards are simply the Creator's method of encouraging him to continue. But as far as I know, he's not affiliated with any recognized church, and I do know that his departure from Asia was involuntary." She leaned forward conspiratorially and whispered the next few words. "It was an open secret in Manila that the American counsel revoked his passport after receiving several complaints."

Sharon glanced toward Abbott, who had finished his wine and was now making his way out of the dining salon. "I would never have thought such a thing. He has always conducted himself around with me with absolute decorum."

"Many rogues have excellent manners, my dear. Take an old woman's word for it." She glanced meaningfully at the table where the Porters were sitting. "And I'd be particularly wary of that young gentleman."

Sharon glanced that way but only for a second. "Mr. Porter? I don't care for his manners at all."

"Nor should you. Haven't you wondered why those two are here? On the Sturtevant, I mean. They could probably buy this ship out of their allowance."

It had struck Sharon as odd. "I suppose they were just in a hurry to get home."

Mrs. Galt shook her head. "That is certainly the truth. Young Mr. Porter boarded the night before the rest of us, you know."

"No, I didn't. Why would he do that?"

"To avoid being seen. I'm afraid our fellow passenger was guilty of some rather indiscrete behavior with an underaged girl."

Sharon flushed slightly. "I've noticed that the Filipino girls tend to be precocious."

Mrs. Galt laughed. "Ah, but it wasn't a Filipino girl that Mr. Porter seduced. She was American and her father is not a forgiving man."

"How do you know all this, Mrs. Galt?"

"I told you. My husband is a close friend of the American consul. And it was the consul's daughter."

Driven by what he admitted to himself was morbid curiosity, Rivers climbed up toward the bridge only to find his way blocked by a rope barrier that had been erected to prevent passengers from entering what was still potentially dangerous territory. He had too much respect for the prerogatives of command to ignore the prohibition, although he could have ducked under it with no difficulty, but his desire to view the damage at first hand was still strong. Retreating a few steps, he climbed halfway up a short stairway, carefully negotiating his way around a badly twisted step that must have been struck by something heavy falling from above, then vaulted the rail and landed softly on the roof of the passenger quarters. At the far end, a short ladder was mounted on the far wall, leading up to a small landing directly in front of and overlooked by the bridge.

From his new vantage point, he could see that the destruction was nearly total. The roof and two of the walls seemed to be missing entirely, and the other two were beyond repair. Even the floor had been destroyed, leaving only charred wood and jagged planks. Considerable water must have made its way down into the ship here during the storm. Rivers had not seen the crew's quarters, but they must be in that general vicinity. He wondered briefly where the bodies had been taken. For that matter, had they even been recovered? It was entirely possible that they had been lost overboard.

Depressed by that thought, Rivers retraced his steps, swinging up onto the gangway and then descending toward the main deck. Partway down, he paused to deal with an errant shoelace, and as he did so, another man appeared below him. It was Fields, moving at his usual rapid pace directly toward the damaged steps. Rivers opened his mouth to call out a warning but it was too late. Fields put a foot down where he expected to find support, then lost his balance and fell heavily, his left leg buckling, saved from a more serious spill when more through luck than planning, his left hand caught hold of the side rail.

"*Scheist!*" he exclaimed, hastily pushing himself back to his feet.

Rivers resisted the temptation to ask Fields if he was all right, remaining silently where he was. The man's expletive had been startling in itself, but more serious was what Fields had revealed while brushing himself off. Inside his jacket, snuggled under his armpit, was a small but very obvious shoulder holster. They had played cards together only two nights earlier, and Rivers was quite certain Fields hadn't been armed at the time. But he was now.

The main pump failed two days later. It was just past midday and the last few passengers were lingering over their lunch, while the others were mostly strolling the deck or playing cards in the lounge. The sky was overcast but not dark enough to dampen their spirits any more than they were already. Captain Burleson had ordered tarpaulins stretched across the ruined bridge, which was now almost completely hidden from view. The radio operator and Heath were buried at sea, but no mention was made of the other fatalities, whose bodies had indeed been lost during the storm.

Burleson was attempting to reassure Reverend Abbott and the Granbys for the twentieth time that they were in no immediate danger, that prospects looked good, and that they should not worry when Ezra Harding came up from below deck, moving so quickly and purposefully that no one watching could have failed to know that something significant had happened.

"We have a problem, Captain," he said tersely, and would have spoken further had not Burleson raised a restraining hand.

"Let's go below and talk about it." He nodded to his companions. "If you'll excuse me?" But he didn't wait for an answer.

Several of the other passengers had been close enough to hear and a few exchanged worried looks, but no one spoke about it.

The number of deck lights at night had been reduced to a minimum to spare the backup generator, so most of the passengers restricted their movement to the lounge and cabin area. That evening, therefore, there were only two sets of eyes that watched as several members of the crew quietly and efficiently began moving food and other supplies into the remaining lifeboats, supplementing the emergency equipment that was already stored there. One set of eyes belonged to Jerry Rivers and the other to Victor Fields, although neither man was aware of the other's presence.

Rivers noticed the change as soon as he came out on deck the following morning. He had never been aboard a foundering vessel before, but he'd seen a few and he knew enough to know that they were in trouble. He went looking for Burleson, but the new captain was notably absent, and his inquiries among the crew were met with shrugs, shaking heads, and in one case, nearly open insolence. Rivers chose to interpret the shifting attitude of the crew as more evidence for what he suspected, that the *Sturtevant* was not going to last as long as Captain Burleson had originally estimated.

Within a few hours, there were murmurs among the other passengers as well. They were obviously lower in the water today than they had been only twelve hours earlier, and their speed had also dropped appreciably. They were restive when lunch was served, and several called out when Burleson finally put in an appearance.

He tried twice to suppress the fusillade of questions simply by waving his arms, but when that didn't work, he resorted to shouting.

"I know you all have questions! If you'll just calm down and let me talk, I'll bring you up to date."

It still took a few more seconds before relative quiet was restored. The tension was almost a physical presence. Burleson remained standing and the seconds stretched uncomfortably until he could no longer pretend he was gathering his thoughts. "All right, here's the situation. The leak was worse than we originally thought. The storm must have increased the stress on the hull just enough to spring the plating even looser than it already was. That's part of the problem."

He hesitated, and people began glancing at one another. What he'd already said was bad enough. What else could have gone wrong?

"As you know, we've been pumping some of the water back out, not as much as we're taking in but enough to give us a few days leeway. Or at least that's what we thought. Last night, just to add to our difficulties, one of the pumps failed. We've been trying to rebuild it, but without any luck so far. So we're taking in more than we expected, and expelling less."

Whatever he had planned to say next was drowned out by another uproar, and this time he made no effort to quiet them down, simply stood impassively waiting for the reaction to subside. It eventually did, although several side conversations continued, but he raised his voice, drowning them out.

"Our chances are still very good. We've stocked the lifeboats with enough supplies to last us for at least two weeks. Captain Corrigan transmitted our last position and course before the storm hit so someone knows where we are. At the moment, we're still headed toward the commercial sea lanes where our chances of encountering another ship are excellent. I know that this is all very difficult and I'm afraid that we're facing some hardships in the near future, but so long as everyone does their part and follows instructions, I'm confident that we'll all be able to look back on this as an unexpected adventure."

This time there was relative silence when Burleson stopped, but it didn't last long. Rivers was about to ask the question himself but Fields beat him to it. "How long do we have? How long before we need to launch the boats?"

Burleson hesitated and for the first time appeared to feel the strain. "If nothing happens to worsen the situation, we'll deploy the boats tomorrow morning. We could safely wait until evening, but I'd rather not take the chance in the dark."

Another uproar. "Will we be able to take our luggage with us? How will the boats stay in touch with each other?" "Can we change our boat assignments?" "What about privacy? How will we bathe or change clothes?" Burleson made a few futile efforts to field the questions, then shook his head.

"All of your questions will be answered later, ladies and gentlemen. The stewards will speak to each of you and tell you what you should bring with you. As you must realize, space for anything other than food or water will be rather limited. I know this has all come as something of a shock, and I suggest that we wait until you've all had a chance to think about what I've just said. Thank you for your attention."

He turned and walked away.

Rivers had another question in mind, but he had decided not to ask it. They had been told that the *Sturtevant* was almost a week away from the commercial sea lane while it was under full power. They were four days short of that mark, and would have to continue propelled only by oars and the ocean current. There were rations for two weeks aboard the boats. Would that be enough?

CHAPTER THREE

Understandably, spirits aboard the *Sturtevant* were considerably lower during the remainder of the day. More than one passenger, and one or two of the crew, spent time standing at the rail, staring out over the now gently rolling sea, as though searching for another vessel to miraculously appear and spare them the hardship which they almost certainly faced. When sunset came, it fell with startling quickness, leaving behind none of the fading red that usually marked its decline. Darkness fell across the crippled ship like a curtain, and even the few conversations that had interrupted the general gloom faltered.

Following the instructions she'd been given, Sharon sorted through her possessions, mildly pleased by her earlier decision to send most of her things home on an earlier ship. She selected only her warmest and most practical clothing, the jewelry and cash still in her possession, toilet articles and a few odds and ends. Her suitcase and most of her remaining clothing would have to remain behind, but the essential items would fit into her canvas zipper bag quite readily. Despite the seriousness of their situation, Sharon felt a mild thrill of excitement. She had traveled through the Orient hoping to soak up a lifetime's worth of adventure before resigning herself to the simplicity of the family farm, but had been largely disappointed. Her father had exerted his influence to ensure that she was never entirely free of friendly counsel and perhaps a hint of surveillance, and although she had been tempted more than once to evade the safeguards he had set for her, in the end she had followed the line of least resistance.

Here at last was something that neither she nor her father could control. It was dangerous, extraordinary, and would allow her to thrill her brothers and sisters with the story, assuming always that it had a happy ending. Although Sharon shared the usual youthful conviction that nothing really serious could ever happen to them, she was smart enough to recognize that the universe did not necessarily require her continued presence. When she put the last items in her bag and fastened it, her hands were trembling.

Despite his greater experience of danger, Jerry Rivers was feeling very similar emotions as he emptied and then slowly repacked his duffel bag. He'd had more than his share of excitement, however, and had hoped for an uneventful, restful, even boring voyage home. He had chosen the *Sturtevant* largely because he knew it would be a longer than usual crossing and he was in no hurry to get back to Boston. His father would welcome him, of course, but it wouldn't be long before the pressure started, pressure to embark on a career that would allow him to eventually take his father's place as company president. His stint in the army would be dismissed as a necessary diversion for a young man, a way to prove his own independence.

Truthfully, Rivers still didn't know what he wanted to do with his life. He had entered the military hoping to find an answer to that question, but without success. The strict hierarchal structure served its purpose, but it discouraged initiative. Rivers didn't want to rethink the thoughts of others; he wanted to do something that originated within himself. Joining the family business was no solution either. Perhaps the prospect of setting out in an open boat didn't frighten him quite so much because he already felt as though his life had been cast adrift.

His hand didn't tremble as he finished packing, but his heart was beating faster than normal.

Victor Fields had no difficulty choosing what to take with him when they abandoned ship. Most of his luggage was merely for show in any case; some of the clothing had never even been worn. The most important item was a packet of letters, wrapped in plain brown paper, which was more valuable to him than everything else he carried combined. He slipped them into an oversized pocket inside his jacket..

Next came his revolver and the two boxes of cartridges he had brought aboard. The weapon had been with him for several years now and he had come to think of it almost as a part of his body. He cleaned it every evening before going to bed, even though it hadn't been fired for several months. On the last occasion when he had used it, the weapon had saved his life, or at least his liberty. The crew insisted that they were optimistic about their chances in the lifeboats, but Fields was less certain. If necessary, he would take whatever steps were necessary to protect his life and complete his mission. No other considerations would be allowed to interfere.

The Porters were equally confident that they had chosen correctly for the simple reason that neither believed that any of their possessions were dispensable and, despite the protestations of Quinn, their steward, they fully expected to bring between them four suitcases, a steamer trunk, and a handful of smaller parcels. Nathan agreed to sacrifice a pair of boots that he'd discovered chafed his ankles but Grace could find nothing non-essential.

"After all, we did pay for passage for ourselves and all of our belongings. And if we do have more than some of the others, I'm sure we can reach some agreement with them. Reverend Abbott only wears that one set of clothes, after all, and Mrs. Galt certainly is past the point in her life where she needs to impress others with the breadth and taste of her wardrobe."

Nathan knew that they might have some difficulty getting their way even with such a logical though perhaps biased interpretation, but he always carried a substantial amount of cash on his person and in his experience most of these seemingly arbitrary rules could be applied with subjectivity given sufficient compensation.

It would not be fair to say that neither of the siblings felt any fear of the outcome. Grace was worried that this further delay would cause her to miss several of the autumn events that she had planned on attending. Nathan, on the other hand, entertained himself with thoughts of being stranded on some out of the way island, populated by half dressed Polynesian girls, and implausibly provided with modern conveniences and a prompt, but not too prompt, rescue.

Captain Burleson was perhaps the most worried of all. A small observation deck had been hastily converted into a makeshift bridge, although there was little that he could do now to affect the *Sturtevant*'s course or fate. The rudder remained immovable and even if it were somehow freed, the ship was proceeding ponderously, low in the water, and was at the mercy of the wind and currents rather than responsive to the hands of her crew. The remaining pumps were beginning to show signs of strain, but they would doubtless last long enough to keep the vessel afloat while their evacuation was being completed. Mercifully, there was only a slight breeze, although he felt – almost smelled – another storm approaching.

Many of the passengers had complained about the arrangements he'd made, either because of the limitations on personal belongings they could bring, or because they objected to individuals assigned to share their lifeboat. Three of them, including Reverend Abbott, were demanding a refund of their money, and several were threatening legal action. More power to them, he thought. Captain Corrigan had few assets that would survive the sinking of the *Sturtevant* and they were welcome to squabble over what remained if that made them feel any better. His own savings were well secured. More secure than he was, in fact.

He reviewed the lists once again. There would be three crewmen in each lifeboat, and seven passengers, except for number four, which would carry eight. Each lifeboat was provisioned for twelve, which provided a little more safety margin. They would need it, he feared, because the summary of their situation which he had provided earlier was more optimistic than he actually felt. Even with the current and wind in their favor, they would have a difficult time reaching a sea lane where they stood a good chance of being rescued promptly. He felt little confidence that the Japanese ship which had received their radio message would pass on the information quickly enough to help them, if at all.

As the evening progressed, the passengers began to gather in the lounge, most of them drinking more than usual. He had considered shutting away the liquor early and closing the lounge so that everyone was rested in advance of the next day's exertions, but at the last minute had reversed himself. They'd be less inclined to balk if they were tired, and there would be little to do once they were off the *Sturtevant* but to sleep and quarrel with one another. Burleson had spent eight days in a lifeboat early in his career, and he had no illusions about what was coming.

For that matter, he expected to get little rest himself.

The evening did not go as smoothly as Captain Burleson had hoped. Several people, Reverend Abbott, Thomas Granby, and Dr. Hudson included, drank entirely too much, and on two occasions hot words led to physical confrontations, although no blows were actually exchanged. Even worse from his point of view, two of the crew broke discipline and over indulged, and Ezra Harding was acting increasingly strange even without benefit of alcohol. He got into a fight with Panera, the cargo chief, and both of them ended up with small cuts and bruises.

It was almost midnight when Burleson ordered the stewards to secure what remained of the liquor. He saw Fields filling a hip flask but didn't object. There was some minor grumbling but no outright resistance, from which he took some hope that subsequent situations could be handled as smoothly. Burleson personally escorted Mrs. Galt to her cabin, attempting to reassure her, but when they reached her door, she turned to him and touched his arm briefly.

"You needn't worry about me, Captain." The title still sounded strange to him. He had never aspired to command his own ship, had always been content where he was. "I'm not a weak woman, mentally or physically, and I've always enjoyed a challenge."

"I hope, madam, that this will be more in the nature of an annoying delay than a challenge."

"But you fear otherwise, don't you?"

He blinked, surprised by her perspicacity. "A captain must always consider the worst possible outcome of a situation. That doesn't make it any more likely."

"No," she said quietly. "Nor any less."

The rest of the night passed uneventfully until just an hour before dawn. One of the remaining pumps began to cycle out of its usual rhythm, stuttered for a few more minutes, then stopped altogether. Burleson took the news with no change of expression and gave instructions that no attempt should be made to repair it.

"It would buy us only a little extra time and we have more pressing issues to attend to."

The sun's ascension was heralded by a blood red tinge that seeped up over the eastern horizon and spread like a stain across that quadrant of the sky. The crew exchanged significant looks, knowing what that portended, but didn't speak of it lest they add to the bad luck they'd already experienced. Burleson ordered the stewards to begin rousing the passengers as soon as there was sufficient light that they could move about without tripping over their own feet, and busied the crew with preparations to launch the boats.

Sharon Bartleby and Jerry Rivers both found themselves in the first boat, along with Winifred Galt. Sharon was glad to be assigned to their company, but less pleased when the Porters joined them. Grace was furious and almost had to be forced to board, accompanied by one suitcase, the largest personal item yet to be loaded, although the rest of her luggage had been left in her cabin, despite her strident threats and insincere cajolery. She glared at Sharon in particular, as though wondering if the crew could be induced to throw her overboard and fill that space with more valuable cargo, but she subsided abruptly, smoldering quietly as she sat at the far end of the lifeboat, staring out to sea. Nathan followed, smiling insincerely, his eyes moving rapidly to measure their new, circumscribed environment.

Reverend Abbott followed, wearing his now much wrinkled dark clothing, in which he had apparently slept. He clutched a well worn satchel that appeared to be quite heavy, or perhaps Abbott's list to that side had another cause. Sharon was indifferent to Abbott and to Victor Fields, the last of the passengers to board, but she did notice the way Jerry Rivers' jaw tightened when he saw Fields stepping into the boat. It seemed there might be some bad blood between the two men, although she couldn't imagine how Fields, who kept to himself and rarely spoke, could have given offense.

The three crewmen assigned to their boat were Toby Walters, who told them he would be commanding by virtue of the fact that he had served as third mate on several earlier voyages. "I've never liked giving orders," he assured them, "and I hope we're picked up before I have to issue any. But until then, you should think of me as Captain Walters, even though I'd prefer you all just call me Toby."

Michael Quinn, the steward, and Ezra Harding rounded out the company. Quinn was a smallish man, and very deferential, but Sharon suspected he was much brighter than he let on. Harding she didn't know at all, but she didn't much care for his looks. His expression wasn't quite fierce but it was certainly unfriendly, and she caught Toby Walters watching him speculatively.

They cast off once everyone was aboard and situated, Harding and Walters using the oars to distance themselves from the ship. "She'll drag down anything within reach when she goes," Walters told them, then hastily added, "but that won't be for at least a few more hours. We'll be well out of danger by then." To Sharon's untrained eye, it looked as though the *Sturtevant* might not last more than a few minutes. Most of the hull was underwater, particularly toward the bow, and now that the wind had picked up again, occasional waves threw their spray across the deck.

Rivers moved cautiously to sit down beside her. "You probably should stow your bag in one of the compartments, Miss Bartleby. It'll be out of the way, and I think we might have some unsettled weather coming." He nodded toward the east, where the sun was now clearly visible within an orange and pink halo.

"Please call me Sharon. I don't think we need to be formal, under the present circumstances."

Before he could reply, Grace Porter turned her head. "I would think, given the situation, that proper manners might be more important than ever." Her voice was heavy with malice.

Winifred Galt was sitting to Sharon's left, her head lowered as though she might be napping. Without raising her eyes, she spoke quite clearly. "Common civility should be sufficient, I would think."

Grace seemed to have been taken aback at this unexpected intervention, but she recovered quickly. "I should imagine you are quite conversant with anything <u>common</u>, Mrs. Galt." She pointedly turned away before anyone could respond.

Rivers acted quickly to ease the tension. "All right, Sharon. I'm Jerry."

"And I am Freddie," added Mrs. Galt.

"Freddie?" Sharon and Rivers responded simultaneously.

"My father always called me Winnie, but my mother insisted that no child of hers would be called after something that came out of a horse's mouth. So I became Freddie. I rather like it."

The last of the boats were in the water before noon, and the entire operation was completed without incident. Mrs. Granby was overcome by her emotions and wept continuously, and Dr. Hudson slipped and twisted his ankle, but there were no other untoward events. The sky began to darken halfway through the process, however, and a light, chilly rain began to fall on them as the crew maneuvered the boats into position relative to one another.

"Will we be staying together?" asked Reverend Abbott.

Walters made a noncommittal gesture. "We'll certainly try. We have flashlights so that we can signal in the dark even if we're out of hailing distance, and even if we lose sight of one another, we should all be carried in the same general direction. If any one of us..." he hesitated and started over. "When the first boat is spotted and rescued, there should be no trouble finding the others."

Each of the boats had a small mast and sail but despite the rain the wind was not strong enough to make much difference. A tarpaulin was spread to make a kind of lean-to behind which the passengers could shelter from the rain, but the wind kept changing directions capriciously and everyone aboard was at least damp. Nathan Porter and Abbott both complained, rather pointlessly under the circumstances. Grace simply curled up into a ball, tucking the hem of her skirt under her legs, and glared, and her obvious discomfort moved Sharon to offer to loan her a pair of slacks.

"What? Do you expect me to change clothing right out in front of everyone?"

Sharon shook her head. "Of course not. You could wrap yourself in a blanket and, you know, manage things under cover." She felt a sudden flash of anger. "We'll have to change clothing eventually and that's about as much privacy as we're going to have."

Grace's eyes widened. Apparently this aspect of their situation had not previously occurred to her.

They never did actually see the *Sturtevant*'s death, although the list to port was quite noticeable as they moved away from the foundering vessel. It receded to a vague outline barely visible through the rain, then faded away completely. For the first hour or so, they remained within easy hailing range of one another, but the gaps widened after that. Two of the boats remained visible, but the other two might have capsized and been lost for all that they could see.

The rain continued intermittently throughout the afternoon, sometimes quite intense. They spent most of their time huddled in their inadequate shelters, shivering, speaking very little, each lost in his or her own thoughts. The three crewman and Jerry Rivers took turns on the oars, and Fields eventually joined the rotation. Reverend Abbott was obviously incapable, and it apparently never occurred to Nathan to lend a hand. No one said anything to him, but more than a few pointed looks were leveled in his direction.

The cloud cover became so thick that they were never exactly sure when the sun went down. The temperature dropped and the rain eased off, but they were so thoroughly soaked and chilled by then that it brought them no relief. Several passengers switched to dry clothing after Harding and Quinn erected a kind of blanket igloo at one end of the boat. Sharon didn't repeat her offer to Grace, who emerged wearing a dry but equally impractical skirt and blouse.

They ate a cold supper with only a few mild complaints, some of them meant to be amusing, and settled back in their places. When the rain finally stopped, dry blankets were passed around and conversation waned, but it was a long time before anyone actually fell asleep.

The morning was bright and calm. There was, of course, no sign of the *Sturtevant*. The four lifeboats were alone on an ocean that now seemed somehow much larger and less welcoming than it had only a day earlier. Several white clouds scudded across the sky, but it appeared that they were in for good weather, at least for the moment. Spirits improved after they had broken their fast, and there was mild though nervous laughter from time to time. Grace Porter even went so far as to speak politely to her companions, and Nathan surprised everyone by offering to take a turn at the oars.

"I was never much good at manual labor, but a Porter always does his share." His share was so awkwardly handled, however, that Fields soon replaced him. Sharon saw the look of smug satisfaction on the younger man's face and wondered if his incompetence was real or feigned.

Although Walters assured them that they were making progress, Sharon stared out at the featureless ocean and had the illusion that they were in fact motionless on an enormous plate of uneven blue glass. The only element that changed was the position of the clouds, which moved very slowly all morning, and thinned to tenuous streamers during the afternoon. They spread their wet clothing out to dry, rearranged their belongings to make more comfortable places to sit, and universally avoided talking about the issue that mattered most to them, their chances of being rescued. By the time the mid-day meal was over, they were all beginning to chafe at each other's company. Rivers had brought a deck of cards and enticed Fields, Reverend Abbott, and Mrs. Galt into playing bridge. Ezra Harding and Toby Walters curled up in the stern and went to sleep while Quinn stood watch, and Sharon sheltered in the shade of the sail and took a nap herself. The day drifted toward night as they drifted toward the unknown.

At some point in the night, they lost contact with one of the lifeboats. Walters did his best to assure them there was no cause for alarm. "The seas were calm and the boats are sound. They probably just wandered beyond range of our lights. We might run into them again at some point, or we might just have to wait until we're rescued. It could even be a good thing. The more we're spread out, the more likely it is that someone will see us." No one asked him why, if that were true, they were attempting to stay together, and despite his efforts to remain upbeat, already lowered spirits were further depressed that morning.

A day, a night, and another day of monotony followed. No one wanted to play cards any longer and conversations were terse and sometimes testy. Harding and Quinn raised their voices to each other one night, loud enough to waken some of the others, but they immediately subsided. Grace Porter had withdrawn into herself, but occasionally lashed out with sarcastic comments. Rivers and Fields ganged up on her brother, who sullenly returned to the oars, managing them more skillfully than he had at first. Reverend Abbott began to experience fits of quiet panic during which he insisted that God was punishing them for some unspecified sins. At one point he became hysterical until Rivers literally shook him into silence. Harding had been watching the man speculatively at first, but his expression toward the end was openly contemptuous. Sharon's depression took the form of constant weariness, and she found herself napping in fits and starts during the daylight hours.

They were all physically uncomfortable as well. It was impossible to exercise and the seating arrangements were far from luxurious. The food was nourishing but unheated and unsatisfying. Walters was rationing their water and they were always thirsty. Although they were able to change into clean clothing each day, at least until they ran out of them, the only way to bathe was to use salt water, which left an itchy residue where it was applied. Harding slipped over the side for an extended soak in the darkness one evening, but no one else imitated him. Burleson advised against trying to wash their clothing in the salt water.

During their third night in the lifeboat, they lost touch with the others. It happened sometime during Ezra Harding's watch, and Walters was not happy about it. Harding insisted that he'd remained alert all the time, but Walters accused him openly of having fallen asleep. Their argument might have escalated into something really ugly, but Quinn said something in a low voice and both men fell silent, glaring at one another.

"The situation really hasn't changed significantly," Walters announced a short while later. "For all practical purposes, we've been on our own ever since we left the *Sturtevant*. As long as we continue as we have been, we should be all right."

No one felt reassured even if they accepted the logic of his words. As long as they could see the lights from the other boats, they knew they were not alone. Now the world had contracted to the length and width of their lifeboat.

That evening, the wind began to pick up again. It was almost refreshing at first, cool and relatively dry. Even Grace had joined in the desultory conversation without offending anyone and it was Fields who seemed to have retreated into his own private world. Sharon noticed that Rivers stared at Fields surreptitiously from time to time and wondered why, since the Englishman had done nothing objectionable that she was aware of.

As darkness fell, the wind became gusty, playful, and the ocean more restive. Although none of them had experienced any seasickness earlier, Sharon, Reverend Abbott, and Nathan all suffered from severe nausea. The small sail strained at its bindings and Walters considered having it taken down rather than risk losing it. Although they could see lightning in the distance, it never came near them, nor did it rain, although spray soaked them just as efficiently. The wind steadied early in the evening, propelling them more quickly through the water, but the cloud cover was so complete that Walters could no longer calculate their approximate position.

He showed them his chart with a large area to the west of South America circled. "We're somewhere in here, just outside the place where we want to be. I think we're heading southeast, which is very close to our best possible route."

The wind finally died away an hour before sunrise. The unsettled weather, frequently punctuated by long peals of rumbling thunder, had made sleep difficult and their spirits as well as their clothing were considerably dampened at first light. There was still enough of a breeze to make the sail billow, but it was calm enough for a meal and, in most cases, a change of clothing. Walters took out his sextant and charts and recalculated their position.

"We're further south than I expected, and not as far west."
He failed to conceal his disappointment.

It was Quinn who spotted the dark blur on the horizon and
called their attention to it. Almost everyone aboard crowded
forward, squinting to see better. "What is it?" "Is it one of the other
boats?" "Is that a ship?"

Without making any suggestions of their own, Quinn and
Harding moved to adjust the sail while Walters retrieved a set of
binoculars from his kit. He stared at the distant object for several
long minutes before lowering them, his face thoughtful.

"What is it?" Nathan was particularly animated.

Walters spoke slowly and thoughtfully. "It appears to be an
island."

His announcement was greeted by general excitement. Even
Grace felt moved to smile and nod, and Reverend Abbott looked
cheerful for the first time since he had boarded the lifeboat.

Jerry Rivers was more thoughtful. "Inhabited?"

"I don't know. It shouldn't be there." Walters picked up his
chart and stared at it closely. "There are islands along the coast, of
course, a good many of them. But we couldn't have come that far
already."

"Something not on the charts then?"

"Well, obviously." There was a flash of anger in his voice,
but Walters immediately softened it. "It's probably uninhabited, but
we should be able to refill our water jugs there. There might even
be fruit or game."

"So we land on it?"

"If we can."

The small dot grew larger during the course of the morning,
but not quickly, and by noon it was obvious that the island was
relatively small. Walters and occasionally the others examined it
through the binoculars. There were high cliffs, at least on the near
side, and no discernible beach or landing spot. A dense forest or
jungle crowned the island. There were no signs of human
habitation, although it was still too early to rule out primitives or
even a civilized installation out of their line of sight.

By midday, the unwelcoming face presented to them was
visible even to the naked eye. Sheer stone cliffs rose directly from
the water, the waves breaking against horizontal columns of stone.

Some variety of large bird was occasionally visible at the summit, flying among the top branches of the trees there, but too distant to identify. A narrow but very picturesque waterfall dissected the cliff, but this side of the island was clearly a barrier they couldn't overcome. Walters adjusted the sail and began coursing counterclockwise around the island. "There might be a beach up ahead."

Initially their prospects looked to be no better, but the summit became progressively lower as they advanced, although the cliff face was itself just as forbidding as ever.

"It looks like it's sinking," said Grace, and the description was apt. The island appeared to be a solid block that had tilted away from them. Like a sinking ship, the western end of the island was rising as the eastern edge slipped under the waves. At its extreme point, they could see trees poking up through the surf, some of them still alive, others long dead.

"Why aren't we heading closer to shore, Mr. Walters?" Reverend Abbott had managed to regain some of his former dignity during the past two hours. They were following a course that was almost parallel to the coastline.

"In due time, sir. I prefer to be cautious in unknown waters. Islands like this often have reefs or treacherous currents that might capsize us. We'll feel our way carefully."

As if to prove his point, the lifeboat suddenly lurched and there was an alarming scraping sound from the bow. Harding scrambled forward with an oar and used it to push them away from the jagged rock they'd struck. "There's more of 'em, sir," he called back and Walters nodded. Quinn was already reefing the sail to reduce their speed.

"Stay where you are Ezra and keep an eye forward."

They finally spotted a beach, less than a hundred feet wide and closely surrounded by jagged rock and thick vegetation. Walters decided to land there, but discovered that it was going to be more difficult than he expected. Jagged spires of stone lurked just under the surface, some very large, others tapering to points the size of a baseball. Rivers, Fields, and Quinn were all ordered to watch for hidden obstructions and fend them off with the oars. On two occasions they were forced to retreat from cul-de-sacs whose gaps were too narrow to allow passage. Walters had second thoughts about his decision but they had gone too far now to retreat easily.

After two wearying hours, they finally broke through the ring of stones into relatively clear water. As they headed in toward shore, Rivers sat down, lost in thought. He had seen something which appeared to have escaped the notice of the others, and he wasn't sure if he should say anything or not.   Just for the moment, it was his secret and his alone, and he wanted to mull that over for a while.

One of the submerged stones had been sculpted into the shape of a dragon's head.

CHAPTER FOUR

The number of hidden obstructions suddenly lessened dramatically and they made much more rapid progress. From closer proximity, it was more obvious than ever that this was more of a ledge than a beach. There was sand, but it was thinly scattered over an expanse of stone that had been polished smooth by the ocean. They ran parallel to the shoreline at first as Walters searched for the safest place to land, eventually choosing a section where the shelf dipped slightly.

"There's no place to tie her up so we'll have to drag the boat out of the water."

It was Grace Porter who surprised everyone by spotting the second boat. "Isn't that another boat up there?" She gestured disinterestedly further up the narrow declivity and almost every head turned in that direction. Sure enough, there appeared to be a second lifeboat snuggled under some low, wiry looking vegetation about a hundred paces up the beach.

"I believe it is, Miss Porter," admitted Walters.

"Is it from the *Sturtevant*?" Mrs. Galt was using one hand to shade her eyes as she squinted to cut off the glare thrown up by the polished white stone.

Walters refused to venture an opinion. "I suppose it's possible, but the odds are that it's been there for some time."

The mechanics of landing were not as simple as they appeared. There was a ridge rather than a gradual slope, and the bow of the lifeboat rebounded sharply when a wave thrust them forward during their first attempt. Harding crouched and jumped forward during their second try, staggered and almost fell on the slick rock. Walters then threw him a rope and Harding helped hold them steady while the others clambered ashore. Only Reverend Abbott lost his footing completely, but his only injury was a bruised knee.

The rest of the operation proved to be more problematic. Despite their best efforts, they could barely pull the lifeboat's nose out of the water. It was just too heavy. Even when Sharon, Mrs. Galt, and a decidedly unhappy Grace Porter added their strength to the effort, they made no further progress. Walters waved them off and shook his head.

"There's no help for it. We'll have to unload the stores first."

"Couldn't we just wait until the tide rises," asked Fields. "You can tell the water comes up much higher than it is now."

"If we do that, there's a good chance that the waves will throw the boat against the rocks hard enough to damage it. Which might explain why the other boat," he glanced upslope, "is still here."

For a moment it seemed that Grace might balk at the prospect of manual labor, but she thought better of it and helped carry some of the lighter items ashore. They left the heavier, bulkier cargo – fresh water and food primarily – until the end, at which point the four women were told that their services were no longer required. Sharon still wanted to help, but Walters just shook his head, so she somewhat reluctantly stood and watched alongside Mrs. Galt. Grace was more interested in the other boat, and wandered off to investigate.

They had just managed to drag the stern onto comparatively dry land when Grace returned, carrying a jagged piece of board. "It's from the *Sturtevant*," she said quietly, showing them the painted legend on one side of her prize. "Lifeboat three."

Everyone gathered around at once and Grace was obviously pleased to be the center of attention. "It's pretty badly damaged."

The news that they might not be alone cheered the group considerably. "That was Ted Bergeron's boat," said Walters. "They must have arrived shortly before we did and they certainly can't be far. Was there any sign of them? A message left behind?"

Grace shook her head. "No, nothing like that. And all the supplies are gone except for a couple of broken water casks."

"Maybe they came in at high tide and the boat was damaged when it hit the rocks. They'd have salvaged what they could and gone looking for shelter. We'll have to look for them, but our first priority is to secure our own boat. We don't want to be trapped here."

Once they had pulled the lifeboat out of the water, dragging it further up the slope was easier than they expected. The rock surface was so smooth that there were few obstructions. Harding and Quinn then secured it to a jagged pillar of stone, wrapping the ropes around it several times. They were almost to the upper reach of high tide, far enough inland to avoid the more violent waves, if any. Most of the men were thoroughly exhausted by then and sat down where they were, but Rivers and Fields were restless and without speaking to one another both climbed up toward the derelict lifeboat.

It took only one quick look to tell them that the damage had not been inflicted at sea. The bottom of the lifeboat was completely shattered and one side was largely reduced to splinters. Two oars lay broken in half, the other two were missing entirely, as was the mast. Whatever had happened had taken place right here, after the boat had been dragged clear of the water.

Fields turned his head toward Rivers and whistled softly. Rivers nodded back. We'd better tell the others."

They spoke quietly to Walters first and he listened without changing expression. "Any sign of how it happened?"

Rivers shook his head. "But I don't think it was accidental. Someone wanted to make certain that boat would never be used again."

Walters nodded, and kept his voice low. "It might not be a good idea to alarm the women just yet."

Rivers disagreed immediately. "On the contrary, I think it would be better if they were alarmed. We don't want anyone wandering off alone until we know what we're dealing with. They'll see the wreckage and figure it out soon enough anyway."

"All right, we'll tell them. Was there any sign of Bergeron and the others?"

Both men shook their heads and it was Fields who spoke this time. "The ground is too hard to show any tracks even above the water line. Once we're up off this shelf, we'll have a better chance of picking up their trail."

"Well then let's get this over with."

Sharon and Mrs. Galt took the news calmly, and Grace seemed indifferent. It was Reverend Abbott who appeared the most alarmed, and he insisted that they put out to sea immediately. Although there was a degree of sympathy for his position, none of the rest of the company was willing to return to that cramped, uncomfortable situation so quickly.

"We'll stay here, at least long enough to refill our water casks and take on some fresh food if we can find it. But we'll remain alert. No one wanders off alone, not even for a moment. We'll post a guard tonight and build a large fire. There may be some form of fruit or berry growing on the island, but I caution everyone not to eat anything until we've had some assurance about its safety. Death by poison can be very painful."

Walters proposed leaving Ezra Harding and Mrs. Galt to watch over their boat, but Reverend Abbott was outspoken in his insistence that they not venture away from shore and Winifred was determined not to be left behind. "My husband and I have traveled by foot through much of Asia, young man. I will have no trouble keeping up to the rest of you." Walters sighed and agreed to the substitution.

At first they saw little vegetation, patches of moss in shady spots, a handful of stunted bushes that had managed to find purchase in a crevice in the hard surface. The slope was deceptively gradual and by the time they reached level ground, all of them felt tightness in their calves and both Porters in particular were breathing heavily. As the sun grew higher in the sky, the temperature rose and it was becoming more humid as well. Walters called a halt and stood staring ahead while the others found places to sit and rest.

The vista ahead of them was formidable. In the distance the forest, more properly a jungle, loomed like a solid green wall. There were enormous trees towering into the sky, most of them wreathed by cascading vines that seemed almost consciously to have grown so that they filled in any gaps in the foliage. It was soil under their feet now rather than rock, and they had been watching for any sign of the other stranded party, but if they had left any tracks behind, they were too faint for untrained eyes to detect.

When Walters roused them to continue, Grace Porter balked. "I'm only going as far as the first shady spot and then I'm through exploring."

"I don't think it's a good idea for any of us to be alone, Miss Porter. We don't know what kind of wild animals might live on this island." He did not mention the possibility of savage humans as well, although the thought had occurred to him.

"That's all right. I'll sit with her." Her brother Nathan waved his hand. "I've never been the outdoors type."

Although he didn't care for the idea of splitting the party further, Walters could see no easy alternative. "All right, but you'll stay where we put you until we return, is that understood? We don't have time to search for our own party as well as the others."

"Yes, sir. Understood." Nathan's voice was openly sarcastic, but Walters chose not to notice his tone.

The jungle did not look any more welcoming from close up than it had from a distance. The Porters took shelter in a shady crevice where a ball of rock had split open like an egg, sheltered from the sun by overhanging branches. A small stream of water running along the ground nearby proved to be drinkable, though warm, reassuring them that they could refill the casks before leaving.

Their number reduced to six, the party continued perpendicular to their original path, looking for a break in the nearly impenetrable wall that faced them. It was Winifred Galt who noticed the first anomaly. "Isn't it awfully quiet?"

They all paused and listened for a few seconds. There was almost no wind to disturb the branches and they were far enough from the water now that they could no longer hear the surf. "That is rather odd," said Rivers. "We saw birds earlier but there's no sign of them now."

A brief silence followed as they all strained to listen. A few insects chirped and clicked, but there was no other sign of animate life. Even the insect sounds seemed muted and Rivers noted, not unpleasantly, that there were no midges or other small flying creatures buzzing around his face. After a few seconds, a branch snapped somewhere deep in the forest, a muffled report that seemed strikingly loud only because it provided such a distinct contrast.

It was Sharon who noticed a second anomaly. "Is that some kind of a snake?" She pointed to a particularly thick mesh of vines that started at ground level and wound around one of the thicker trees, constricted so tightly that they could see where the tree's bark had become distorted, rising until they lost sight of it in the canopy of thicker branches overhead. There was clearly more than one variety twisted into the coil, but one strand stood out because of its coloration, which was almost an unusual dark bluish green, and its texture. Although it was obviously vegetable in nature, the vine's outer surface was covered by interlocking, thorny plates, almost like the scales of a reptile.

Walters leaned closer but made no effort to touch anything. "No, it's a vine, all right. But certainly a peculiar one. I don't think I've ever seen anything like it. Take a look, Mike."

Quinn joined him and bent to peer at it from close at hand. "Ugly looking thing. I imagine it could scratch you up pretty good if you fell into a patch. The corners of each section look nice and sharp."

"I don't fancy trying to push in through this." Fields spoke up for almost the first time since they'd left the beach. "Maybe we'd be better off returning to the boat."

Rivers glanced at him and noticed an odd wrinkle in his jacket. Was it the shoulder holster? No, it looked too large for that. And why was Fields wearing his jacket in this heat?

Walters seemed to have lost much of his enthusiasm for exploration. "Well, we still haven't found the others and they have to be around here somewhere. There's fresh water that'll do in a pinch, but it's brackish. I'd like to find a faster moving stream with cleaner water."

"Could they have been lost in the storm?" asked Mrs. Galt. "I mean, could their boat have been thrown up on shore by a wave after they were all...gone."

Walters shook his head. "No, ma'am. That boat was broken up right where it is."

"But why would they wreck their only chance of getting away?" A possible and frightening answer occurred to Sharon as soon as the words were out of her mouth. "Oh! There might be someone on the island already. Someone else, I mean."

Walters nodded, sighed, and tapped the pistol strapped to his waist. "If there are savages here, they might have caught the party by surprise. But I don't think that's likely. The island is too small to support much of a population, so there's probably some other explanation. All the same, I think we should be cautious and stay together."

Sharon realized that he was trying to reassure her and might not have been entirely truthful. Although the implied condescension rankled, she recognized that his intentions were good and decided to let it pass for the moment.

They resumed their trek, parallel to the jungle's edge now, still unable to find a break in the wall of thick vegetation that faced them. They did come upon a second narrow stream, however, and Walters knelt and tasted it. "It's fresh and cool." He sounded genuinely optimistic this time.

A moment later, Rivers found some footprints.

"Someone's been here before us," he said quietly. "Someone wearing boots."

The others joined him and stared down at the disturbed soil. In two places there were discernible signs of a modern boot heel and in another one full print and part of another. .

"Where do you suppose they went?" Rivers scratched his head absentmindedly as he stared around.

"Probably the same way we've been headed," replied Quinn. "Trying to find a way in."

Walters glanced at the sky. "We'll go a little way further, but I don't want to leave the others alone any longer than is necessary."

The Porters were not having a good time. Although they never quarreled in public, they were not as fond of one another as appearances might suggest, and they tired of each other's company very quickly. Nathan had brought one of the canteens from the boat, so they had sufficient water, but he insisted that they needed to ration it even more strictly than usual, and Grace immediately recognized it as another of his attempts to assert his supposed brotherly authority over her.

"I'm thirsty, Nathan. Hand it over." She wasn't, actually, but it was the principle of the thing.

"You've just had some. We'll wait a bit longer and each have another drink."

"Oh for Christ's sake, give me the goddamned canteen or I'm going back to the boat and get a drink there."

"I don't think you appreciate the seriousness of our position, Sis. And your language is most unladylike."

"Oh, stick it up your ass, Nathan." She rose from the rock where she'd been sitting in the shade and walked out into the sunlight. It wasn't particularly hot, but the humidity made her clothing stick to her skin and she was beginning to itch. She needed a bath, a long, luxurious one, and she wasn't likely to get one in the foreseeable future. Grace's tolerance for discomfort was extremely low, and she was also bored. The sinking of the *Sturtevant* had actually been somewhat diverting at first, but after the first few hours in the lifeboat, it had become tedious, dirty, and perhaps worst of all, demeaning. It was bad enough to have to share the open deck of a large ship with the likes of Reverend Abbott, the tasteless Mrs. Galt, and that snippy Bartleby girl, but to have to spend days shoulder to shoulder with them and common crewmen was insupportable. And she had noticed one of them, Harding, watching her when he thought she wasn't looking, and sometimes watching Sharon as well, and Grace recognized the hungry look in his eyes.

"Where are you going? We shouldn't wander off."

"I'm not wandering and you're not my babysitter. I just need to stretch my legs. I won't go far."

They had been sitting in the shelter of a mound of very large stones, some of which were so regular in shape that they appeared almost to be artificial, although what should have been corners had long since been eroded by wind and water. Grace began idly picking her way around the periphery, watching her footing carefully because the surface was loose and uneven in some spots, jagged and treacherous in others.

She was so intent on her footing that she didn't notice the blood until she was about to step in it. Even then, she didn't realize what it was at first. It had dried into a syrupy brown stain splattered across a relatively smooth stretch of rock. The smell was what made her hesitate, although she didn't recognize that either at first. Her eyes followed the discoloration, a fan shaped spray, back to its source, an object lodged in a crevice as though it had been placed on a shelf for safekeeping.

The object was a human leg.

For the first time in her life, Grace Porter screamed in fear rather than in rage.

Reverend Abbott heard the scream and immediately jumped to his feet, staring up the slope toward where the party had disappeared from sight. Harding glanced up from where he was squatting, but without changing expression.

"Did you hear that?" Abbott sounded as though he had been aroused by the trumps of doom.

"Course I did. I'm not deaf." Harding had always avoiding interacting with the passengers as much as possible, partly by choice, partly because Captain Corrigan had given orders to that effect. He had signed on the *Sturtevant* to get away from people and had not been happy when it had become profitable to move people as well as freight. He had attempted to find a berth on another ship, but his reputation preceded him and no other captain working the Asian coast was desperate enough to make him an offer.

So he had remained on the *Sturtevant* where things were arranged so that he stayed out of the passengers' way, and they were kept out of his.

"Should we go and help?" Abbott looked as though that was the last thing he wanted to do, and he was visibly relieved when Harding shook his head.

"Probably just saw a snake or something. You can go off if you want to, but I'm staying put."

Abbott shook his head. "No, no. You're right. They told us to wait here until they got back. I'm sure they're not in any real trouble." And he sat back down abruptly, turning his face away from his companion.

Quinn had a sharp eye and spotted the opening even though the others had passed it first. "Look, there's a way in through here." Sure enough, the vines were thinner where he was pointing, could easily be pushed aside, and beyond them was a relatively clear space, narrow, possibly an animal trail. The clear space stretched away from them for several meters, then angled off out of their line of sight behind a stand of trees.

Quinn had a sheath knife and had just begun hacking away some of the obstructing foliage when the scream came, quite distinct despite the distance they had traveled. There was never any question in their mind that it was Grace Porter.

"Damn that woman!" Rivers said not quite under his breath. He was certain this was going to be a false alarm, but knew they couldn't ignore it.

"We'll have to check it out." It was obvious that Walters suspected the same thing, though he said nothing.

"Some of us could stay here and look around," suggested Quinn.

Walters shook his head. "No, I don't think it's smart to split the party any further. Mark the spot so we can find it again and catch up to us, Mike."

It seemed to take much longer to retrace their steps than it had to make them the first time, but it was almost entirely downhill in this direction and they actually made good time. They had been traveling at an angle up the slope of the island, which seemed much more pronounced from near at hand than it had from a distance. Some of the oldest trees had trunks which were ever so slightly curved, as if they had started their lives in one position only to have it shift ever so slightly as the years passed.

Grace was almost composed by the time they reached her. Her voice was level and her face was once again set in its usual haughty calm, but her hands were clutched into fists at her sides and her eyes were shifting nervously, never resting on her companions but moving beyond them, to the edge of the jungle. Her brother was standing beside her, attempting to look solicitous, but he was pale and there was an audible tremor in his voice when he spoke.

"Grace found something back there." He waved one hand to indicate the general direction. "A dead body, or part of one."

Walters glanced away, then back. "All right, we'll look into it. Miss Bartleby, would you and Mrs. Galt please see to Miss Porter?" Grace clearly neither required nor desired any sympathy from the two women, but Walters' purpose was obviously to keep the women away from whatever unpleasant sight awaited them. Sharon was more than mildly offended. She had helped butcher livestock back home, and she'd helped pull Abner Strahn out of the thresher when he'd gotten his arm torn off. A little blood was not going to cause her to faint. At the moment, there was no way to politely assert her independence, however, so she nodded rather curtly and watched as the four men started away. Nathan made no effort to join them until Walters paused. "Mr. Porter? Would you show us the way, please?"

The smell of blood reached them before they saw the dark stain. Nathan stopped and turned away. "It's just through there, nudged into a crack in the rock."

It was a human leg, complete from mid-thigh to the toes although scraped and torn in several places. The shoe was completely gone but most of the pants leg was still in place, and Quinn let out a muffled gasp and crouched, examining it closely. "I know this material, Mr. Walters. These pants belong to Mr. Bergeron."

And so presumably did the leg.

Rivers had seen a few detached body parts while serving in China, but somehow this isolated example, in this quiet setting, seemed more shocking than anything he'd experienced before. He felt his stomach begin to rebel and turned away, fighting for self control. As he did so, Fields pushed past him, bent low to study the grisly remains. "Looks like it was hacked off. There's some cutting, with an axe maybe since it sheared right through the bone, but the rest of it is just torn away."

Quinn looked even sicker than Rivers and that perversely made him feel better. He moved to Fields' side and confirmed the description for himself. "What in God's name happened here?"

When Walters spoke, his voice also quavered a bit. "Let's fan out and search the area, see if there's anything else that might help. But be careful." To illustrate the seriousness of the situation, he unholstered his pistol and held it ready in his hand.

Thoughtfully, Rivers turned toward Fields, but the other man still appeared reluctant to admit that he too was armed.

They found more signs of the other boat party very quickly, although fortunately no more disconnected body parts turned up. There were bloodstains, however, several of them, sometimes quite extensive. "Someone died here," said Rivers, standing above a rocky alcove whose floor was so a dark smear. The others remained silent except for Fields, who looked around curiously for a few seconds.

"Where are the flies?" he asked quietly. No one had an answer. Small crawling insects moved around the edges of the bloodstains but there were no flies. They hadn't seen a flying insect since landing on the island.

Bits and pieces of supplies and equipment began to turn up. There were cans of food, some intact, some smashed, and once a canvas bag filled with women's clothing, although it was slashed open and stained with blood. "Who was in Bergeron's boat?" asked Rivers, but no one could remember exactly. Walters thought the Granbys had been with him, and he knew the two crewmen by name, Blake and Maltby. A few minutes later they found Dr. Hudson's medical bag, lying open and with most of the contents strewn about. There was another puddle of blood here, but a small one.

"What the hell happened here?" Walters was sweating heavily and not because of the heat. He took out his handkerchief and wiped his forehead while the others continued to search nearby. They had almost reached the end of the patch of jagged rock, the ground leveling off in front of them for a short distance before reaching the jungle. He let his eyes trail along the horizon, then gave a sudden start. "Captain Rivers? Could you come here a moment?"

"Right here, Mr. Walters. What is it?"

"Look out there and tell me that I'm not imagining what I think I'm seeing." He pointed into the distance.

Rivers followed his finger with his eyes and for a second or two, he had no idea what the other man was referring to. But then he saw it and his eyes widened as he whistled softly. "Well, what do you know?"

They had pretty well completed their search of the immediate area, and a small pile of canned goods, a pocket knife, some assorted clothing and personal items, and a badly damaged medical kit had been stacked in a pile on a smooth, flat stone. Walters had also found Bergeron's pistol, with four rounds in the chamber. The other two had presumably been fired. He handed the weapon to Rivers without comment, and the two of them then gave Fields and Quinn a chance to catch their breaths before telling them of their latest discovery.

"There are some ruins not far from here. They look to be very old and in bad shape, but if there were any survivors of whatever happened here," he gestured vaguely, "they might have taken shelter there. That's probably where they were heading when they were attacked, if that's what happened. I think we should look it over before returning to the others."

"Do you think they're still alive?" Quinn sounded as though he might be on the verge of tears.

"We know that at least one of their party died here, presumably Mr. Bergeron. The others, or at least some of them, might have taken shelter there. Or possibly the others, or some of them, were lost at sea before they reached the island."

Fields shook his head. "Bergeron never dragged the boat that far ashore on his own or even with a couple of helping hands."

Walters nodded. "That's true. But the fact remains that we don't know how many are still alive or where they are. We're not equipped for a large scale search, and I wouldn't want to split the party up that way in any case. But I think we should at least go as far as the ruins. If we don't find anything, we come straight back."

"Then let's get to it," said Quinn, getting to his feet. Fields looked less certain, but he followed suit. But another voice delayed them further.

"You gentlemen haven't forgotten the rest of us, have you?"

They turned to see Nathan Porter approaching, one hand raised to shade his eyes from the sun, which was by now quite high in the sky.

Walters was visibly annoyed. "Mr. Porter, I had hoped that you would stay with the women. There is clearly some kind of dangerous animal at large on this island."

Undismayed, Nathan waved his hand dismissively. "Oh, I didn't abandon them. They insisted on coming along, as a matter of fact." And no sooner had he spoken than three figures emerged from behind a shoulder of stone.

Walters made an exasperated sound but bowed to the inevitable and waited quietly until they were all together. Grace Porter was clearly out of sorts, and Sharon seemed unusually somber, but Winifred Galt was in good spirits. "We don't intend to be a burden to you, Mr. Walters, but it was just too dreadful sitting there without any idea what might be happening."

Rivers quickly summarized their findings, trying to downplay the more suggestive details, but he doubted that he fooled any of them. Even Grace, despite the mask of thoughtless indifference, possessed a perceptive and agile mind. She was the one, in fact, who spurred them to action. "All right, if we're going to check the ruins, let's get it over with. You gentlemen might enjoy playing Robinson Crusoe, but I've moved beyond childish delights."

And so it was that the eight of them set out. The ruins were fairly close to the outlying fringes of the jungle and in fact thick vines had grown like dark veins through the whitened bones of the building, which seemed even larger as they grew closer. The largest building was constructed from carved stone, not surprisingly, cut into enormous pillars and lintels, with a roof, now partially collapsed, that looked from a distance as though it had been fashioned from aluminum or some other metal, although that was clearly impossible. The damage was also more obvious as they drew closer. Some of the columns had fallen, although these were all in front and didn't compromise the main structure, although they did block most of the original entrance. If the floor had ever been level, it was so no longer. The entire structure was tilted forward to match the slope of the ground, and its collapse had been in the direction gravity would have pulled it. There were gaps between the pillars facing them, but for the most part the rear wall was solid, built of the same material as the roof.

They were halfway there when they began to see blood again.

CHAPTER FIVE

There were only a few spatters, widely separated, but that was enough to tell them that they were on the right track. Several sets of eyes went immediately to the crumbling building.

"Whatever happened, they probably tried to make it to shelter." Rivers squinted in an attempt to see more clearly, but the structure of the building was carved from white stone that shimmered in the sunlight. He had left the safety on the pistol, but it was still in his hand, at the ready.

They had crossed about half the distance when they found a man's shoe lying all by itself. Walters crouched and examined it but was oddly reluctant to touch it. "No blood, no sign of violence." He hesitated. "Nothing inside."

"Might have come off while they were running." Rivers let his eyes scan the surrounding area. He considered calling out, then realized that they had all been talking in hushed tones since they'd found the first patch of blood. It might be a good idea not to advertise their presence any more than was absolutely necessary, although if anyone hostile was still out there, they were standing in plain sight.

"No one came back for it," Sharon pointed out.

"Which means either they were prevented from doing so, or they didn't want to risk it." Unobtrusively, Rivers disengaged the safety. His heart was pounding.

Walters stood up. "I think it might be a good idea if we kept moving."

No one argued the point, even though Grace was clearly experiencing some discomfort. Sharon glanced down at her feet and noticed the stylish but impractical shoes and suppressed a smile.

Although the building had seemed enormous from a distance, it proved to be partly an illusion resulting from the blocky nature of its construction. The edges of the roof were no more than two stories high, with the peak a few meters above that, forty meters wide and just over twice as deep. From closer at hand, they could see that while the damage was substantial – the entire structure was tilted downhill to their right and partially collapsed, the roof appeared to be mostly intact and there were no obvious breaches in the walls. Vines sprawled across the structure in several places and smaller plants had sprouted where the wind had deposited sufficient soil.

There were no entrances on the side facing them, so they moved downslope and turned the corner. The edges of a flight of ruined steps were visibly under the debris, but most of the multiple narrow entrances here were covered with crumbled stone and debris. There were at least three points of entry, all partially blocked, one a very tight fit even for the smallest of the women, the other two manageable as long as they kept their heads down. Walters was the only one carrying a flashlight, so he and Quinn were the first to go inside, while the others waited nervously, Rivers with the pistol ready at all times.

"All right, come on in!" When Walters gave the all clear, Rivers nodded for the three women to enter first, then Fields, and himself last. There had been no further sign of the other party, and no hint of what might have attacked them. The lack of a clear threat bothered rather than reassured him.

The footing was uncertain at first, crumbling stone and drifting sand, but once inside, Rivers was surprised to find the air relatively cool, and when his eyes adjusted, he could see surprisingly clearly. The roof only appeared to be intact. There were numerous small cracks and holes, enough to admit sufficient light that Walters had turned off his flash.

"I think this was a temple of some sort," said Mrs. Galt. "That over there looks remarkably like an altar."

Fields glanced around. "No place for worshippers to sit."

"Maybe they knelt on the floor," suggested Sharon. "Or the furniture might have been taken away."

"It looks like a hole in the ground to me," announced Grace, who had already seated herself on a fallen column. She lifted one leg and removed her shoe, massaging the sole of her foot. "And there's nobody in here but us."

Walters nodded. "It doesn't look as though they made it here, or stayed if they did. But we ought to look around just in case."

"Well, let's get it over with so we can go." She sounded irritated, but there was genuine weariness in her voice as well.

"And just where do you suggest we go to, young lady?" Winifred Galt sounded tired also, but angry as well. "It seems to me this is the most sheltered place available to us just now. Or would you prefer to sleep in a tent out there where whatever attacked the others can drop in for a visit?"

"I assumed we'd be leaving this place as quickly as possible."

Nathan took his sister's part. "We are leaving, aren't we? In the boat, I mean?"

Walters hesitated. "We still don't know what happened to the others. Some of them might be alive and need our help."

Both Porters immediately objected and Fields seemed to side with them as well. "We're hardly equipped to ride to their rescue. If they've survived, the best thing we could do is find outside help."

The passengers were evenly split on the issue, while Quinn and Walters seemed reluctant to commit themselves. Walters finally raised his arms and shouted for them to settle down. "My primary obligation is to protect the people placed in my charge, which means the six of you and the two watching the boat. As much as I'd like to continue the search, we're too few in numbers and too ill equipped to accomplish anything. It does seem to me that the best thing to do is to reach the authorities."

That led to a renewed flurry of argument, but Walters cut it off immediately. "Please! Hear me out. Our original intention was to refill the water casks and gather whatever additional food – fruit or game – might offer itself. That must still be our first priority. If we discover anything useful about the others while we're doing that, we'll reconsider our options at that time, but in the absence of a compelling reason to stay, we will put back to sea at the earliest possible opportunity. And whatever we do, we remain cautious and no one goes off alone."

There was a restless stirring, but no one spoke up this time. Walters waited a few seconds to let his decision settle in, then continued. "Unfortunately, I don't see any way that we can avoid staying here tonight." The Porters immediately began to protest but he shook his head at them. "It is very unlikely that we can get everything done, relaunch the boat, and navigate through the rocks before night falls. The passage back to the open sea is going to be tricky enough in the daylight. I won't risk it in the darkness."

Nathan appeared to recognize the sense in what Walters was saying and subsided, but Grace continued to look furious although, for the moment, she remained silent.

"Given that necessity, I feel that Mrs. Galt's suggestion is a good one. We're reasonably sheltered here. We can build a fire and perhaps block the other entrances to keep wild animals out," he blinked nervously as he mentioned that possibility.

"What about the boat?" asked Fields. "We don't want to wake up in the morning to find that it's been smashed up like the other one."

"We'll have to post a guard. Two guards. We'll take shifts."

"No offense," said Nathan. "But do you really think that little popgun you're carrying is enough to deal with whatever attacked the others? Whatever broke that boat up was big."

"Or there were several of them," suggested Fields.

"We'll build a fire. Animals avoid fires."

There was some grumbling, but no one could suggest anything more appealing. Rivers recommended a thorough search of the temple, if that's what it really was. "We don't want to find out later that some kind of animal is using it as a lair."

The subsequent search only took a few minutes. There were small piles of rubble in the central room, and the six smaller vestibules, three on each side, contained little other than rotting wood, crumbling stone, and in one case a pile of animal bones. "Not human," said Rivers. "And pretty old. Whatever lived here hasn't been around in a while."

They did make three interesting discoveries. Mrs. Galt found a piece of the roof that had fallen in, and when she handed it to Rivers, he noticed right away that it seemed to be made of the same hard, thorny substance that covered the strange vines. "Light weight and durable," he remarked. "They probably used some kind of adhesive to hold the individual pieces together."

Nathan made the second discovery, the crumbled remains of a statue lying behind the altar. It was too far gone for them to be able to visually reconstruct the body, but the head was reptilian with exaggerated features, similar to a Chinese dragon, but with an oddly different cast. Rivers blinked several times when he saw it, remembering the very similar carving he'd seen lurking under the surface of the ocean as they'd come ashore. He wondered if it had been the top of a statue of some sort, as he'd originally believed, or perhaps a spire at the summit of a building. If so, it was significant. Buildings on such a scale were not erected by hunter-gatherers. There had been a higher civilization here, with some grasp of technology, and in considerable numbers. Something had clearly destroyed that civilization, perhaps the same upheaval that had caused the island to gradually subside into the waters. He knew very little beyond the names of Atlantis and Lemuria but could they be more than just legends?

Quinn made the third and most startling discovery. There was a second, smaller chamber at the rear of the temple, but the collapse was much more dramatic there. The rear wall had buckled and even some of the columns had split or shattered, a good chunk of the roof was down and that part of the structure was open to the sky. There had been two entrances, one of which was completely blocked, the other partially filled with rubble. Walters tried to poke his head inside but couldn't maneuver his shoulders through the gap. Sharon offered to take his place, but he refused and turned to Quinn, who quickly stepped forward.

Crouching with his body twisted awkwardly, Quinn was small enough to slither through the gap and crawl into the open space beyond. There was a second or two of silence, then a gasp. "Oh my god!"

The others came closer, Walters calling insistently, but Quinn didn't answer at first. Almost a minute passed before he reappeared at the opening, pushing through to rejoin them with such haste that he snagged his clothing and scratched one cheek and both hands.

"What's wrong?" "What did you find?" The questions came from every side while Quinn leaned over, hands on his thighs, breathing heavily.

"There's a body in there," he said at last, his voice strained. "It's Dr. Hudson."

No one spoke, waiting for Quinn to find the words. "He's only wearing one shoe. It looks like the one we found."

"What happened to him?" asked Walters.

"Some kind of animal, I think. He's all torn up. And parts are...gone." His body twitched as though he was going to be sick, but Quinn forced himself to breathe slowly and regularly.

Walters glanced around. "He must have been attacked on the way here, crawled inside and died."

Quinn slowly stood up, his face nearly expressionless. "No, he was killed in there. There's blood splashed all around. The roof's open. Something must have come in that way."

Rivers nodded. "All right, then we block up this doorway completely, just to be safe. Are you sure he was alone?"

"There's no sign of anyone else. There's so much blood...I don't know. I suppose there could have been others. But they're gone now if there were."

"What about Hudson's body?"

Walters shook his head. "We can't do anything for him now."

They worked as quickly as possible during the balance of the afternoon, filling water casks, blocking all but one entrance to the temple, building fires and stockpiling dead wood there and alongside the beached lifeboat. Reverend Abbott was near panic when he heard about Dr. Hudson, but Ezra Harding betrayed no visible reaction. Although Abbott contributed little to the subsequent effort, he at least managed to stay out of the way, and even Grace condescended to gather some firewood. There was a surprisingly large number of fallen branches in the area, probably blown there by a storm. None of the plant life growing nearby bore fruit, and they had seen no indication of wildlife, so they were forced to use up more of the supplies they'd brought with them..

By dusk, Walters declared that they'd accomplished enough for the day. "We can finish up in the morning before we launch. Good work people."

Sharon had found herself a relatively soft spot in one of the side chambers and was carrying armsful of leaves in to make herself even more comfortable when she was approached by Grace, whose expression might almost have been termed friendly. "Leave that until later. I've got a better idea."

"Like what?" Sharon halted, but didn't drop what she was carrying.

"Like a bath. There's a little pool of water down the slope a little way. I found it while I was looking for firewood."

"We're not supposed to go off alone."

"We won't be alone. We'll be together. Look, we can take turns, one in the water, one keeping watch. It'll only take a few minutes and we'll be back before it starts to get really dark."

It sounded appealing, but risky. "I don't know if that's such a good idea."

Grace shrugged impatiently. "No, it's probably not. But I'm hot and itchy and I haven't been clean in days. Once we're back in the boat, it's salt water sponge baths at best for God knows how long. This might be our last chance for a long time."

Sharon thought about it. "All right, give me a minute." She added the leaves she was carrying to the pile she'd already accumulated. It wasn't much of a substitute for a mattress, but it was better than nothing. She had a towel tucked in her bag and she extracted it, rolled it up, and stuck it under her arm. When she emerged from the room, Grace was still there, looking somewhat impatient, and her eyes widened when she saw the towel.

"I didn't think to bring one," she explained. "I'll just have to sun dry."

"We can share it," offered Sharon. "We won't need it at the same time if we take turns."

For a split second, Grace's features seemed to soften, but then they returned to her usual careless indifference. "All right, let's get moving. We want to be back before it gets much darker, and before anyone notices we're gone."

They had no difficulty slipping past Quinn, who was nominally on watch. Rivers and Nathan were currently guarding the lifeboat, and the others were either resting or making their individual sleeping arrangements. Grace led the way and, as she'd promised, it was only a short distance. It was a very small pond, a backwater actually, closely surrounded by a dense patch of neck high bushes with dark, spatulate leaves whose points ended with sharp thorns. They had to pick their way through them carefully, but once they had done so, they were effectively concealed from casual viewers. The water was shallow but quite dark, covered in large part by broad leafed floating plants, some of which had pale yellow flowers. There was no trace of a current, at least on their side, and no indication that anything mobile lived in the waters.

"You first," said Sharon. "You found it."

Her offer was unnecessary. Grace was already shedding her clothing. Sharon turned away, ostensibly to fulfill her role as lookout. She wasn't particularly shy; she'd gone skinny dipping in mixed company back home, but sensed that Grace might somehow be offended and didn't want to disturb their current peaceful co-existence. A moment later she heard a gentle splash and ripple and a sigh of undisguised pleasure and smiled to herself. Even the anticipation began to feel good.

Rivers had finished arranging the pile of wood to his liking. They'd started a small fire which was burning nicely, and would enlarge it once darkness fell. He joined Fields, who was sitting atop a smooth, sloping rock, settling into place beside him.

"Keep that weapon of yours ready, Rivers. I have the feeling we're being watched."

"Anything specific?" He turned and looked inland, but saw nothing that he hadn't already seen before.

"No, but I have a feel for this sort of thing. I spent some time in South America. The jungle is always watching you. It's full of eyes. And empty stomachs."

"All right, but I only have four rounds left in any case." He slid the pistol out of his pocket, weighed it in his hand, and put it back. "How many do you have?"

Fields swiveled his head, saying nothing, his expression unreadable.

"I saw the shoulder holster back on the *Sturtevant*," Rivers explained.

Fields nodded. "I occasionally work as a courier," he said slowly. "Sometimes things have to be delivered to dangerous places. Sometimes what I'm carrying is of value to some dangerous people. I don't like to advertise the fact that I'm armed."

"Under the circumstances, I think you might want to at least let Walters know. He's in charge, after all."

"Perhaps you're right." There was an uncomfortable pause. "Five rounds loaded, another twenty in a clip in my pocket. It doesn't have much punch though. It'll stop a man, but only with a body or head shot."

"I don't think it's men we have to fear just now."

"No, probably not."

They fell silent then, both men lost in their own thoughts. One of those rattling around in Rivers' head was that Fields had lost most of his British accent since they'd come ashore. And he remembered that Fields had cursed in German when he thought he was alone. Interesting.

The water was cool but not cold, and it felt absolutely wonderful. Sharon half swam, half floated, moving her arms and legs back and forth. She could almost tread water but it wasn't quite deep enough. The footing was silty and clouds erupted where she disturbed it, but there was relatively little rock. Once she was confident that she wasn't going to fall over, she ducked her head for a second, then stood and smoothed her long hair back over her head. It would have been better if she'd had shampoo or even some soap with her, but she would take what she could get.

Grace was on the shore nearby, already partly dressed, rubbing her own hair vigorously. She was a redhead and this was the first time Sharon had seen her hair not meticulously coifed or hidden under a hat. It looked much better this way, more natural. And Grace had emerged from the water smiling, almost playful, looking younger than she had before. Sharon was twenty-five and she had thought Grace must be closer to thirty, but now she wondered if she might not in fact be the older of the two.

She ducked her head again, this time working the fingers of both hands through the long tresses, spreading them so that the water could wash away the accumulated dirt and oils of the last few days. When her breath gave out, she raised her head again, feeling more refreshed than she had in days.

Something moved at the edge of her vision.

Instinctively she ducked down so that only her head was above water level. Grace had been looking in her direction and noticed the sudden change because she came down to the edge of the water, still holding the towel, her head turning to follow Sharon's line of sight. "What is it?" she whispered.

"Something moved over there. Where that big rock sticks out of the bushes."

There was nothing visible now, no obvious threat, but the serenity of the moment was lost. "Are you through with that towel?"

"Here." Grace handed it to her and Sharon wrapped it around herself as she stepped up onto the shore. Grace immediately turned away and started walking briskly toward the rock.

"Grace, no!" Sharon felt a sudden sense of alarm, but the other woman never hesitated. "Damn it!" she cursed under her breath and began drying herself while she walked to where her clothes lay. She leaned over and began wringing the worst of the water out of her hair, then toweled herself briefly and began donning her clothing, all while watching Grace out of the corner of her eye. Grace had reached the rock and climbed up onto it, staring out over the wall of brush, her head slowly turning from left to right.

With her shoes on and the towel wrapped turban style around her hair, Sharon started to walk along the edge of the water, but Grace promptly turned and jumped down, headed back toward her.

"Did you see anything?" Sharon's voice was a hoarse whisper.

"Oh, yes. I certainly did. It was Harding, the sailor, having himself a little peepshow."

"Oh!" The idea bothered her, but she felt relieved as well. She had feared that it might be something worse. Her relief swamped her indignation, at least at first. "What should we do about it? Tell Walters?"

Grace shook her head, her mouth twisted into an evil smile. "Oh, no. That would be too easy, and we'd have to tell them we were naughty. We'll deal with Mr. Harding in our own way, when the time is right."

Walters was unhappy with the situation on so many levels that he hadn't even considered them all consciously. He was uncomfortable being in command under the best of circumstances, which these most decidedly were not. Remaining on the island overnight seemed to him foolhardy, even though he still believed he had made the best decision. He wasn't confident about the arrangements he had made to safeguard the lifeboat, but thought he'd probably done the best he could. Fields and Rivers would take first watch, Nathan Porter and Quinn the second, and he and Ezra Harding would take over for the final stretch. Reverend Abbott was, in his opinion, useless, and he would not even consider using the women, although Sharon Bartleby had offered.

He was also considerably annoyed to discover that his orders to stay close to the temple seemed to have been generally ignored. There was no sign of either of the two younger women, Ezra Harding had disappeared, and he'd just caught Nathan wandering off on his own.

"I've got some personal business to attend to," the young man had answered indignantly.

It had taken a few seconds for his meaning to penetrate. "All right, but stay close, please. We still don't know what's out there."

Harding reappeared just as Walters was considering raising the alarm, but he shrugged and said he hadn't gone far and no, he hadn't seen the two young ladies. Walters knew him well enough to recognize at least an evasion if not an outright lie, and was about to press him further when he saw the others climbing up the gentle slope in his direction. "Thank God," he breathed, then went off to berate them for disobeying his instructions.

Darkness fell surprisingly quickly, but the sky remained clear and star speckled with a nearly full moon. The fire helped cheer the party as well, although shadows that danced in the distance as the flames flickered were sufficiently unsettling that they retreated inside the temple very quickly. The three women were supposed to take turns tending this fire through the night, but Walters knew that he would not sleep easily under the circumstances and that he would waken frequently to check it himself.

The noises began only minutes after darkness fell, a muted buzzing and humming that made them all pause at first. The contrast with the silence of the day was startling, but once they had a chance to adjust, they realized that what they were hearing was the sound of flying insects. It was surprisingly comforting to hear the return of something approaching the ordinary and only a few continued to wonder at the absence of similar activity while the sun was up.

Each of the three women had been given one of the small rooms and they retreated there promptly, except for Mrs. Galt, who was on fire watch. The men were distributed among the remaining three, although Walters had made his own place at the rear of the main room. The responsibility of command felt like an enormous weight and he wondered if he would be able to get to sleep at all.

Fields and Rivers felt the change as night fell. Both men had been alert to the possibility of danger throughout the day, but it intensified now. They exchanged looks the first time they heard some unseen winged insect buzz through the air nearby, and Fields added a few pieces of wood to the fire and stirred it up so that sparks rose into the air, extending the light further. The only other sound was the slap of waves against the shore and, occasionally, a light gust of wind that stirred loose sand. The full moon washed the ground with pale light for some distance and by mutual consent they sat back to back, each watching half their perimeter.

"We're not alone," said Fields after a few minutes.

"Yeah. I can feel it too. Any idea where they are?" Or what they are, he thought, but didn't say.

"No, but they're watching us."

A branch snapped and crackled in the fire and both men jumped. Rivers laughed nervously, but Fields did not. "So where are you really from?" asked Rivers after a moment.

"What do you mean?"

"You're no more British than I am, Fields."

"I went to school in Kent, and attended Oxford, though I didn't stay long enough to get my degree."

"That's not an answer."

"Perhaps it is all the answer I am prepared to give."

"Fair enough."

The silence stretched for a long time.

"I was born in Holland," Fields said at last. "But I have never considered myself a Hollander. My mother was Flemish, my father German. Prussian, actually."

"So what's your official nationality? What does your passport say?"

Fields laughed shortly. "According to the passport I am carrying at present, I am British. The truth is more complicated than that."

"And where do your loyalties lie?"

"My primary loyalty is to myself. Second would be my employers, under ordinary circumstances. At the moment, I am rather more inclined to value the continued welfare of my companions, since my own is so intimately tied to theirs."

Rivers wanted to ask about the packet Fields had concealed within his clothing but decided now was not the time. "Is Fields your real name?"

"Yes, as a matter of fact, though it is not the one I was born with. I am not a criminal, Captain Rivers, though I suppose it is true that I have not always acted entirely within the law. Is there some purpose to this conversation or is it just idle curiosity on your part?"

"I like to know the people watching my back, that's all."

"Well, I'm not going to cut your throat in your sleep if that's what's bothering you. I've spent most of my adult life avoiding violence, which is not to say that I'm not efficiently violent when the situation demands it."

"All right, I can live with that. How are you with that pistol of yours?"

"I hit what I aim at."

"That's all I ask."

"You have resigned your commission?"

"Yes. Whatever I was looking for, the army didn't have it."

"You worked in military intelligence, didn't you?"

Rivers jumped imperceptibly. "How did you know that?"

"Nothing sinister. I overheard you make reference to it when you were speaking to Dr. Hudson the first night we were aboard."

Rivers remembered the conversation and relaxed slightly. "I tried to track Japanese troop movements. Without much success, I might add. They're very good at concealing their intentions."

"A valuable skill in other human endeavors as well."

"I understand you've had some experience working with our Japanese friends as well."

This time it was Fields who stiffened. "What do you mean?"

"The party that saw you off when we left port made a considerable impression."

"Ah yes. They were very insistent upon seeing that I boarded successfully."

"Businessmen?"

"After a fashion. With the Japanese, the roles of business, politics, and even the military often blur together."

"Some of the men I served with believe that there is going to be a war in the Pacific."

"I wouldn't know. I never involve myself in political issues."

The first watch passed uneventfully, but neither man ever felt any temptation to sleep. The sensation that they were not alone remained strong, and they took turns adding to the fire to make sure it didn't burn down and reduce the circle of illumination around them. Once Rivers thought he saw some dark shape move in the distance, but it might have been a shadow, or a trick of his imagination.

Things were similar uneventful at the temple, where the fire burned just outside the remaining usable entrance. Mrs. Galt sat huddled in the shelter of the opening. It was still quite warm but she felt chilly, perhaps because she too sensed that other eyes were watching. A pile of fresh wood was conveniently at hand and she didn't feel at all sleepy, although her body ached, particularly her feet and calves. She had always been an active person, but the last few days had been a severe drain on her strength.

A sound startled her suddenly, coming from behind, and she twisted around in alarm, although the source was immediately apparent. Reverend Abbott, still fully dressed, was lumbering across the broken floor toward her. He didn't appear to be distressed, but he was moving quite rapidly.

"What's wrong, Reverend?" she whispered, not wanting to waken the others.

"Ah, um, I need to go outside for just a moment."

She smiled, covered it with the back of her hand. The Reverend's fastidious nature never ceased to amuse her, but she resisted the temptation to tease him. "Can't you wait until morning? Mr. Walters asked that we stay inside until daylight."

"No, I'm afraid this can't wait. Please, just let me by."

She backed away slightly so that he could slip through the opening. "Stay where I can see you, at least."

Abbott stopped and turned to look at her. "Indeed, madam, I think not. I won't be a moment, I promise."

Although she still had misgivings, she was not about to physically restrain him, and after all, he would stay very close to the fire she was sure. She edged away from the entrance to allow him passage, and he nodded politely to her as he passed. There was no brush nearby, but a hummock of stone stood only a few meters away and Abbott made directly for it, disappearing around the side. The hollow beyond had by common usage become their latrine.

Mrs. Galt had barely had time to shift into a more comfortable position before Abbott started to scream.

CHAPTER SIX

The scream cut off so quickly that for a few seconds she wondered if she had imagined it. It was only when Walters joined her, followed closely by some of the others, that she realized that she had really heard it.

"It was the reverend," she whispered. "Over behind those rocks."

"What the hell was he doing out there?" Walters' frustration and a hint of fear were both audible in his hoarse whisper.

"Answering the call of nature."

"He could have done that inside."

She shook her head. "No, he couldn't. Reverend Abbott was most particular about things of that nature. Priggish, in fact."

"Did you hear or see anything else?"

She shook her head. "It's been very quiet. I thought I might have heard something earlier, something like wings, but it only lasted a few seconds."

"And I don't suppose he took a torch with him either." He made an exasperated sound when she shook her head. "Ezra! Michael! Get yourselves some fire and let's go see what's out there." He already had his flashlight in his hand, but he picked up one of the rough torches they'd fashioned earlier, thrust it into the flames, and waited for the fire to take hold. The other two crewmen emerged from behind him and followed suit.

"You're not really going out there, are you?" Sharon had crept up behind them. "It might be a trap."

"Oh let them go." Grace Porter didn't sound the least bit alarmed. "He's probably fallen and cracked his skull. You're not going to talk them out of it. Their masculine egos won't let them just sit without knowing what's happened." Sharon turned in her direction but her expression of disapproval was hidden by the shadows.

"Where's your brother?"

Grace shrugged. "Still asleep if he has any sense. And I'm planning to do the same." She disappeared into the interior.

All three men had blazing torches now. Harding moved forward first, with his arm extended to light his way. Walters followed promptly with Quinn taking up the rear. They were only a short way from the entranceway when Sharon abruptly picked up another of the torches and extended it into the fire.

"I don't know if that's such a good idea, Sharon." Mrs. Galt was watching her disapprovingly.

"I'll be careful." And a moment later she was hastily following the others.

It was not difficult to catch up with the three men, who were proceeding cautiously but deliberately counterclockwise around the mound of rocks. Walters was in the lead now, his torch over his head while he probed the shadows with the flashlight. Harding was half crouched an arm's length behind him, Quinn still further back. The latter gave Sharon a disapproving look when she joined him but said nothing. The party moved with a stealthiness that underscored the seriousness of their situation even more effectively than the muffled scream which had wakened her.

The first words spoken were a curse, almost inaudible, as Walters came to an abrupt halt. He moved the light back and forth while the others strained to see what had attracted his attention. "There's blood up ahead," he whispered at last. "A lot of blood."

They were moving again and Sharon realized she was gripping her torch so hard that her fingers hurt. A narrow passage loomed ahead, providing the kind of seclusion that Abbott would probably prefer, and as they reached the entrance Sharon saw the dark stain to her left, caught the smell a moment later and turned her head away, wrinkling her nose. It was flesh blood, still dripping from where it had spattered.

Walters came to a halt and turned to look back, and he grunted with displeasure when he saw Sharon. "Quinn, you stay here and make sure nothing comes in behind us. I would prefer that you wait here with him, young lady."

The smell of blood seemed to strengthen with each passing second and Sharon nodded her head quickly. She had no intention of going further.

Walters and Harding pushed on, edging around a protruding ridge of stone so that they could no longer be seen, although the shadows cast by their torches continued to dance back and forth. The silence stretched like a taut spring, ready to release a flood of violent energy in a split second. Despite a cool breeze, the night was hot as well as humid and Sharon was perspiring freely. She felt mildly dizzy and put one hand on the rock face to steady herself.

"Are you all right, Miss?" Quinn's voice betrayed his own tension.

"I'll be fine."

The two men returned quickly but it still seemed to her an endless wait.

"There's no sign of him," Walters said quietly. "The blood ends just around that bend. Whatever attacked him carried him off."

"Mightn't he have run off himself? Trying to escape, I mean."

Walters shook his head. "No, Miss Bartleby. There's no point in holding out any false hope. No man loses this much blood and runs away. We need to go back to the temple now and remain inside until morning. Maybe we can figure out what happened in the daylight. Whatever it was must have left some tracks somewhere."

She didn't want to accept that Abbott was dead, that there was nothing they could do to help him, but she couldn't think of an alternative. It seemed like an act of cowardice to abandon the hunt so quickly, but she saw the sense of it, and felt a great wave of relief.

Harding suddenly turned around and lifted his torch higher.

"What is it?" Walter angled the flashlight toward the distant jungle.

"Something's watching us."

Abbott's scream was not audible where the remaining two members of the party were tending the fire. To all outward appearances, both men appeared relaxed, but an educated eye would have noticed that they always stood or sat so that they could reach their weapons quickly, and that their eyes were constantly moving, sifting through the shadows that pooled around them. The moon was nearly full and the sky relatively clear so that they could see quite well even without the fire, and there was little cover near where the beached lifeboat and the pile of supplies stood safely above the high tide mark.

"What do you suppose happened to the people in the other boat?" asked Rivers, breaking a long silence.

Fields shrugged. "Some kind of animal, I guess. I've seen wild apes attack a hunting party that intruded on their territory. They can be pretty vicious. And we don't know how many of them made it ashore to start with."

"Would apes have carried off the bodies?"

"It's hard to predict what apes will do. They're almost as unreliable as people." Fields laughed at his own joke, but it sounded forced. "Or it might have been some kind of big cat, maybe a pack of them."

"You haven't said anything about natives."

"No, but that doesn't mean I've ruled it out. Someone lived here at one point, obviously. But I would have thought we'd have seen some sign of them by now if they were still in the neighborhood."

"They could be hiding. Burleson's weapon," he patted the pocket where it rested, "had been fired. They might be afraid of us."

Fields didn't answer. Instead he rose very slowly to his feet and his hand slipped inside his jacket. Rivers understood the significance immediately and withdrew his own weapon, moving slowly to close the gap between himself and his companion. "What is it?" he said quietly.

"I think something just moved out there. Something big."

They retraced their route to the temple entrance without incident, except that Quinn's torch had flickered out. Walters just shook his head in response to Mrs. Galt's questioning look.

Sharon tried to soften the blow. "We don't know what happened to him. He may have run off in a panic." Neither woman took any solace from that possibility.

"No one else is to leave the temple until daybreak," insisted Walters, but Quinn responded quickly.

"It's almost time to change the guard on the boat."

Walters bit his lip. "Right. I'd forgotten. You and Mr. Porter will both take torches and you, Mr. Quinn, will take my pistol. Mr. Rivers will bring back the other weapon when you relieve them and they will both carry fresh torches. If Reverend Abbott had done so, he might still be.." he had been about to say "alive", but hesitated. "He might still be with us and not off on his own."

"Will do, sir."

But waking Nathan was not as easily managed. The younger man thrashed his arms around and turned over at the first attempt, and cursed fluently when Quinn persisted. It was only during the third attempt that he seemed to understand what was wanted of him, and he balked even then. "Let someone else do it. I'm very tired."

"There is no one else, sir. Harding and Mr. Walters are taking the last shift. You and I are responsible for this one."

"Fine, then you go. I'd make rotten company in any case, Quinn."

The steward hesitated, battling with his long experience of catering to the desires of the passengers placed in his charge. "We're not supposed to go outside unaccompanied, sir. You'll have to come with me." When there was no response, he sighed. "Once we're there, I can watch while you rest, sir, if that's what you wish."

His answer was an unintelligible grunt accompanied by no hint of movement.

"Sir, if I go there alone, Mr. Rivers and Mr. Fields will just make a scene about it when they return, and you'll have to go anyway." He paused. "And by yourself. It would really be better if we walked down together."

For a few seconds it appeared that Nathan would ignore this as well, but then he stirred, slowly and with evident irritation. Quinn stepped back and waited for the younger man to get to his feet. "I think this is best, sir."

"Let's get it over with," came the testy reply. "I'm not happy with you and I'll remember this, Quinn."

"I imagine you will, sir, and I'm very sorry." But as he turned away, his expression suggested that he was anything but repentant.

The two men stared into the darkness so intently that it was almost painful. On two occasions, Rivers thought he caught a glimpse of a large shadowy figure moving purposefully just beyond the limit of relatively clear vision, but it might have been wisps of cloud passing in front of the moon. The breeze had grown steadily stronger during the previous hour and the waves rhythmically slapping the shore had become increasingly frothy. They had both jumped once when something passed through the air above their heads, a muffled, transient sound that might have been the flapping of wings. It stopped almost immediately, and if it was some kind of nocturnal predator like an owl, it had opted to continue its journey by gliding.

They had begun to relax slightly when they saw the two bright lights in the distance, soon identified as a pair of torches. "That must be our relief," said Fields, whose eyes immediately shifted back to the spot where he'd first sensed movement. "What do you think we should tell them? Quinn is solid enough, but the Porter kid is useless."

"Maybe he'll do better if he's a little bit scared." Rivers slowly returned the pistol to his pocket. "We'll tell them the truth, but keep it low key."

Fields nodded and holstered his own weapon, and this time when he opened his jacket, Rivers caught sight of the packet he'd seen earlier, now firmly strapped to Fields body.

"Whatever's in that package must be very important."

Fields glanced down and quickly zipped up his jacket again. "Like I said, I work as a private messenger."

"For your Japanese friends?"

"At the moment."

"Official documents?" He was fishing openly now.

"Possibly. I make it a policy not to look at what I carry. I can't let anything slip if I don't know it to start with. And I speak Japanese but, well, reading the language is a whole different proposition. I just deliver the package and take my pay.

"If our luck doesn't change you might not have a chance to do that."

Fields looked directly at him, clearly taking Rivers' measure. "Perhaps not. But if we do get out of this, I intend to complete the job I agreed to perform." He stood up abruptly. "They're taking their time, aren't they?"

It was clearly a change of subject, and Rivers decided not to press the issue.

The changing of the guard went smoothly despite Nathan's obvious unhappiness with the situation. He acknowledged their greeting with a grunt and immediately moved to a sheltered cavity, leaning against the stone and closing his eyes. Rivers glanced at him sharply, Fields with obvious distaste. Both men were startled by the news of Abbott's disappearance

"Are you going to be all right here with him, Quinn?" asked Rivers.

The steward nodded. "I've stood second watch before, sir. I won't need his company to stay alert." Rivers told him about what they'd seen, or rather, what they hadn't seen but suspected. "It might be nothing, but then again, it might be some kind of big cat. Be sure to keep the fire going and don't let the boy wander off," Rivers nodded toward Nathan, who appeared to have fallen asleep.

"No, sir. I've brought some fresh torches with me. Please take care on the way back."

"Don't worry, Quinn. We'll be very careful." With a last look at Nathan, who was already beginning to snore softly, Rivers lighted his torch. Field had already done so and when both were blazing strongly, they nodded to Quinn and set off inland. Quinn watched them go, then walked slowly around the lifeboat, inspecting the immediate vicinity carefully. The ground was hard and unmarked, with only the slightest traces of drifting sand and little other debris. If something crept up on them in the darkness, there was little chance that it would give itself away by stepping on a dead branch or anything similar. He retreated to the low hump of rock where Nathan was sleeping, climbed on top of it and began slowly turning, watching for any hint of movement.

A particularly large wave slammed into the shore. The tide was coming in.

The two men reached the temple without incident, ran their torches into the sand to extinguish the flames, and nodded to Sharon, who had replaced Mrs. Galt at the fire. She was adding wood as they arrived and glanced up only long enough to smile at Rivers before returning to her work.

"Any sign of the reverend?" he asked, but she shook her head and said nothing.

Once inside, Rivers was overcome by such a sudden wave of fatigue that he almost dropped where he stood, but he forced himself to move to the smaller chamber where Quinn had been sleeping just a short while before. He still felt mildly anxious about leaving the steward on guard with such an unreliable partner, but there was nothing he could do about it, and moments later he was sound asleep.

For the first hour, Quinn told himself that he was better off with his partner asleep. Although he had always taken pride in the fact that he treated every passenger with equal respect, that didn't mean that liked them equally well. Neither of the Fosters were ideal passengers. The sister was spoiled, insensitive, demanding, and occasionally found fault with his performance simply to have something to complain about. At least she was attractive to look at, he mused. The same thing could not be said about her brother, who was less inclined to waste the steward's time, but treated him even less like a human being. Grace Foster would have given him an excellent tip when the voyage was concluded, simply to prove how far above him she was. Nathan would have left a pittance, if anything, to demonstrate his contempt.

The first hour passed uneventfully, but Quinn began to grow anxious. On several occasions, he had spun around, convinced that something had crept up behind him, and even though there had never been anything to indicate they were not alone, he became firmly convinced that something prowled just beyond the circle of light. He built up the fire and stirred the coals so that more sparks rose into the air, spreading their flimsy light further, but if anything had been lurking just beyond the limit of illumination, it had retreated quickly enough to remain in concealment.

Although he tried to convince himself that it was just his nerves and that he should ignore them, he became increasing edgy and his anxiety turned to resentment that worsened every time he saw Nathan sleeping in his cubbyhole. Less than an hour after the torches held by Fields and Rivers disappeared from sight, he crouched over his temporary partner and shook his shoulder.

"Mr. Porter, you need to wake up."

Nathan opened his eyes reluctantly and awkwardly pushed Quinn's arm away. "Is it time to go back yet?"

Quinn suppressed his own rising temper. "No, sir. But I need you to wake up. I think I saw something prowling around." It wasn't entirely true, but it did the trick. Nathan pushed himself to his feet, brushing himself off.

"What was it?"

"I don't know. It was out past where the light falls. You have younger eyes, sir, and might be able to see it more easily than I could."

At first, Nathan actively cooperated. He followed Quinn's instructions and seemed to be conscientious about watching his assigned area. Almost an hour passed in which neither man saw even the slightest hint that they were not alone, although Quinn still couldn't shake the feeling that they were being watched. The air had grown even more humid and perspiration plastered their clothing to their skin, and dripped into their eyes. Quinn licked his lips and tasted salt.

"This is bullshit!" Nathan turned around abruptly, his arms on his hips. "There's nothing out there."

Although his tone was belligerent, Quinn could hear the uncertainty in Nathan's voice. The younger man was frightened, and his fear made him more assertive. "I hope you're right. But remember what happened to the reverend."

"The silly old fool probably wandered off in the dark and fell into a hole somewhere." Porter walked over to one of the canteens and began drinking, then spit some of it out. "Even the damned water is warm."

Quinn was about to say something when there was a sharp crack from behind. He turned and saw that a large part of the blazing fire had collapsed, sending a spiral of ashes into the air. The circle of light around them contracted quickly. Leaving Nathan to his own devices, Quinn began to methodically rebuild the fire, adding wood slowly. When he was finally satisfied that it was bright enough again, he stood up and turned back to Nathan.

Who was nowhere to be seen.

It was halfway through Sharon's watch before she began yawning uncontrollably. The first time she caught herself nodding off, she took a long drink of water and that helped for a while, and the second time she stood up, stretched her arms above her head, and began walking back and forth. The fire lit up the entire area but she still stayed quite close to the temple, moving along the front wall but stopping short of each corner. Although she had neither seen nor heard anything remotely alarming, she was reluctant to get any farther from the fire, as though some bogeyman lurked just out of sight, waiting for her to come within reach.

Twice she had heard what sounded like the whirring of wings, a large insect or small bird, once directly overhead, once off to her left. In neither case had she seen anything, and the sounds had ended almost as soon as she noticed them. She had removed one of the heavier pieces of wood from her stockpile, just the right size and shape to serve as a crude club, and she carried it with her when she walked and kept it near at hand when she sat. She would have felt better if it had been her father's shotgun.

She had just returned to the fire when the sound came again, lasting just a second or two, but this time a flutter of movement at the edge of her vision made her turn her head. Whatever it had been was gone or hidden in the shadows, but she was convinced that it hadn't been her imagination. Thoughtfully she removed a blazing stick from the fire, holding it in her left hand, while her right closed around her makeshift cudgel. Moving very slowly, she started in that direction, stopping when she reached the slight bulge caused by a collapsed portion of the temple's front wall.

The silence was definitely disturbing. Sharon knew what the night should sound like and this definitely was not it. Tightening her grip, she stepped sideways and away from the wall, swinging the firebrand quickly to illuminate what lay beyond. Almost immediately a dark shape rushed at her face.

Mr. Porter!" Quinn cupped his hands around his mouth and shouted, his voice wavering but distinct. A wave crashed against the shore and he turned in that direction, then felt a sudden sense of relief as someone answered.

"Over here." It was faint but tinged with Nathan's usual supercilious tone and his distinctive Boston accent.

"Where are you? What are you doing? It's not safe out there!" Now that his initial alarm was allayed, Quinn felt growing anger. Passenger or not, Porter had no right to wander off in violation of the orders Walters had given them.

"I'll be back in a minute! I'm just rinsing off!"

"We're not supposed to separate!" Quinn waited for a response, but the only sound was another wave coming aground. The steward cursed under his breath and took a step toward the shoreline, hesitated, torn between his responsibility to a passenger and his instructions to remain with the lifeboat. "Mr. Porter!" he shouted. "I must ask you to come back here at once!"

Another branch split in an explosion of sparks and Quinn jumped, but there was no other answer. Cursing under his breath, he picked up one of the torches and lit it, although it was barely smoldering when he removed it from the dancing flames and stepped down onto the ground. If he moved quickly, it would only take a minute or so to reach the water now that the tide was in. He could jog down there quickly, locate his quarry, and order him back to his post.

Having made his decision, Quinn decided there was nothing to be gained by waiting. The torch flared when he started forward, then sputtered, spitting sparks. He slowed immediately, not wanting to extinguish his only light, then speeded up again when he was certain that it would not blow out. He was halfway toward his goal, concentrating so intently on the condition of his torch that he paid insufficient attention to his footing, when he reached a slippery spot and both feet went out from under him.

The torch was torn from his hand as he came down heavily on his back.

Sharon flinched away instinctively when the shadowy object rushed at her, raising both arms in front of her face. The flaming torch struck brushed against something and she heard a faint, high pitched sound that cut off almost immediately. The temple wall saved her from a bad fall, but she banged her knee and slid down to a sitting position before she regained her balance. Her sleepiness evaporated in an instant and she stood up warily, moving the torch slowly as she examined her surroundings. There was no sign of whatever it had been – an insect or nocturnal bird in all likelihood – and the night was quiet once again.

For a moment she considered waking up Walters and telling him what had happened, but then she thought about it more objectively. She hadn't been harmed, and whatever it was – most likely a bird, she thought – it had seemed at least as frightened of her as the reverse. If she woke up Walters before his watch with such a pitiful story, he'd listen politely and tell her she did the right thing, but it would be condescending and she'd know that he really thought she was just being hysterical and acting like a child.

She did retreat to her original position by the fire, and she knew now that she wouldn't have any difficulty staying awake for the remainder of her watch. In that sense at least, the night flyer had done her a service. Whatever it was certainly hadn't been large enough to be responsible for the attacks on the earlier party or Reverend Abbott. This reasoning should have made her feel better but it didn't. There was plenty of firewood left to last the night through, so she built the fire up until the heat made her back away. The island of light flickered and grew brighter.

Nathan Porter wasn't sure if this had been such a good idea after all. He had pulled off his clothing and laid it across a waist high stone, then moved cautiously down to the water line. The first wave was gentle and washed around his feet and ankles, a bit chillier than he had expected. It felt delightful. He was hot and sticky and hadn't had a decent bath since embarking on the *Sturtevant*. The water wouldn't be deep here; the slope from where they originally came ashore was quite gradual, and it was smooth enough that he felt confident of his footing. He had no intention of going much further anyway, just far enough that he could lie down and let the breakers wash up over him.

When Quinn called to him, he answered, although he was tempted not to. Whatever had happened to Abbott seemed inapplicable here. Possibly a wild animal had jumped him and carried off the body, but more likely he'd gotten disoriented in the darkness and had wandered off and gotten lost. The blood was unsettling but perhaps he had fallen and cut himself when he panicked and rushed off. Besides, wild animals didn't hunt near the sea shore, did they?

When Quinn called again, repeating his insistence that Nathan return, he had simply ignored him. The water felt so good pouring over his legs that he laid down on his back and closed his eyes, shifting slightly into a more comfortable position. A wave surged up over his feet, then his torso, and for a second or two he was completely immersed. As it fell back, he opened his eyes and smiled, cool for the first time since coming ashore.

Quinn had apparently given up and was no longer calling to him. Nathan sat up slowly and glanced back toward the fire. It was concealed partly by a knob of stone, but the flames were reaching much higher now than they had been when he'd slipped away. Another, smaller bit of flame separated and started to move away at a slight angle. Nathan frowned, then relaxed, recognizing that it was a torch. Apparently Quinn was taking his advice and coming down for a quick bath of his own. Couldn't blame the man. He was obviously unlikely to act on his own volition, but was intelligent enough to respond to the suggestions of his betters. Nathan considered him a tolerable enough servant under the circumstances, although he would never have employed him for a longer term than necessary. He was insufficiently deferential, kept his peace but betrayed himself by a faintly judgmental look inadequately hidden in his eyes. Nathan knew that look well. He had seen it in his father's eyes more times than he could count.

Nathan got to his feet and raised his arms, letting the wind dry his body. That was when he started to have second thoughts, because the salt immediately made him itchy and he realized belatedly that he would only make matters worse if he dunked himself again. He told himself that it had been worth it for the brief moment of cool relief, but began to dress hurriedly anyway, brushing as much from his skin as he could. A quick glance back toward the fire made him frown. The second, smaller light had disappeared.

"Quinn? Are you there?" He fastened his belt and slung his shirt over one shoulder. The itching sensation in his crotch was getting worse and when he ran his hands down his arms, he felt more of the crusty, salty residue. "Where are you?"

Quinn wasn't really hurt by the fall but he had the wind knocked out of him and it was several seconds before he could sit up. He was vaguely aware that Nathan was calling him, but at the moment the necessity to draw breath overwhelmed all other considerations. He did look around for his torch, but there was no sign of it. His weapon was still in his pocket; he felt its reassuring pressure against his thigh. The torch must have fallen some place out of his line of sight, or perhaps he was close enough to the incoming tide that it had been extinguished. The darkness seemed closer somehow, almost a physical presence. He tried to get up but his head was still spinning and he paused with one knee still down, waiting for the unsettling sensation to go away.

Another wave crashed against the sloping shoreline and he glanced in that direction. As he did so, there was a hint of movement, barely seen despite the relatively bright moonlight. He squinted his eyes, trying to peer through the darkness, all senses alert, but there was no sound out of place, no hint that he wasn't alone. But he knew with absolute certainty that something was out there, between him and the waves, and that it wasn't Nathan Foster.

He climbed unsteadily to his feet and took one step back toward the fire. Foster's welfare was no longer his primary concern. His heart was beating fast and his difficulty breathing no longer had anything to do with his mishap. Michael Quinn was terrified, and his only thought was to retreat to the safety of the light. He had even forgotten the pistol in his pocket.

But he would not have had time to use it even if he tried, because death came to him swiftly out of the shadows, striking silently and efficiently. He died without making a sound except for a soft surprised exhalation that no one was close enough to hear except for his killer.

CHAPTER SEVEN

Nathan Porter was still barefoot, picking his way carefully up the slope when he heard Quinn cry out. The sound only lasted for a second, cut off in mid-cry, and was followed by a return to utter silence. He paused, not entirely certain what it was that he'd heard. "Quinn? Are you there?"

His voice sounded unnatural and his mouth was suddenly dry. He stopped moving, stood with his head cocked forward, waiting for a reply that never came. The only sounds were wind and water and although they both sounded entirely normal, he was convinced that there was something wrong, something hidden within the ordinary, something alien. For the first time in his entire life, Nathan was genuinely terrified, and the rush of adrenaline sharpened his senses even as it made his head swim.

There was something wrong with the wind, an undercurrent that didn't fit, an irregularity in the rise and fall. He stood there for a full minute, then another, and it came to him suddenly. There was another sound intermixed with the wind, a deeper, moist sound. The sound of something breathing, and quite close to him.

Nathan began to retreat toward the ocean.

The feeling that he was not alone continued to grow and he back stepped more quickly. A cloud swept across the moon and deeper darkness fell like a cape. Nathan's breath caught in his throat and he stumbled, nearly losing his balance. It would only take a small thing to push him across the border into open panic, and that one thing happened a moment later.

He heard a muffled sound, as if something very large had let out a single explosive breath. It was enough to tip the balance. Nathan turned on one heel and began to run toward the ocean, slowing only when he reached the waterline, splashing and stumbling as he continued to run away from he knew not what. Pursued or not, he continued until it was impossible to run, then bent forward and threw himself into the water, convinced that at any moment something would grab him by the ankles and pull him back.

The water was very cold.

Although the fire at the lifeboat was not within a direct line of sight from the temple, there was a faint glow just barely visible, a glow that slowly faded during the waning hour of the second watch.

Walters and Harding came out of the temple, nodding toward Sharon, then stepped away from the fire. Harding's head moved slowly back and forth as though he was sampling the night air, searching for some foreign scent.

Grace had another half hour to sleep before her shift started. Sharon was still wide awake and doubted her ability to fall asleep, and she had reservations about Grace's ability, or willingness, to keep watch. She was wondering whether or not she should stay up and keep her company, but her thoughts were interrupted when Harding stiffened suddenly and spoke out loud.

"They've let their fire go out."

Walters made a disbelieving sound and moved to the end of the temple to see for himself, but there was no question. Not even the faintest hint of light showed down near the beach. "Shit!" The expletive from the normally soft spoken Walters struck Sharon even more forcibly than the implications of what Harding had said.

Walters checked his pistol, the one he'd loaned to Rivers earlier, spinning the cylinder, then turned to Sharon. If you hear gunfire, rouse the others immediately, understand?"

Sharon nodded and clutched her cudgel.

The walk from the temple to the lifeboat had a nightmarish quality to it. Each man held a torch, but the wind had picked up considerably and was so brisk that they were forced at times to shield the flames with their bodies to avoid having them blown out. Walters was tempted to call out for Quinn, but felt an odd reluctance to do so, as though the sound of his voice might upset some precarious balance. Harding was his usual silent self, but Walters could read his tension in the way the lanky sailor held his body.

Their worst fears were partially realized before they reached their destination. Harding nearly tripped over an object in his path, which turned out to be one of their water caskets. More precisely, slightly more than half of one. Despite his growing alarm, Walters picked up the pace, and a moment later confirmed what he somehow had already known. The lifeboat was directly in front of them, a short distance from a bed of glowing coals. Almost half of the bow was missing, and pieces of polished wood with jagged ends were scattered all around.

Walters called out then. "Quinn? Mr. Porter? Where are you? Can you hear me?"

His voice wavered but he felt no embarrassment. He doubted Harding felt any better than he did despite the man's outward calm.

No one answered, but his voice had been low and would not have carried far. Walters walked over to where they had piled up the provisions, which would have been loaded into the lifeboat at sunrise. He made a disgusted noise when he saw the ruins. Most of the containers had been torn open and the contents strewn about, although there were several that seemed to have escaped more than cosmetic damage.

"Ezra! Get the fire going."

"What for? There's nothing much to watch over now."

"Because I told you to!" Fear and anger boiled together in his voice. Harding gave him a thoughtful look, but held his peace and began gathering the scattered firewood and feeding small branches into the coals.

Moving very slowly, swinging his torch in a wide arc to either side with every third step, Walters approached the rock where the two guards had been stationed overlooking the fire and the lifeboat. He was looking for splashes of blood or any other indication of what might have happened, but there was no sign of violence here. It didn't make him feel much better.

He set the torch down in a sheltered spot, then cupped both hands around his mouth. 'QUINN! MICHAEL QUINN! NATHAN PORTER! CAN YOU HEAR ME!"

At first there was no reply, not even an echo, but just as he was about to renew his call, he heard what might have been a voice in the distance. It was almost inaudible over the tumultuous surf, but Walters felt renewed hope and called again. This time there was no doubt. The answer was faint, almost inaudible, but undeniably human.

Harding had stirred the watch fire to active life, and the sight of the growing flames restored some of Walters' flagging nerve. He found one of the unused torches and replaced his own, which was near the end of its life. "There's someone still alive, down by the shore. We'll have to go find them. They may be injured."

Harding made a noncommittal sound which Walters chose to interpret as assent. He turned and started toward the breaking waves, not looking back to see if Harding was following. If he had, he might have caught a glimpse of the strange look on the other man's face, sly, thoughtful, and not entirely friendly. Harding had always followed orders because that's the way it was aboard a ship. But they weren't at sea any more and he hadn't decided yet which, if any, of the old rules still held. But after a brief hesitation, he threw two more pieces of wood on the fire, then swept up his own torch and followed.

Walters called out again as he advanced and this time the answer came more quickly, still faint but clearly human. They were very close to the water now and some of the stronger waves sent ripples across the sand within range of their light. The next reply was recognizable; it was Nathan Porter's voice.

"Mr. Porter, are you all right?"

"Cold. Very cold."

Walters and Harding exchanged looks. It was obvious that Porter was in the water; either he had waded out voluntarily or he'd been overtaken by the tide. But what had induced him to leave the fire? And where was Quinn?

"Can you move? Can you see our light?"

There was a long pause before the answer came. "I can see it. I don't know if I can make it that far."

Walters cursed under his breath. "All right, wait a minute!" He turned to Harding. "I'll have to go after him. Take my torch. I'll use its light to find our way back to you."

Harding hesitated, then shook his head. "No, sir. I'll go. I'm a stronger swimmer than you."

"I can't ask you to do that, Ezra."

"You didn't ask. And you know I'm right." He thrust his own torch forward and after a second or two, Walters nodded and accepted it. "All right. But be careful."

Ezra slipped out of his clothing quickly and efficiently and set it on top of a dry rock. With a final, unreadable look at Harding, he started forward into the water. Walters watched him go, but lost sight of him when the other man leaned forward and began to swim.

When Sharon heard someone moving inside the temple behind her, she assumed that it was Grace Porter. It was time for the shift change. But when a figure emerged from the opening, it was that of Jerry Rivers.

"Captain Rivers? You should be sleeping, shouldn't you?"

"It's Jerry, remember? What's going on? I heard Walters get up and come out here a while ago."

She quickly explained what had happened. "Mr. Walters said for the rest of us to stay here."

He was silent for the next few seconds, his face set, but then he nodded. "For the time being, that seems the best course." He brushed off the surface of a large piece of rubble and sat on it.

"Aren't you going back to sleep? You've been up most of the night." She didn't want him to go.

"Not until I know what's going on." He shifted his legs, trying to find a more comfortable position. "Do you mind the company?"

"No, of course not."

"Your shift is almost over anyway. I could watch for you and wake up Miss Porter when it's time."

"No, no. I'll do my part. I've been up all night with sick cows more than once. I won't collapse from exhaustion if I don't get a full eight hours." An uneasy pause followed. "They've been gone quite a while."

"It seems longer when you're on edge. Walters is a cautious man. He'll take his time looking the situation over before he acts."

"Both of our weapons are out there now. If something attacks us here, we'd have to throw stones."

"It's not quite that bad. Animals are afraid of fire." He glanced in her direction, trying to measure her character through the darkness. "And we're not completely unarmed. Fields has a pistol."

"Oh!" She thought that over for a moment. "I didn't know."

"He's not advertising the fact. Our Mr. Fields has his own agenda. At the moment, it coincides with our own, but once we're out of this, I don't think we should count on him."

"Are you saying he's some kind of criminal?"

"No. I don't know exactly what he is. But you must have noticed that his accent has slipped lately."

She hadn't, but now that he pointed it out, it seemed obvious. "Do you think he's dangerous?"

"Not now. Like I said, we all want the same thing, to get off this island and back to civilization."

"But what if...?" Sharon never finished her question because just then she was struck hard on the back of her head and something tugged at her hair. She cried out in terror and lurched forward, stumbled and fell toward Rivers.

Walters paced restlessly back and forth. He had stuck one torch into a rocky crevice so that it stood like a beacon and carried the other with him. The last two times he had called he'd gotten muffled responses from Harding and nothing at all from the Porter boy. The temptation was to stare out to sea, trying to distinguish some movement within the darkness, but he didn't think the danger would come from that direction. If so, Porter could hardly have survived as long as he had, alone and without light. There was no sign of Quinn and even though he lacked any evidence to support his belief, Walters was certain that the steward was dead.

He moved slowly in a counterclockwise search pattern with the stationary torch as his base, looking for tracks on the dry ground. There were a few sandy patches but for the most part this was smooth rock. A troop of elephants could have marched past and he would be none the wiser, but he continued to search anyway. He had to do something.

Every minute or two he glanced at his watch. Harding had only been gone fifteen minutes but it felt as though hours had passed. Walters had been slowly increasing the radius of his circle from his beacon, and on his next circuit he found another torch lying on the sand, thoroughly soaked. It was unquestionably one of those they had fashioned earlier, and its presence offered a possible hint to what had happened. Quinn or Porter or both had taken torches with them when they left their post. Had they been attacked even though they carried fire? The possibility made his hackles rise.

His thoughts were interrupted by a muffled shout. He turned toward the ocean and saw movement, which quickly resolved itself into the shape of a man. One man half carrying, half dragging another out of the foaming surf.

Walters ran to meet them.

Both men were soaked through, but Harding appeared to be in good shape. Nathan kept trying to get his legs planted under him, but his knees buckled at each attempt, and his flailing arms seemed uncoordinated. Walters took one arm and helped lead the younger man to the brighter circle of fire, where he quickly looked him over. Nathan was clearly exhausted and only occasionally coherent, shivered uncontrollably and could not seem to focus his eyes, but there was no sign of any significant injury, no blood stains, no broken bones.

"Where did you find him?" he asked Harding.

"Holding onto a rock. I don't think he'd have lasted much longer, sir."

Walters turned back to Nathan, slapped his cheek lightly to get his attention. "Mr. Porter, can you tell us what happened? Where is Quinn?"

Nathan opened his mouth, but couldn't speak. He was sitting on the ground now, his hands pressed down beside his hips, barely keeping his balance. He shook his head, closed his eyes for a second, then tried again. "Dead. He's dead. It killed him."

Walters and Harding exchanged looks and the latter picked up the planted torch and began examining their surroundings, but without moving more than a few meters from the others. "Are you sure, Mr. Porter?"

Nathan nodded, slowly at first, then vigorously. "I couldn't help him. I ran into the water and started swimming. I thought I was going to die!" His voice was thin and uneven, but stronger than it had been before.

"What was it? What attacked you?"

"A demon," whispered Harding, but neither man heard him.

Nathan shook his head. "Couldn't see it. It came out of the darkness. It was fast and it was big." His voice started to crack and he reached up and grabbed Walters by the arm. "We have to get out of here before it comes back!"

"Do you think you can walk, sir? We need to have our hands free." Walters showed him his right hand, which now held his pistol.

"I think so. Can you help me up?"

Harding came closer as Nathan got to his feet. "Quinn had the other pistol," he said quietly.

"We'll never find it in the dark. Let's get back to the others."

"What about the boat?"

Walters shook his head. "There's no point guarding it now, is there?"

Rivers raised his arms as Sharon toppled forward, but he didn't have time to prepare himself and they both fell sprawling.

Her long hair was moving with a life of its own and his immediate thought was that a bat had gotten entangled in it. He didn't relish the thought of putting his hands anywhere near a possibly rabid and certainly terrified animal, but there were plenty of fist sized rocks nearby.

"Hold still! I'll get it!" He really didn't expect her to stop thrashing around, but Sharon surprised him with her nearly instantaneous obedience. He raised a rounded stone and brought it down as hard as he could, aiming directly for the still indistinct shape struggling to free itself.

There was a sharp crack, as though he'd hit a piece of pottery rather than a living creature, momentary resistance then collapse. It was still moving, but feebly now. "Get up!"

Sharon sat up, shaking her head vigorously, and as she did so something dark and approximately the size of a small bird dropped out of her hair, jerked convulsively a few times, then became still. Rivers froze with the stone raised over his shoulder, prepared to strike again if necessary. His face slowly twisted into a mask of revulsion as he focused on what flopped and twisted on the ground.

Sharon was frantically dragging her fingers through her hair to make sure nothing remained there, and several seconds passed before she turned around. When she saw what lay on the rock, she flinched back but she didn't look away. "What is that thing?"

"I don't know." There was a tremor in Rivers' voice. "Some kind of bug."

"That's pretty big for a bug."

In fact, it looked more like a crab, although four of its six limbs were wings rather than legs, and the ends of the remaining two were funnel shaped rather than pinchers. The stone had shattered most of what might have been its face, but enough remained for them to see that its eyes were prismatic and that it had an extended beak. The exterior of its body was very hard, like that of a beetle, but there were internal bones as well, although they appeared to be very fragile, possibly hollow.

"What is that stuff?" Sharon pointed to a lump of softer material, half concealed under one edge of the shell.

Overcoming his revulsion, Rivers leaned down, squinting. "It looks like webbing. I think this is some kind of spider."

"Spiders don't fly. Sometimes they jump, but they don't fly."

"This one does."

Nathan seemed to recover much of his strength once they started moving, and by the time they were halfway back to the temple, he had shrugged off Walters' helping hand, rather brusquely in fact, and was keeping up to them without assistance. They stopped once, briefly, when Harding spun about abruptly, waving his torch back and forth.

"What is it, Ezra?"

"Heard something. We're not alone."

"Take this for a second." Walters handed his torch to Nathan and took out his flashlight. His other hand still held the pistol. He probed the darkness for several seconds, but nothing seemed out of the ordinary. "I don't see anything. Maybe our lights scared it off."

"Maybe." But Harding didn't sound entirely convinced. Walters took back the torch and they continued their retreat from the beach.

The rest of the walk was uneventful. Walters was only mildly surprised to see Rivers standing beside Sharon as they approached. There was a flurry of questions, mostly involving Quinn. Nathan seemed to have lost all of his strength again now that they had reached relative safety and he disappeared inside the temple without saying a word. Walters brought the other two up to date.

"Any chance of salvaging the boat?" Rivers didn't sound hopeful.

"I'll know better after the sun comes up, but I don't think so. We can probably save some of the supplies, unless whatever it is comes back."

"We could try to retrieve them now." Rivers didn't sound as though he liked his own suggestion.

"Too risky. We still don't know what's out there."

"Is there any chance that Quinn is still alive?" asked Sharon.

Walters sighed. "I don't think so, Miss. Mr. Porter says he saw something attack him, but he can't tell us what it was. And there was no sign of him."

"He might have been hurt. Unconscious."

"I know that." Walters sounded angry for a second, then moderated his tone. "We just can't risk looking for him in the darkness, not until we know what we're dealing with."

Harding had wandered over to the fire and he suddenly started. "Lord help us!" He stepped back quickly

That led to a brief recounting of Sharon's adventures with the spider creature. "You said this thing was flying?" Walters looked skeptical.

Sharon and Rivers both nodded.

They never did waken Grace Porter for her shift. Harding and Sharon both went off to try to get some sleep, but Walters and Rivers sat up and tended the fire, talking occasionally, mostly caught up in their individual thoughts. Fields joined them just as the sun came up and Walters brought him up to date. He accepted the news calmly. "Looks like we're in for an extended stay. We probably should try to find safer living quarters."

"What's wrong with this?" Walters nodded toward the temple. "The walls are solid and we're near fresh water. There's only one entrance now that we've blocked up the others so it's easy to defend if we're attacked."

It was Rivers who answered. "One entrance means one exit. If something decided to camp out here and wait for us, we'd have to fight on its terms. We have water nearby but we're going to have to go into the jungle for food. And soon, unless we find a lot of our stores survived the attack."

"All right, I see your point. But what if there's nothing better?"

"Then we make do with what we have. There's a hole in the roof in the rear chamber. We could probably widen it enough to make another exit."

Fields smiled. "But another exit means another entrance to be guarded."

"There is that," Rivers admitted.

The others were up soon after, and the story of the previous night's events had to be told again. Mrs. Galt looked saddened and concerned, and even Grace seemed affected by the loss of Quinn. They had brought most of their remaining food to the temple but no one had much appetite for breakfast. Fields took out a pocket knife and bent over the flying creature's corpse while the others were making an attempt to eat. When he was done, he had a thoughtful expression on his face.

"I don't suppose anyone here has a background in biology." He glanced around quickly, obviously not expecting an answer. "I'm afraid my formal education has been in other areas, but I've traveled a good deal in my time, and our little visitor back there is like nothing I've ever seen before."

"Some of these islands are very isolated, Mr. Fields," replied Walters. "I've seen some pretty strange things myself."

"I imagine you have." Fields raised his hands and displayed what appeared to be a three inch wide piece of black mesh. "Any idea what this is?"

"That's a piece of its web, isn't it?" asked Sharon. "We know it's some kind of spider."

"I don't think it's webbing. I think it's a net. Look at this." He set the webbing down on a piece of rubble and picked up another small object. The others came closer and it was Sharon who first recognized what he was holding.

"That's one of its claws."

Fields shook his head. "Not a claw. Look closely." He turned it around so that they could see that he'd cut open the reverse side. The interior contained a thick, tubular structure surrounded by what appeared to be very delicate bones or stalks of cartilage, all nearly as dark as the webbing. "The other one was damaged so badly that I couldn't see how it worked, but this one is fine. Watch now."

He moved his other hand to the base of the object, closed two fingers around a think stalk of tissue, then pushed down. As he did so, the small bones or cartilage were forced out through the end of the funnel shaped structure, opening up into a lattice almost ten inches from side to side. Between the spikes of the lattice were bits and pieces of the black webbing.

"While it was alive, I imagine it generated webbing to fill all these gaps."

"My God!" Sharon whispered, the first to understand the implications.

"Congratulations, Miss Bartleby. You're quick off the mark. Anyone else?"

Rivers thought he understood, but he remained silent, letting Fields have his moment in the spotlight. Field waited only a few seconds before continuing. "This creature is undoubtedly a night feeder. I believe that it launches itself into the air and then quite literally drops this net below its body. As it flies, it scoops up any insects in the area, to be killed and eaten later. Let loose a few dozen of these things on an island this size and wait a few weeks and what do you have?"

"A severe shortage of flying insects." It was Mrs. Galt who spoke this time. "Very clever, Mr. Fields. But it doesn't really help us much. I'd be more interested to know what attacked Reverend Abbott and Mr. Quinn."

Fields shrugged elaborately. "I couldn't venture a guess, madam. But I suggest that it might be something as radically different from anything we've seen before as this is from your common household spider. Oh, and one other thing."

They all waited. The usually reticent Fields seemed to be enjoying his brief stint as the center of attention.

"I can't be certain because Rivers there bashed its head in quite efficiently, but I poked around in the...ummm...remains and I think I can say with some confidence that our little friend here had six eyes, three on each side."

The general mood remained subdued but Walters efficiently organized a search and salvage operation as soon as they had eaten. "So far no one has been attacked during the daylight, but we can't assume that means we're safe. We will stay within sight of each other at all times and one of us will be armed and on watch while the rest are working."

Nathan seemed well enough although it had been difficult to waken him and he was clearly shaken and sullen. Walters amended his order and told Nathan to remain at the temple to keep the fire banked but alive. After a grudging acquiescence, Nathan sat down with his back to the temple wall, discouraging further conversation.

They spent the balance of the morning scouring the vicinity of the lifeboat. The destruction was even more extensive than Walters had thought. Either he had been fooled in the poor light or whatever creature was responsible had returned later to inflict further damage. They managed to find one intact water cask and scattered packets of food and other supplies, including one of the two medical kits, a coil of rope, and Mrs. Galt's purse, which had been snagged on a rock and not carried out to sea. None of the other personal baggage survived so they had only the clothes they were currently wearing. The food they had saved plus what was back at the temple was enough to last them no more than three or four days. There was no sign of Michael Quinn or the weapon he had been carrying, not even a bloodstain. Rivers found a patch of sand that had been disturbed since the tide had receded, and thought he saw the hint of a very large clawed foot, but it might have been a vagary of the current, or his imagination. He decided not to alarm the others and scuffed it away with his foot.

It was hot, and by mid-day they were all tired, discouraged, uncomfortable, and to one extent or another, frightened. It took two trips to carry everything they'd found back to the temple, but only because they didn't have containers with which to gather the many small packages. There was no sign of any other form of animal life in the immediate area, but at one point Rivers spotted three dark shapes in the distance, flying above the fringes of the jungle. He pointed them out to Fields.

"Think they're more of our spider friends?" asked Fields. But he realized that couldn't be the case even before Rivers answered.

"They're too big, and they're flying by day. It's too far to make out any details, but there's something odd about the way they're moving."

"Yeah, I noticed it too. Can't quite make it out though."

"I think I know what it is." He paused, unconsciously dramatizing the moment. "I think they have too many wings."

CHAPTER EIGHT

The atmosphere was subdued as they sat around eating their next meal. They had reduced the portions as a precaution but no one seemed to have much of an appetite. Walters had told them quite frankly that there was no chance of repairing the lifeboat, at least in the near future. "We might be able to find suitable trees in the jungle, but we don't have any tools other than three pocket knives. And frankly, I doubt that any of us has the necessary skills to shape and fit boards."

"What about a raft?" asked Mrs. Galt.

Walters shook his head. "We'd still have to bring down the trees somehow, and cut them to length. There are eight of us, which means a pretty big raft, because we'd also have to load aboard enough food and water to last us for a long while. And we don't have enough food, or any way of preserving it if we can find some, or a sufficient number of containers to hold the water."

"How long would we have to survive once we left the island?" asked Sharon.

Walters just shook his head. "We have no way of knowing. We can't steer the raft the way we could the boat even if we fashion a rudder and sail and the wind and current could take us anywhere, even away from where we want to go. It could be days, or weeks, or months."

"Well we certainly can't stay here," insisted Nathan, finally emerging from his near stupor. "Something out there has already killed two of us and we still don't even know what it is."

"It's some kind of animal, Mr. Porter," Nathan answered soothingly. "Whatever it is appears to be afraid of the fire, and doesn't come out in the daylight. As long as we're careful, we should be all right."

"Tell that to Quinn!"

Nathan's attitude finally stirred Walters' own anger. "As to that, Mr. Porter, would you mind telling us exactly what happened last night? Why did the two of you leave the fire and how did you get separated?"

That stopped the young man short. He visibly recoiled and his eyes began moving furtively. No one watching him could have expected anything other than a lie, and they would not have been disappointed. "It all happened so fast. We got separated and then something got him. There was nothing I could do to help so I ran.

It was just lucky I was close to the water and knew enough to swim out where it couldn't get me too."

"Why did you leave the lifeboat? Why didn't you stay near the fire?"

"I just went to rinse off," was the sullen answer. "Quinn said it would be all right. He came with me, with a torch. We were going to take turns, just long enough to cool down. But while I was in the water, he must have heard something and went off to see what it was. The next thing I knew the torch was gone and I heard him shout something and then it was coming for me and I ran. You would have too."

The words came quickly, tumbling over one another, and no one present believed that Nathan was telling the complete truth, even though his lingering terror was equally obvious.

"And you never saw what it was?" Walters softened his voice.

"No, maybe a shadow, but I'm not sure. But I heard it. It was breathing real hard and I heard a clicking sound coming toward me."

"Clicking? What do you mean clicking?"

"I don't know! I only heard it for a second and then I ran, like I told you. I wasn't going to stand there and get killed like Quinn just to satisfy my curiosity, was I?"

Walters turned away without answering, turning his attention to Rivers. "We need to know more about this island," he said evenly. "Are you up to a little reconnoitering?"

Rivers nodded. "I'll take Fields." Fields glanced up when he heard his name mentioned, but didn't object.

"All right. You should take this." Walters held out the pistol. Rivers glanced at it thoughtfully, then shook his head.

"No, you keep it. We'll be all right."

Walters looked dubious and kept the weapon extended. Fields broke the silence by standing up. "It's all right, Mr. Walters. Hang onto your weapon. I have one of my own." He made it appear from inside his jacket, then made it vanish just as quickly. Walters gave him a very strange look for a moment or two, then nodded.

"Take care, gentlemen. We can't afford to lose anybody else."

They started off at an angle that would bring them quite close to the fringe of the jungle, this time in the direction of the low end of the island. Objectively the landscape looked just the same as it had before, but they saw it with altered eyes today. Now it was more than just unknown. There was danger as well, indistinct but certain. Whatever had killed two of their companions most likely was concealed somewhere within the densely packed mass of trees, vines, and foliage.

Within half an hour they had moved beyond the nearly barren scrub to a stretch of low, rugged looking grassland sprinkled with hardy looking bushes and occasional trees, singly or in small clumps. The landscape sloped slightly upward and from time to time they had to make detours around rough patches, but for the most part the first hour passed uneventfully. They startled a small, furry creature at one point, and although they never saw it clearly enough to identify before it disappeared into a cluster of barbed bushes, it appeared to be perfectly ordinary. Fields thought it might be some variety of ground sloth.

"At least it only had four legs."

The temple was invisible behind them, concealed by a humpbacked hill, when they passed around a spur of jungle and were greeted with a new vista. There was a much larger stretch of similar terrain which sloped gently downward in front of them before rising again to what appeared to be a very steep, rocky ridge on the far horizon. Beyond and to their right a cone shaped rise dominated the scene, its summit jagged, obviously an old volcano, now canted to one side as the island beneath it slowly subsided into the ocean.

The dead volcano was impressive, but another feature was even more remarkable. They were buildings ahead, more than a score of them, some almost as large as the temple. It was difficult to judge their condition from this distance but many appeared to be virtually intact, although others had collapsed into piles of broken stone. They were gathered in three concentric circles around what must have been a plaza of some sort, a circular space surrounded by a shoulder high stone wall, which was now interrupted by several gaps of varying sizes. In the very center of the plaza stood a statue and the statue was that of a man, about five meters tall, standing with his legs planted firmly and two arms raised above his head.

And with two more arms folded across his chest.

Walters wasn't thrilled with the prospect of reopening the rear exit from the temple, but they still had to do something about Dr. Hudson's body, which they had temporarily walled up inside. He and Harding climbed onto the roof of the temple, picking their way carefully from one support to the next, to examine the situation from above. When they reached the rear wall and peered down, they exchanged guarded looks. Dr. Hudson's body was gone and only a smear of dried blood showed that it had ever been there.

"Something must've taken it out this way," observed Harding unnecessarily.

" I don't like this, Ezra. I don't like it at all."

Walters tried to estimate how much work would be involved turning this into an acceptable emergency exit, but in the end he gave it up as a bad idea. They would have to split their numbers to guard both entrances at night, and there simply weren't enough of them to keep that up for any length of time. If attacked, he supposed they could clear a route from the inside, but he didn't much like the idea of leaving their refuge in such a vulnerable position. Their chances would be better if they made a stand inside. But that bothered him as well, because they couldn't last through a prolonged siege. He sighed. Maybe the scouting team would find something better.

"All right, let's go back down."

Sharon and Mrs. Galt, with the grudging assistance of Grace Porter, had cleaned a portion of the main chamber of the temple. The altar now served as a table where they had carefully arranged all of their surviving supplies and equipment. It made a depressingly small pile. The floor had been swept clean with cut branches and the entrance had been cleared to make the footing less treacherous.

Harding and Nathan spent an hour replenishing the stack of firewood, but their efforts were less successful this time. They had exhausted the dead wood in the immediate area and, lacking the means to cut down anything substantial, were forced to range farther from their base. Harding was further hampered by Nathan's insistence that he needed to rest frequently because of his ordeal the previous night. The older man was openly contemptuous, but either Nathan didn't notice or chose to pretend that he hadn't.

About mid-afternoon, Sharon mentioned the swimming hole to Walters. "We didn't see any fish, but we were only there for a few minutes, just enough for a quick rinse."

Walters refrained from pointing out that they shouldn't have gone off on their own, and agreed that it was worth investigating. "There has to be some form of game on the island. You can't have predators without prey." He waited until Harding and Nathan returned, told them to watch over the other two women, then let Sharon lead him to the pond. The walked the entire perimeter without seeing anything other than a few insects skating on the surface.

"We'll have to make up a fishing pole and try later. Frankly, miss, I think we're going to have to go into the jungle if we want fresh meat."

They started back to the temple, and as they approached they heard raised voices in the distance. Walters took out his pistol and cautioned Sharon to stay close to him. Then he started to jog toward the disturbance.

Rivers and Fields approached the nearest building cautiously, but not because they thought it might still be occupied, at least not by people. There must have been streets or paths at some time, but they were so completely overgrown that it was impossible to tell where they had been. Whoever had lived her had moved on, or died out, long before. The building they chose was in better shape than most. The roof seemed to be intact and the walls were solid and even. There was moss growing all over one side and thick vines climbed the walls and crawled across the roof, but there seemed to be no structural damage.

There were several windows, narrow slits that could not have let a great deal of light in. The doorways were empty, yawning holes with no indication that there had ever been a means of closing them off. Dirt had drifted inside, and there was mold and some fungus growth on the floor and interior walls. Inside they found several smaller chambers opening off a truncated central corridor, but all of the rooms were empty except for wind blown debris and dust. .

"Didn't these people have furniture or tools?" Fields kept his voice low, as though afraid to waken the dead.

"Maybe they took everything with them when they went away."

"Went away where?"

Rivers didn't have an answer.

They found little difference in the next three they inspected, and after that they only glanced through the doorways of the buildings they passed. By unspoken agreement they headed next to the dominant statue in the middle of cluster of buildings. From close at hand, it was less impressive other than its size and odd subject matter. The carving was crude and had an unfinished look, as though it had been erected hastily. All four of the hands had six fingers but the feet were just indistinct blobs with no detail. None of the buildings varied in any obvious way and none of them bore any symbols, decorative or otherwise. Even the temple had been devoid of any distinguishing features and it was not at all clear that it actually was meant to serve any religious purpose.   The statue seemed out of place, an anomaly inconsistent with the rest of the architecture.

Years worth of debris had piled up around the base of the statue, a mound of dust and dead leaves and broken branches that had been worn almost smooth by the wind. Almost. Fields poked at an irregularity and then started digging around it with his fingers.

"What have you got there?"

"Just a second. I've almost got it loose." He used both hands to grip the object, braced his feet and began to wiggle it back and forth. Clumps of dirt broke fractured and fell around his feet. Then he jerked backward slightly as it came free and he stepped back.

The object in his hand was a human skull.

The first thing Walters noticed when he came within sight of the temple was that Grace Porter was standing on top of a raised stone, brandishing a short, thick piece of wood above her head. She was shouting something, but he couldn't make out the actual words. Since she didn't seem in imminent danger, he put his weapon away, but he didn't slow his pace.

A few more steps gave him a more comprehensive view. Just beyond reach of the makeshift club, Ezra Harding, naked to the waist, had both fists clenched and was looking up at Grace with an angry expression. He was bleeding from the scalp, and a dark smear had run down the right side of his face. Mrs. Galt was standing a few meters away, her hands clasped in front of her, looking uncharacteristically uncertain. There was no sign of Nathan.

Grace and Harding were both shouting, and neither turned in Walters' direction until he raised his own voice. "What the hell is going on here?" He stepped between them, glared at each in turn, and then they both resumed shouting at the same time. Walters gestured angrily and Harding fell silent, although Grace ran on for another few syllables before she ran out of breath.

"Miss Porter, would you please tell me what the problem is? Calmly and without raising your voice, if you don't mind?"

Her expression didn't soften, but she took a deep breath and spoke evenly, though with obvious suppressed fury. "I caught that man sneaking up to watch me while I was...engaged in some private business." Her eyes fell for a second, but almost undetectably. "It's not the first time he's tried to sneak a look when he shouldn't have!" She glanced at Sharon, who had arrived in Walters' wake. "Tell him about what we saw when we were swimming, why don't you?"

Walters glanced at Sharon, who dropped her eyes, not wanting to contribute to what was already an unpleasant scene. He must have read some inkling of the truth from her posture, because he turned quickly to Harding.

"What have you got to say for yourself, Ezra?"

Harding seemed to be caught somewhere between embarrassment and defiance. "I didn't mean no harm. I was just checking to see if the lady was all right. You said no one was supposed to go off on their own, and she did, so I was looking after her."

"I was just around there," Grace said indignantly, nodding toward the crevice that had become their makeshift latrine. "And he sneaked around so that he could watch me. I only noticed him because I thought I heard something and I turned around and looked." The memory obviously made her uncomfortable. "And besides, as I said, this wasn't the first time. Go ahead, tell him." The last was directed to Sharon, who felt her face grow warm.

"Do you have something to add, Miss Bartleby?" Sharon dropped her eyes, not knowing what to say. Walters spared her the ordeal by turning back to Harding. "All right, people. This is how it's going to be. Right now we need each other if we're going to stay alive and that means putting up with things we don't particularly like. So we're going to forget this little incident and go back to what we're supposed to be doing." He paused and turned to Ezra. "You, Ezra, will keep your eyes to yourself in the future and will stay away from the ladies – all of them – unless it is absolutely necessary. And you, Miss Foster, will put down that club and refrain from assaulting Harding or anyone else. Is that understood?"

There was more authority in his voice than he had ever displayed before, enough to penetrate even Grace's seemingly impervious armor. She didn't answer except with a barely visible nod, but she did lower her arm and drop the piece of wood.

Walters breathed a long sigh that was half exasperation, half relief. "All right, let's get back to work."

They uncovered three more skulls after only a few minutes of probing the mound, one of them that of a child, but no other bones. There was no obvious damage to any of them. "At least they didn't have their heads bashed in," Fields observed.

"But the placement suggests some sort of sacrifice." Rivers looked up at the six-limbed figure, whose face displayed no discernible expression. "This has got to have some kind of religious significance."

Fields stepped back, craning his head to look upwards. "There's something wrong here."

"That's kind of an understatement, don't you think?"

"No, I mean look at it. Doesn't it look kind of slapdash to you?"

Rivers took several steps backward to get a better perspective. Now that Fields mentioned it, the statue did seem unusually crude, particularly compared to what they'd seen before. The buildings might be crumbling with age and neglect, but they had been well constructed. "Okay, I see it. What do you suppose it means?"

"I don't know. But I get the feeling our handy friend here is a recent addition. Something they put up after their civilization began to decline, maybe, and they'd lost some of the skills of their ancestors."

Rivers glanced around. "That can't be. This is the central point for everything. The other buildings are arranged in circles around this spot."

Fields shrugged. "Maybe they tore down whatever was here before and replaced it with Franz here."

"Franz?"

"He looks a little like a kid I grew up with. Big, brutal, and not too bright."

"Okay, Franz he is." Rivers set down the skull he'd been examining. "What do you suppose happened to them?"

Fields shrugged. "An isolated society like this, it could be any of a number of things. A couple of years of famine, a new disease, or maybe just general decay. Their numbers may have been dropping for generations until they just reached a point where there weren't enough of them to carry on." Fields glanced toward the broken backed mountain. "But I'd guess that whatever happened to this island didn't help any. You've noticed the way the whole land mass is tilted, haven't you?"

"It looks like someone lifted one side and submerged the other. But it didn't happen all at once. There are younger trees growing out of the salt water in some places. That must have been dry land only a few years back."

"So the island is still sinking?"

"Looks like it. But at least it's going down slower than the *Sturtevant* did."

"So where did everyone go?"

Rivers glanced toward the jungle. "Maybe they're not gone. Maybe they've just moved back into the jungle."

Fields gave him a sharp look. "You think it might have been the natives who killed Abbott and Quinn?"

"I wouldn't rule it out. Animals usually don't do such an efficient job of covering their tracks."

"Point taken." Without thinking, Fields moved one hand closer to his pistol. "What now?"

"Let's get going. We have a lot of ground to cover if we want to get back before dark. And we do want to get back before dark."

They were less thorough examining buildings on the opposite side of the settlement. Although the lack of furnishings made it difficult to discern their function, they must have been primarily if not entirely residential. The internal architecture varied very little, one central room or corridor flanked by four to six smaller chambers. The sun was well past its highest point when they reached the far side and stopped beside a small stream, which provided relatively cool, fresh tasting water.

"How much farther do you want to go?" asked Fields.

Rivers wiped his forehead and looked around. "I wonder if we'll be able to see the opposite coast of the island from that ridge." The higher land ran like a rough wall from the left to right in front of them, gradually rising at the far right until it disappeared into the side of the canted volcanic cone.

"How long do you think it'll take us to get there?"

"Half an hour or so, another fifteen, twenty minutes to climb it."

"We'll have to shake a leg to get back on time."

"We can wait until tomorrow if you want."

Fields shook his head. "No, I'd like to know how big a cell we have to pace in. Let's go for it."

It took a little longer than Rivers had estimated. The ground began to slope upward as though they were climbing out of the bottom of a shallow bowl and the surface was rougher, with potholes, shattered fragments of rock, and treacherous patches of slippery sand that shifted under their feet. The ridge itself proved to be steeper than expected, and although they searched along several hundred meters of its length, they were unable to find anywhere that promised an easy ascent. Eventually they were forced to climb using both hands and feet, and Rivers banged his knee and Fields cut the palm of his right hand before they finally reached the summit.

The view beyond was breathtaking. As Rivers had guessed, it provided them with a panoramic view of one section of the opposite coast. Whitecaps smashed into a line of jagged rocks almost directly below them, at the foot of a cliff face that was clearly beyond their ability to descend. The daunting terrain extended for as far as they could see in both directions, although it was possible that more favorable conditions existed beyond the band of jungle that blocked their view to the west. The crumbled slope of the dead volcano looked as though, if anything, it became even more formidable a barrier.

"Well, we're not going down there, that's for certain."
Rivers shook his head and turned away, then sat down with his back
against a smooth surfaced rock.

Fields slid down to sit with his knees up and head back,
apparently out of breath. "I'm getting too old for this sort of thing."

Rivers laughed. "You're what? Thirty?"

"Thirty two on the outside. A lot older than that where you
can't see."

Not knowing how to respond to that, Rivers said nothing at
all. They sat quietly for several minutes, and it was Fields who
finally broke the silence.

"I guess we'd better be heading back."

They both knew they would have to hurry to reach the
temple before darkness, but by unspoken consent they walked along
the ridge a short way eastward toward the volcano, looking for an
easier place to descend. Fortunately they found one fairly quickly, a
stretch where a large section had collapsed providing a rough and
dangerous but negotiable downward slope. They picked up their
pace as soon as they hit level ground, but were forced to detour
around a stretch of treacherous looking bog they hadn't encountered
on the way out. This brought them even closer to the base of the
mountain, close enough for them to see that someone had carved an
elaborate staircase out of the stone, leading up from the grassy plain
until it disappeared where dark shadows cloaked the mountain's
skirt.

"Staircases usually lead some place," observed Rivers.

"Probably a cave," replied Fields. "Should we go look?"

Although the destruction of the lifeboat meant that they
would only have to keep a single fire going that night, their efforts
to replenish the fuel supply had not been remarkably successful.
This far from the jungle, only low brush and occasional stunted
trees grew, and the former burned too quickly while felling the
latter required tools they currently lacked. Unhappy with the initial
progress made by Harding and a subdued but still uncooperative
Nathan, Walters suggested that Grace and Sharon try looking closer
to the jungle.

"But I want you both to stay well away from the trees. Keep
a safe distance at all times and if you even think something is

wrong, come back immediately. I'll be along to check on you shortly."

Sharon suggested a more systematic search pattern and Grace cooperated and in fact gathered nearly as much as her partner. They began accumulating what they found in small piles at increasing distances from the temple, but in a line that approached the jungle obliquely. When they reached the farthest point from their encampment, they would start to reel in the line, moving the wood from the last pile to the next to the last, and so forth, until they were close enough that the others could come out and help gather it all in before darkness fell.

Since it was impractical for them to carry on a coherent conversation, each was left alone with her thoughts, and for the first time Sharon began to think about what it would like to be stranded here permanently or at least for years rather than days. There was always the chance of discovery and rescue, of course, but she interpreted the fact that Walters was not saying much on that subject as indicative of his pessimistic appraisal of their chances. They were already well off course when the storm hit, and would soon be officially overdue, so presumably someone would know that they were missing. She had no doubt that someone would come looking for them eventually, but that didn't mean that they would be looking in the right place. This was an uncharted island in a remote part of the ocean far from where they were meant to be. The search was likely to be perfunctory and unsuccessful.

So if they were stuck here, what were their chances of survival? There was fresh water and they had shelter, and if people had lived here in considerable numbers in the past, there must be a source of food sufficient for the eight of them. They wouldn't be comfortable, but theoretically they could survive. They could, that is, if they were allowed to do so. The one unknown factor in the equation was whatever had already killed two of their number, as well as the earlier landing party, and killed them without even revealing its nature.

Was it an animal or were they not alone here? Someone had built the temple. Maybe their children were still around, and maybe they objected to having outsiders squatting in their property.

She was carrying an armful of firewood back to their cache when Grace appeared, similarly laden, from the opposite direction. "Drop what you've got and come look. I found the mother lode."

Grace was looking inordinately pleased with herself, and now that her hair was falling loose rather than tightly coifed and her face was bare of makeup, she looked five years younger, barely more than a child. Sharon wondered about her own appearance and as soon as her hands were free, she pushed her hair back from her face and shook it out.

"Stop preening and come see!"

Grace led her up a gentle but considerable slope, at the crest of which they stood above a shallow ravine that stretched back all the way until it disappeared into the jungle. It was completely dry but had obviously been a watercourse at some time in the past, perhaps still functioned as such during the rainy season. It was heavily congested with uprooted trees and severed branches, some still bearing leaves although they had long since turned brown. The only greenery consisted of vines which snaked through the wrecked vegetation, appearing and disappearing along the length of the trench. They were predominantly the odd bluish green variety which they had noticed earlier. "There's enough here to last us for weeks!" said Grace enthusiastically.

"At least. This is great, Grace." The discovery didn't really cheer her very much, but she didn't want to spoil Grace's good mood. She'd been alternately irritable and sullen ever since the incident with Harding, but there were hints that a genuine person existed somewhere under all that pretense and haughtiness.

They began harvesting firewood together, working their way along one side, leaving questionable pieces that they would previously have gathered up. It only took a few minutes to accumulate enough to fill their arms and they made four trips back to add to their closest cache in less time that it had taken previously for one armload. While she was working on her fifth armful, Sharon spotted the animal.

It looked very much like a sloth, about eighteen inches long without the tail, and it was very obviously dead. The eyes were open and fixed, and a grayish tongue extended out of one side of its narrow jaws, lying flaccid and vaguely obscene. The corpse was tucked into an elbow of the vine and most of its body was concealed by the large, six pointed leaves. Curious, Sharon set down the wood she was carrying and moved closer. Very cautiously she reached out and pressed her fingers against the stalk of the plant, intending to push it up and away to give herself a better view. The surface of the vine felt very strange, almost as though it was covered with a layer of hair or very fine wires, and she turned her head to look at it just in time to see the supposedly inert plant react to her presence.

A section of the vine suddenly flexed, a movement that reminded her of a snake, and then snapped back toward her. As it did so, something thin and dark separated itself from the surface, and a sharp, burning pain made her draw her hand back quickly. "Damn it!" She retreated several steps, clutching her wounded arm. A bright line of blood extended almost the length of her forearm and began dripping onto the ground.

CHAPTER NINE

Both men were curious about where the steps might lead, but Fields glanced toward the sinking sun and sighed, and Rivers didn't need to be reminded that they were still a long way from shelter. "Next trip," he said aloud, and then he and Fields turned away, walking as quickly as they could down the slope in the general direction of the six limbed statue. The lengthening shadows stretching across the abandoned community were perfectly ordinary, but their imaginations were already beginning to evoke nebulous, threatening shapes..

By the time they reached the low point and had started up the opposite side, it seemed as though the sun had accelerated its decline. They began to alternate walking and jogging, and by the time they crested the rise, both men were breathing heavily. Neither suggested taking a break, even though both could have used one. Fields lost his footing once and had what could have been a very bad fall, but he got back to his feet immediately and shook his head when Rivers gave him a questioning look.

When they rounded the protruding tip of the jungle, they could see a faint glow in the distance. Walters and the others must have already built up the fire, perhaps to provide a beacon. The sun was completely gone now, just a pink glow indicating where it had disappeared, and full darkness would fall within minutes. There was no way that they could make it to the temple before then, so they were forced to stop long enough to fashion a pair of makeshift torches from broken branches with one end wound about with dried leaves and vines and used two of Rivers' matches to ignite them. Carrying the torches would slow them down, but it was too risky to continue without the protection of fire.

The most direct path back to the temple took them away from the fringes of jungle, but there were uneven patches where they had to concentrate on their footing. It was tedious and nerve wracking and they lost more time when they discovered their torches were burning more quickly than expected and had to find suitable materials to replace them. It was shortly after they had resumed their march that Rivers put one hand on Fields' arm.

"We're not alone." His voice was barely audible.

Fields nodded and they both stopped and stood back to back, raising their torches and moving them very slowly, trying to illuminate their surroundings. They had reached a flat section of sand and ankle high grass and except for a few stunted trees and a scattering of rounded stones none of which were as much as a meter high, there was no cover for a considerable distance in every direction.

"I don't see anything," said Fields.

"Doesn't mean they're not out there."

"So what do you want to do?"

"Let's keep moving, but don't lose that pistol of yours."

They had only gone another hundred paces or so when Fields came to an abrupt halt. Rivers instinctively moved to cover his back. "I think I saw something move," Fields whispered. "Something big."

When Grace saw the blood, she pressed both hands to her mouth and turned away, and Sharon felt a fleeting moment of contempt. It wasn't the first time she had cut herself; cuts and bruises were a fact of life on a farm. The wound didn't hurt particularly, but it was bleeding profusely, even when she pressed down hard. She opened her hand for a second to assess the damage. The thorn had punctured her flesh cleanly but the wound had been torn open for an inch or two when she pulled back.

"Grace, I need your help."

"I'll run and get someone. We're not that far away."

"No, you will not run and get someone. You're going to help me stop the bleeding and you're going to help me right now." She was speaking firmly and calmly, but a sudden wave of dizziness caused her to sway slightly. Furious, she told herself to stop acting like a silly girl. That was Grace's job.

"What...what do you want me to do?"

"I want you to take off my belt and tie it around my arm. Once we have the bleeding stopped, we can go back to the others and use the first aid kit."

"I don't know if I can do that." Grace still had her face averted and took a step away from Sharon.

"Don't be ridiculous! Of course you can do it." Sharon was beginning to feel light headed. Was she going into shock? She hadn't lost that much blood. "Do you really want Captain Rivers and the others to think you're just an hysterical girl?"

That seemed to strike the right note, because Grace raised her head and turned back, even took a cautious step forward.

"Come on," Sharon said soothingly. "It's not that hard. You just have to tie the belt around my arm so the bleeding stops and then we'll walk back together." Grace nodded, took a deep breath, and started to move.

It wasn't the neatest or most efficient job, but Grace managed to fasten the belt as instructed, and didn't falter even when a spurt of Sharon's blood landed on the back of her hand. They couldn't get the bleeding to stop completely, but it slowed considerably, and by then Sharon was feeling so faint that she didn't dare delay any longer to adjust the makeshift tourniquet. "I'm a little unsteady, Grace, so you'll have to take my arm. The other one."

They started back toward the temple, and after every third or fourth step, a small drop of blood fell to the ground beneath them.

Sharon never quite passed out during the nightmarish walk back to the temple. When they were close enough Grace began shouting for help, and after what seemed an eternity, Walters and Harding came out to meet them. Sharon saw their faces blurrily and didn't recognize them until Walters spoke, and then she finally did faint, slipping out of Grace's grasp and crumpling to the ground. That was the last thing she knew for a while.

Harding carried her back to the temple while Grace told Walters as much as she knew about what had happened. They laid her down outside where the light was better and Mrs. Galt brought out the first aid kit. "I'll see to this. My mother was a nurse and she taught all of us children how to tend to a wound."

Sharon was pale but didn't appear feverish, and the wound itself appeared to be clean. Mrs. Galt didn't trust appearances, however, and proceeded to thoroughly and methodically apply antiseptic. She was puzzled by the profuse bleeding but knew that it would help flush away any foreign matter, and when she finally stitched and bandaged and wrapped the arm, she felt satisfied that she had done all that could be done.

"How is she?" asked Walters, who had been looking on throughout the process but who had not spoken until now.

"As well as can be expected. She'll need to rest. How did it happen?"

"We don't know. Miss Porter wasn't with her at the time. Some kind of animal bite maybe?"

"That's no animal bite. It's a puncture and tear, like you'd get if you fell on an old board and had a nail stick you. I've cleaned it out and closed it up. She should be all right if there's no infection I missed. I don't understand why she's unconscious though. She didn't lose that much blood, and Sharon is a strong girl."

"It's probably better if she sleeps a while."

"Yes, if it's a normal sleep." She leaned over and lifted one of the unconscious girl's eyelids. "But look at her pupil. I'd say she's been drugged."

Rivers and Fields stood straining with all their senses, but there was no sound that didn't belong, and the shifting of shadows at the limit of their circle of light was too faint to identify.

"We have to keep moving," Rivers said at last. "These torches won't last forever."

"How much further do you think?"

"Less than half an hour in daylight. Maybe twice that now."

"We're going to need more torches."

Rivers was about to agree, but suddenly had a moment of inspiration. "Stay with me. I've got an idea."

Although they didn't see or hear anything, both men sensed that they were being watched. They moved slowly and carefully, not wanting to risk a slip and fall, at a slight angle away from their original route. Fields hadn't asked what Rivers intended, but he did finally speak in a hoarse whisper. "I'm going to be running out of fire pretty soon now."

"Just a few more steps."

A few paces ahead of them, a good sized tree had been snapped in half by some storm in seasons past. Next to a truncated trunk the bulk of its twenty foot length lay on the sand, slowly rotting away.

"I've got a new torch for us," said Rivers, lowering his own and pressing it into the tangled branches.

The dead tree caught fire quickly, so quickly in fact that the two men were forced to retreat a few steps to keep from being singed. Fields was still looking back the way they had come and he gave a shout of satisfaction. "There IS something out there. I knew it."

Rivers turned to look where he was pointing, but apparently too late. "I don't see anything."

"It's gone now. I didn't get a good look at it but it's big and it wasn't anything human. Some kind of animal, but a big one. It was down on all fours, like a wolf maybe, but the biggest one I ever saw. It was only visible for a second and it was moving away. I think there were a couple more of them further off, but that might have been a trick of the light."

"Well, as long as they're running away from us rather than toward us, I'm happy."

They made up four more torches and lit two of them while the fire spread and engulfed the entire tree. It was throwing off a great deal of heat and light, but was burning so quickly that they knew its protection wouldn't last. The other fire, the one at the temple, was sending sparks high into the air now, a welcome beacon. The others must have seen the burning tree, interpreted it correctly, and were doing their best to help.

"The ground is smoother from here on," said Rivers. "We should be able to make better time."

"Then let's get moving." Fields sounded more confident, but he still had the pistol ready in his free hand.

Harding and Nathan both went with Grace to bring in the accumulated firewood, while Mrs.Galt sat with Sharon. When the sun began to lower, she attempted to rouse the unconscious girl, but Sharon was so groggy that Walters had to help move her inside the temple, and she fell asleep again almost the moment she lay down. Although she had no fever, her pulse was lower than usual and Mrs. Galt left her long enough to brew some strong tea.

"I want to get a stimulant into her as soon as possible, Mr. Walters. This isn't a natural sleep."

"I'll leave that in your hands, Mrs. Galt. I'm afraid we may have another problem. The sun is starting to go down and there's no sign of Rivers or Fields."

"I have every confidence in Captain Rivers. I'm sure they're all right." But she wasn't sure whether she was reassuring Walters, or herself.

The light faded slowly but it didn't seem that way to Walters. He was standing on a broken column, staring into the distance, when Grace Porter came out of the temple, followed almost immediately by her brother. "Any sign of them?"

Walters shook his head, barely visible in the gloom. "Not yet. I thought I saw a speck that might have been a fire, but it was gone so quickly. I just don't know."

"We shouldn't have split up like this anyway," said Nathan, with just the faintest hint of a whine. His mood had not improved since his rescue the night before. "What if we're attacked while they're gone?"

"We have to know more about our situation, Mr. Porter," Walters answered calmly. "The food we have won't last much longer and we need to find a place for a permanent camp."

"What about this?" Nathan spread his arms to indicate the temple and its environs. "We have shelter here. We can hunt in the jungle. There must be some kind of animal life, and fruits and berries, whatever it is that people stranded on islands eat."

Walters closed his eyes, waited until he was sure he could trust his voice. "We're too exposed here. Reverend Abbott disappeared only a few feet from where you're standing," he'd almost said "died". "We have fresh water but we don't have a food source and we'll use up the nearby firewood very quickly. This may turn out to be our best bet, but if there's a more suitable site elsewhere, we need to know about it, and as quickly as possible."

While he'd been talking, Grace had climbed up onto a rocky perch of her own. She was turning slowly, surveying the horizon, when she stopped. "What's that over there? Is that a light?"

Walters turned to look and Nathan even deigned to show sufficient interest to climb up beside his sister. It was very faint and it seemed to flicker and die from moment to moment, but the tiny glowing point in the distance certainly could have been a small fire. "They'll have made themselves torches," said Walters. "I think that's them."

"Why aren't they moving?" asked Nathan.

"They probably are. If they're headed straight toward us, we wouldn't be able to tell."

Mrs. Galt appeared a moment later. "Mr. Walters, she's awake."

"How is she doing?"

"Better, I think. Her head's clearer, but she's very weak. The arm is a little bit uncomfortable, but I just changed the dressing. There's no swelling or discoloration."

"I'm glad to hear it. Where's Harding?" He glanced around, the question meant generally. He hadn't seen his former crewmate for at least half an hour.

"He's sleeping. Do you want me to wake him up?"

"No, let him rest while he can, Mrs. Galt. He'll take second watch tonight."

Grace, who had been staring intently out into the darkness, suddenly became animated. "They're moving! And there are two of them. They're very close together, but if you watch you can see the light split in two sometimes."

Walters felt considerably relieved, although the two men were still too far away for his liking. It was almost completely dark now and they had a long way remaining before they were back.

"Should we send someone out to meet them?" asked Mrs. Galt.

"No. We'd just increase the danger. I think we should build the fire up a little, thought, to light their way." He didn't really think it would help the two men, but it would give the others the feeling that they were contributing something.

Mrs. Galt went back inside to look after Sharon and Nathan wandered off as well, without bothering to give an explanation. Walters and Grace stood silently, only an arm's length apart, watching the slow progress until their vision blurred and they had to look away. From this distance, it appeared that the two men were moving very slowly, but he had no doubt they were making the best time they could.

Half an hour later, Grace broke a long silence. "I think they've stopped."

Walters had squatted down and was resting his eyes, but he stood up immediately and quickly located their distant light. It was hard to tell but he thought she might be right. "Maybe they needed to rest."

"Would you?" Grace was openly skeptical.

"No, I guess not. We'll just have to wait and see what happens."

What happened was spectacular even from a distance. The light began to grow, slowly at first, then leaped skyward, shooting sparks, then spread horizontally. "They've started a fire, a big one." He began to massage his jaw, a habit which he believed helped him to think more clearly.

"Why would they do that?"

"I have no idea, Miss Porter, but I imagine they have a good reason." He was silent for a moment. "Watch for them to move away from the fire. I'm going to throw some more wood on ours." He jumped down and began adding a new layer of branches all around the perimeter of the already healthy blaze, jumping back from time to time when sparks exploded from the suddenly ignited wood.

The wait after that seemed endless, even though it lasted only about twenty minutes. When the two men finally reached the temple, Walters had to resist the temptation to rush over and throw his arms around one or the other. Grace felt no similar need for restraint and was soon embracing a tired and mildly embarrassed Jerry Rivers, while Fields looked on with considerable amusement.

"What happened?" asked Walters.

"The return trip took a little longer than we expected, but we did make it to the far side of the island, and we found a few surprises along the way."

"And we also had company for part of the trip," added Fields.

Walters raised an eyebrow. "Company?"

"We didn't see them clearly," explained Rivers. He glanced at Fields, whose face was neutral, and added, "but there's a good chance they were the same things that got Abbott and Quinn."

"Some kind of animal?" asked Grace.

Rivers and Fields exchanged looks again before Rivers answered. "They looked like wolves or big cats. We also found the ruins of a good sized town. It looks like whoever lived there has been gone a long time."

Mrs. Galt had heard their voices and came out to greet them. She brought some of the ration packs with her and the two men ate in fits and starts while they described what they had seen. When they were done, Walters asked if they thought one of the buildings in the town might be safer than the temple, but neither man was ready to commit themselves.

"We need to look them over more thoroughly before deciding that," said Fields. "They're smaller but some of them are in pretty good shape and they might be easier to defend."

Rivers glanced around. "Where are the others?"

That led to a recounting of Sharon's injury. "She seems to be doing well now," Mrs. Galt reassured him. "But she'll probably be weak for a couple of days. And we'll have to find out exactly how she was injured so that it doesn't happen to any of the rest of us."

Fields went off to sleep almost as soon as he was through eating, and Rivers wasn't far behind, although he did look in on Sharon first. Now that it was over with, the exertions of the day caught up to him quickly and he felt exhausted. Nathan was theoretically taking the first watch, but Walters intended to keep an eye out as well, at least until Harding took over. He was determined that the younger man should assume his share of the responsibilities for the group, but was reluctant to rely on him. Nathan's composure had deteriorated steadily ever since Quinn's death, and Walters didn't need to be a psychologist to know that Nathan's account of that incident had not been entirely accurate.

He also looked in on Sharon, who was sleepy but apparently otherwise alert. She insisted that she was comfortable and apologized for causing so much trouble. When he asked how she had hurt herself, she seemed confused.

"We found a ravine filled with dead wood and some of that strange vine was growing there. You know, the one with the odd bluish green coloring. I had just touched it when something moved and either I snagged myself on a thorn or something bit me. It hurt like the devil and started bleeding so quickly that I didn't have time to investigate."

"Don't worry about it, miss. The important thing is that you're all right. When we have a chance, we'll look into it. You just rest now."

"All right, thank you." She closed her eyes, but opened them almost immediately. "One thing I did notice, or at least I think I did."

"What's that?"

"I know this sounds crazy but I think the vine moved by itself. I think it was reacting to my touch." His face must have betrayed his skepticism because she shook her head. "Yes, I know how unlikely that is, but there are plants that react to touch. My mother used to have a Venus Fly-Trap in her greenhouse."

"It's certainly possible," he reassured her. "In any case, we'll look into it later. You just get some rest."

Nathan was sitting by the fire, idly adding wood from time to time. Walters would have preferred him to have been more actively alert, but as long as he kept the fire going and stayed awake, it was unlikely that anything could reach the temple entrance undetected. They had cleared away more of the rubble during the day and the immediate vicinity of the entrance was now devoid of any significant cover all the way to the hump of rock behind which Abbott had died. The breeze carried the stink of their latrine toward the temple but it was mostly overpowered by the acrid wood smoke. If they were forced to remain where they were, they would have to make other arrangements.

"If you're not going to sleep, there's no point in both of us staying up." Nathan's voice was low and he didn't look at Walters when he spoke.

"I just want to take a final look around. I have third watch."

"I don't see why we don't just block the doorway at night. It's hot enough without keeping a fire going all day and all night."

"It's stuffy enough inside as it is. And I don't relish the thought of climbing out of a hole every morning to see what's waiting for us."

"Whatever's out there doesn't show itself in the daylight. We'd be safe enough."

"Hasn't shown itself in the daylight doesn't mean it won't change its habits in the future. There are enough of us to keep watch."

"Whatever."

Walters suppressed the urge to snap out a critical remark. He had spent years catering to the often childish whims of passengers without losing his temper and their altered circumstances had not yet broken down his inhibition. It was best to keep things as amicable as possible, he told himself, but he also made a mental note that Nathan Porter bore close watching. He felt a sudden sense of his own inadequacy. He'd already lost two people under his care, and another one lay injured. Nathan was almost openly rebellious, and he was still disturbed by the incident involving Harding. He'd been cast adrift in an open boat once before, but they'd been picked up at sea after only a few days. There hadn't been time for the usual societal restraints to slip in that case, but now they seemed to be coming loose all at once. And although he pretended optimism in front of the passengers, he knew that their chances of rescue – at least in the short term – were very slim indeed.

Suddenly feeling very weary, he went into the temple and made himself comfortable just inside the entrance, leaning back against the wall. He wasn't sure if he could sleep yet, but at least he could rest.

Nathan Porter had not slept well the night before, and his frequent naps during the day hadn't done much to remedy matters. It was not fatigue that sapped his energy but a growing sense that they were doomed, and a deeper feeling that he had been responsible for Quinn's death. He'd been troubled by dreams, dreams in which Michael Quinn often appeared, never saying anything, but always staring at him accusingly. Sometimes the steward seemed perfectly fine; at other times he was drenched in blood. Alternately he dreamed that he was running along the beach, or swimming through the water, and that he was being pursued by something he never clearly saw, something monstrous and menacing that was always coming closer although it never quite caught up.

Awake, he told himself that he was being foolish. He was not responsible for Quinn's death. Nathan had not asked him to risk himself, had gone off on his own. Quinn should have stayed by the fire as he'd been told. If he had done so, he would still be alive. Nathan had been all right, after all. He'd been in the water and Quinn's killer, whatever it was, hadn't ventured in after him. He was a survivor and Quinn was not. That's the way it was. Some people were meant to live and some were meant to die. It was a fact of life and those who tried to alter their fate or that of others were doomed to failure and frustration.

He had pursued the same line of reasoning several times and could find no flaw in it. It always reassured and cheered him when he reached the logical conclusion, but his mood never lasted and he found himself churning through the same questions again and again. Frustrated with himself, perversely angry with Quinn, he threw a piece of wood onto the fire so forcefully that a flurry of sparks rose into the air with a sharp popping sound. One blazing forked branch toppled from the opposite side and slid across the rock hard ground, coming to rest almost a meter from the main fire.

Swearing under his breath, Nathan climbed to his feet, brushed off his pants, and walked around the perimeter of the blazing wood. When he reached the wayward branch, he tried to kick it back the way it had come, but it defied him and flew away at an unexpected angle, back toward the temple wall. More annoyed than ever, he went after it. As he leaned down, intending to pick it up by the portion not yet alight, movement attracted his attention..

Something small and dark moved at the edge of the light, hidden in the flickering shadows.

"What the hell?" Nathan picked up the burning branch, took one step forward and raised his misshapen torch. The circle of light expanded quickly, and once again something small and dark scurried away. Interested but not yet alarmed, Nathan returned to where he had been sitting and exchanged the burning branch for one of the torches, holding it in the flames just long enough to set it alight.

Then he went to investigate.

Walters had thought he was too worked up to sleep, but he had been wrong. Only a few minutes after sitting down, his eyes closed and his head fell forward. His dreams were more peaceful than Nathan's. He was back home, or what had once been his home, a cottage on the coast in Southern California. His wife was standing in the garden. Mary had loved working with the soil. She had grown most of the vegetables they ate and there were always flowers in bloom. Walters had worked on a coastal freighter then, smaller than the *Sturtevant* but in better condition. He was never gone for more than a few days at a time, and the pay had been pretty good. They had been talking about starting a family. But then came the sickness and the long stay in the hospital and when it was over, he had not been able to look at the house or the garden without seeing her. It had been too much for him and he had sold it all and signed on when Captain Corrigan advertised for a crew to work the Asian market with him. He had tried to leave all the old memories behind, but they lingered in his dreams as vividly as ever.

The dream enfolded him so closely that he was considerably disoriented when someone shook his arm violently, shouting unintelligibly. He reached up and caught the other's arm, his eyes focusing slowly. "Mr. Porter? What is it? What's wrong?"

There was more animation in the young man's face than he had ever seen before. Nathan took a deep breath, but his voice still crackled with tension. "You have to come see this right now, Walters. I think we may have a problem."

Someone emerged from one of the inner chambers, rubbing his arms and shaking his head. "What's going on out here?" It was Rivers, and a moment later Harding, Fields, and Mrs. Galt had all joined them, all asking the same question.

"If you'll all just be quiet for a minute, I'll tell you." Nathan's voice was tinged with hysteria.

"What is it then?" asked Walters, who was now standing. "What's going on?"

Nathan glanced around nervously. "You'd better all come outside. I think we're being attacked."

CHAPTER TEN

Nathan refused to answer their questions, insisting that they had to "come see" for themselves. As they stepped outside, he urged them to take lighted faggots from the fire. "They shy away from the light, but they don't go far."

Half a dozen steps from the entrance, he pointed his own torch at a small dark mass on the ground. "I stomped on that one. The first time it was like standing on a stone, but I broke the shell eventually. It still kept moving but not as fast after that."

Several of the party crouched and Rivers poked at it with his flaming stick. A sticky fluid burst into smoky flame that guttered out almost immediately. "What is it? Some kind of crab?"

It was hard to tell because Nathan had destroyed most of its features in the process of killing it, but there was a rough surfaced, hard shell that was approximately circular and six limbs, although its claws split into three parts rather than two. The body measured about two inches across. When Rivers pushed it over onto its back, his frown deepened. Instead of the smooth bottom plate he'd expected, the underside was covered with curved hooks ending in sharp points. "Do you suppose this is what attacked Sharon?"

"No," Mrs. Galt answered immediately. "Not unless they get much bigger than that. Her puncture wound was deeper."

"This way," Nathan called impatiently. "There are more of them."

Sure enough, a second mangled body lay only a few steps away, and beyond that another. "I killed six of them before I reached the corner," he explained. "They were all headed straight toward the fire."

"That doesn't make sense," said Fields. "Not if they're afraid of the light."

Nathan was in the lead, and he stopped abruptly. "There! Look!" Ahead of him, another of the crab creatures appeared at the limits of their light. But this one was moving. "There weren't any on this side of the building when I went to get you. They're still coming this way. Follow me."

He stooped and swung his torch at the newcomer and it skittered away with surprising quickness. They could hear its claws clicking on the hard ground. The sound stopped as soon as it was beyond the light.

Nathan advanced slowly, swinging his torch back and forth. A second crab appeared and ran off as quickly as had the first, and a third came around the corner just as they reached the end of the front wall. This one froze for a second, giving them a closer look at what for lack of a better word Rivers thought of as its face. It projected out of the point where the upper shell met the lower plate, and looked more like the head of a turtle than a crab. There were two powerful looking jaws surrounding by a fringe of tiny cilia that seemed to move with a life of their own, as though tasting the air. There was no sign of anything that might have been eyes.

Nathan brought his foot down hard. There was an audible snap as the shell burst, but when he lifted his foot, the creature still managed to scrabble away from the light. He leaped this time, came down heel first, and this time the only movement was reflexive jerking of the legs. "You have to move fast or they hide in the shadows. As soon as you take the light away, they come right back."

"If they won't come any closer to the fire, we're still all right," said Walters. "We haven't seen any around before so I don't think we'll see them once the sun comes up."

"Wait! You need to see the rest." Nathan waved the group forward with such energy that Walters didn't argue.

Once they were past the far end of the building, they understood Nathan's excitement. A line of the creatures, at intervals ranging from one foot to one meter, extended off as far as their light would reach. "Now watch this!" Nathan cocked his arm and threw his torch arching through the air. It hit the ground, throwing sparks in every direction, and slid another few feet before coming to a stop, burning steadily. This almost doubled the distance they could see, and the line of crabs continued through and beyond, disappearing once more into the night.

"Where are they coming from?"

"I bet I know." The voice surprised them because it was Grace, who had caught up to them unnoticed from behind. She pushed past them to the front of the group, staring off into the night. "That's the path Sharon and I took when we went looking for firewood today. They've followed us back."

Rivers was about to argue the point, but Mrs. Galt forestalled him. "They followed the blood trail. Sharon was bleeding profusely. It was so hard to stop the bleeding that I wondered if the drug that made her so sleepy mightn't have included some kind of anticoagulant. They can sense it somehow, maybe smell it."

"So how do we discourage them from coming this way," asked Walters. "Can we could build some kind of wall across their path."

"They'd just climb over it or go around it." The creatures had all scurried away from the light except for one that stolidly continued in their direction. Rivers took a step forward and kicked it, sending it flying into the shadows. "And I wouldn't trust the light to keep them away either, not permanently."

"What about laying an alternate blood trail?" asked Fields. "Send them off on a wild goose chase."

Rivers shook his head. "I don't know if that would work. We'd have to completely eradicate the old one first. And what if it isn't the blood but something mixed in the blood, whatever kind of drug it is, that they're following?"

"Sharon has lost enough blood already," said Mrs. Galt huffily. "I don't think we can expect her to give us more to experiment with."

"Nor would we ask her to," said Walters. "But I think we need to build a second fire on this side of entrance. That may discourage them and at least it will narrow the path they have to follow. Whoever is on watch will have to take care of the braver ones." He glanced at Nathan's feet. "Perhaps dropping large stones on them will prove more efficient than stamping them to death. Or kicking them into the fire."

Even as they spoke, two of the crabs had ventured out into the light again, staying near the edge but moving parallel to their original path. The distant torch was burning out quickly, and it didn't require much imagination to think about what lay beyond.

"This might be a temporary problem," said Rivers. "As soon as the scent wears off, they won't have any way of finding us."

"Unless they have memories." Fields picked up a small stone and threw it at one of the visible crabs, but he missed. "And can communicate with each other."

It only took a few minutes to build a new fire and Walters suggested that everyone go back to sleep, but only Grace and Harding did so. The others were too animated to rest right away and sat around talking. Fields went off by himself, although only as far as the corner of the building and never out of the sight of the others, and eventually came back with one of the creatures trapped between two stout sticks. Its legs continued to move frantically but the oddly shaped head had been retracted inside.

"Heavy little guy, this one," said Fields, holding it near to the fire and slowly turning it so that he could examine the details of its external body. "Those things on the underside are flexible. It caught hold of one of these sticks and it's not letting go."

"Be careful," cautioned Walters. "We don't know what they might be capable of."

"I don't think it's going to spit poison at me, but I see your point. Let's find out how it responds to fire at close hand." He twisted his arms and dropped his captive right on the outer edge of the fire.

It reacted even before it struck the ground, twisting its body around as though it had some sort of internal gyroscope. When it landed, it was right side up and the legs were already moving, carrying it out of sight so quickly that it caught them all by surprise.

"Well, they're even faster than we thought." Fields didn't sound pleased with his discovery. "At least with the proper motivation."

All but Walters had drifted off to bed by the time Nathan's shift ended. Harding appeared without having to be wakened, silently nodding as he took his post. Only one of the crabs had tried to negotiate the passage between the two fires, and Nathan had dropped a flat rock on it and then stood on top of it for good measure. Walters returned to his spot just inside the entranceway, settled down, and this time almost instantly fell asleep.

The seaman's internal clock is as reliable as any mechanical contrivance and Walters raised his head only moments before he was due to relieve Harding and take the last watch. He stood up slowly, unkinking his muscles, and told himself he was getting much too old for this kind of life. It was time to return to the land, even if that meant wrestling with memories that had been too painful for him in the past.

Harding was in the same position he'd first taken up his watch, as though he hadn't moved once during the four hours he'd been on duty, but he was alert and stood up as soon as Walters emerged.

"Any problems?"

Harding shrugged an answer, then decided to elaborate. "Heard them moving out there somewhere, but they stayed clear of the fires." Both of which were neatly tended and burning crisply.

"All right, get yourself some sleep. We have a lot to do tomorrow."

Harding acknowledged that with what might have been a nod but which was so faint that it might have been nothing at all. Walters had worked with Harding for more than six years, but he suddenly realized he didn't know the man at all. They'd never even had a companionable drink together, and as far as he could remember, Harding had never chummed around with any of the others aboard. He watched him appraisingly as he disappeared into the temple, vaguely troubled.

He felt no inclination to sit down again just yet, so he added a couple of unnecessary pieces of wood to each fire. The purr of the flames was loud enough to drown out any slight noises from outside the encampment, but twice he thought he heard what might have been tiny claws scraping across stone. On both occasions he paused, listening intently, and then searched the immediate area almost to the limit of the firelight, but on neither occasion did he see any sign of an intruder.

He sat down and tried to map out a plan for the coming day. Food was his primary worry at the moment. They had supplies enough for two or three more days, but they had yet to find anything on the island that they could eat. It might be possible to fish from the shoreline, and they would certainly have to look into that, but sooner or later they would have to investigate the jungle. It would also be advisable to evaluate the ruins the two scouts had located today, and possibly even the cave. Given tonight's unwelcome visitors, relocating made more sense. Walters tried to divide the party up in his mind into two groups so that he could address both problems, then fretted over his lack of resources. Fields and Rivers both seemed reliable, and Harding could probably be counted on as well, but he didn't trust Nathan. Mrs. Galt was more resourceful than he'd expected, but her physical limitations limited her usefulness. Sharon seemed a real trooper, but she would be questionable until her strength returned. Grace was more problematic. Her vacillation between spoiled child and responsible adult made her too unpredictable to be trustworthy.

Frustrated, he tried to stop worrying about it. He stood up and checked the fire, adding another few pieces of wood. A long brand fell off the opposite side, burning at one end, and he walked around and picked it up, but hesitated before throwing it back in. Instead he raised it to shoulder level, having decided to see whether or not the crabs had retreated after being frustrated in their pursuit of the blood trail. He had taken only a few steps in that direction, however, before he heard a low sound from ahead and to his left. Walters froze immediately, straining to hear, but the sound died away quickly.

Not so quickly that he didn't have a good idea what it was.

Very slowly, he raised the burning branch higher. The sound repeated itself, softer and ending more quickly. He took another step forward with the same results. "Damn me!" he whispered aloud, then took three quick steps. This time he was too fast for them.

Perhaps two hundred of the crab creatures were arranged in a semi-circle facing him, standing packed tightly together just outside the circle of illumination. They began to retreat again as the light from his makeshift torch fell on them, but then stopped abruptly, as though realizing that they'd been discovered and that there was no point in scuttling off into concealment. Walters froze, facing them, and felt his mouth go dry.

The standoff lasted for a minute, then another. Walters slowly began to lower his arm, and as he did so, there was the clicking of claws again as the host advanced to retake the ground they'd ceded to him. His arm started back up and they halted, but they didn't back away this time.

Nervously, Walters glanced behind him, as if he expected them to have sent a contingent around to the rear to cut off his retreat. The ground was clear, however, and he retreated a step. The clicking resumed.

Suddenly angry as well as unnerved, he fell back quickly to the nearest fire, then tossed the flaming branch out into the darkness. It landed near where he'd been standing, and this time they did fall back, climbing over one another in their haste to get away from the flames. That helped restore his confidence, and he pulled another faggot from the fire, singing the hair on the back of one hand as he did so. He threw this one approximately the same distance, but slightly to one side of the first. When it fell, spitting sparks, there was another flurry of movement.

Reassured, he began taking fresh wood from the stockpile, holding each piece in the fire until one end was burning well, then tossing it out into the darkness, successive throws describing a progressively wider arc. By the time he had completed the semicircle, some of the first few were burning down, so he replaced them with fresh pieces. Still not satisfied, he began carrying burning brands to his new perimeter and tossing them out even further. The clicking was almost continuous now, and it was perhaps his imagination that made him think they sounded increasingly angry. Twice he wound up his arm and threw burning missiles as far as he could, out past the corner of the temple, and on both occasions he was afforded brief glimpses of hordes of shelled creatures moving frantically to safety. There must have been hundreds of them by now, perhaps thousands.

He fell into a routine, replacing charred pieces with fresh ones, maintaining a double perimeter. After a while he wasn't even thinking about what he was doing, and he was only dimly aware that he had depleted their stockpile considerably more than seemed possible. He had allowed the two main fires to burn lower, although they still crackled healthily, and the surrounding area was littered with charred nubs and drifting ash by the time the first light of dawn began to dispel the gloom. He stopped then and looked around, and to his surprise, found that the besieging army had decamped during the night, that he had been flinging his flaming missiles unnecessarily for some time.

His legs were shaky as he walked to the corner once again, looking back along the path they'd been using, but for as far as he could see, there was no sign of the enemy. They had abandoned the field completely.

Rivers was the first one up, but the others followed fairly quickly, even Sharon, who seemed a bit shaky but whose color had improved during the night. "Freddie is a good nurse," she explained, but Mrs. Galt demurred.

"Young people bounce back quickly. If it had been me lying there yesterday, you wouldn't get me out of bed for a week."

Even Nathan seemed in better spirits, and Grace actually helped prepare their plain but welcome breakfast. Walters had to explain the mess he'd made during the night, twice in fact, and that dampened spirits a little.

"Do you think they're gone for good?" asked Mrs. Galt.

"I have no idea, but I do think we should seriously consider relocating to one of the other buildings. Scavengers tend to have long memories."

"Won't that make it harder to find us? Rescuers I mean," said Nathan querulously. "We'll be farther from the shore. If a boat comes past, we'd never even see it."

"At this point, we're more likely to be spotted from the air than the sea," explained Walters. "We can pile up some rocks, make an SOS on the beach if you'd like. But as long as we keep a fire going, anyone flying over will know that someone is here and they'll investigate."

"Well, if we're going to move, we ought to get started as soon as possible, shouldn't we?" Rivers phrased it as a question, looking directly at Walters, and it was clear he was making certain no one thought he was challenging the latter's authority.

Walters nodded, recognizing and appreciating the gesture. "I think that's best. We can leave the two large water casks here until later since there's a fresh stream where we're going. We also need to start thinking about foraging for ourselves. Mr. Rivers informs us that there is some game where we're going, but we need to find a wider range than that."

Harding hadn't spoken since rising, but he did now. "How about them crabs? There's plenty of them around. I like crab meat just fine."

The rest of the company showed varying degrees of distaste, but Walters took the suggestions seriously. "That's a possibility, Ezra. We'll have to try to trap one of them."

But no one looked very happy at the prospect.

It was Rivers who suggested that one other matter needed attention. "Someone ought to go look at that place where Sharon was injured. It might be important to know just what happened there."

Walters was impatient to be gone, but he gave a reluctant nod. "All right, why don't you take care of that while we're getting the supplies ready." He glanced around. "Mr. Porter, I'd like you to go with him."

Nathan was clearly surprised, and just as clearly displeased. "Why me?"

"Because he can't go alone and you can be spared." His contempt for the younger man was thinly masked this time and the tension level went up a notch.

For a few seconds, it seemed Nathan would balk, but instead he smiled, not pleasantly, and stood up, sketching a hasty salute. "Yes, sir. Whatever you say, sir."

Insulted or not, Nathan's attitude improved once they were away from the camp, and he even made some small talk with Rivers, who responded minimally, lost in his own thoughts. They kept watch for the crabs, but there was no sign of them except for one empty shell lying along the path. Rivers crouched and poked at it with a twig. "It's fresh but scoured clean. Must have been an injured one, killed and eaten by his friends."

"We may have to do the same," said Nathan lightly. "Eat the crabs, I mean. Not our friends."

Rivers decided not to respond. He stood up, shaded his eyes with one hand. "Your sister said we need to watch for a rock shaped like a heart and turn right. Let's get moving."

They found the ravine with no difficulty, and it was exactly as it had been described to them. Rivers stood on the rim, looking down thoughtfully, then caught Nathan by the arm when the younger man made as if to climb down. "Wait. Let's be cautious until we know what we're dealing with."

He looked around until he found a dead branch long enough for his purposes. Once he had both feet planted securely, he told Nathan to watch closely and began probing the tangle of dead wood and living vine below. He could feel the tension in the back of his neck, but when repeated probing failed to generate any reaction, he allowed himself to relax slightly.

"No sign of life?"

Nathan returned his glance with a negative head shake. "Maybe whatever was in there is gone now. Some kind of animal or even a big insect."

"Could be." Rivers crouched and let the branch rest against the bluish green vine, pushing it slightly so that he could look under it. As he did so, something struck the end of the branch so violently that he almost lost his grip. "Well, that was interesting."

He pushed the vine again, and again the end of the pole was batted to the side. "Can you see what's going on?"

"No, nothing." Nathan sounded puzzled, began to move to his right, trying to get a better angle. "It looks like somewhat swatted the end away."

"Felt like it too. Let's try again." He pushed harder this time, and got a much more violent reaction. Like some gigantic serpent, that entire section of the vine twisted, and this time the branch was almost knocked from his grasp. "What the hell is it?"

"I saw it!" Nathan sounded elated. "It came right out of the side of the vine. It looks like a barb or a thorn, but it's three of four inches long."

Nathan took the branch and repeated the experiment while Rivers watched, and now that he knew what to look for, he spotted it right away. "I'll be damned," he whistled softly. "I'll bet that vine just sits there until some animal comes and brushes against it, then jabs it. If it isn't killed outright, it's so drugged that it can't go far."

"But how does that help the vine? It doesn't have a mouth or anything."

"I don't know. My guess is it has some kind of symbiotic relationship with the crabs. They're probably hidden in there, in the darkness. Maybe they eat whatever the vine kills and then, you know, share it with the vine."

"You mean the vine eats their shit, right?" Nathan seemed amused by Rivers' avoidance of the cruder term.

"Yeah, that's what I mean. Let's get back to the others. I don't think we can learn anything else here."

They were underway half an hour later. Both Rivers and Walters offered to lighten Sharon's load but she waved them both off. "I'm fine, gentlemen. If I can't keep up, I'll let you know."

They set out in a rough double column, with Walters and Rivers leading, Fields and Harding bringing up the rear. Nathan muttered a bit about the hastiness of the decision but quieted down when his sister glared at him. They followed almost the exact path as the scouts had the previous day, passing the now blackened stump of the tree they'd set afire. From that point on, their attention was divided between the view ahead and the jungle wall to their left, which loomed like an insubstantial but unnerving threat.

Although they didn't move as quickly as the two men had managed the day before, they reached the outskirts of the abandoned town slightly before mid-day. Mrs. Galt suggested that they split up so that they could investigate the separate buildings more quickly, but Walters shook his head. "We go in pairs at a minimum and no one gets too far from the others. There may be wild animals lairing in some of them."

They found no traces of any such thing during the hour or so required to do at least a quick survey of every building except the two that had completely collapsed. Not once did they find a significant variation in architecture, and the closest they came to finding any other artifact was a broken length of wood that had apparently functioned as a handle for some kind of tool, perhaps a shovel.

It was Mrs. Galt who noticed an architectural feature the others had missed. "These windows have been altered. Look, you can see the original outline. These are all newer stones, added later."

Once she had pointed it out, it was obvious. The windows had originally been much bigger, but had later been reduced to narrow slits. "Why would they do that?" asked Grace. "It keeps out most of the light."

"Maybe they were interested in keeping something else out as well," suggested Fields.

"Our friends the crabs?" asked Sharon.

"Or something worse," said Fields. "The crabs didn't kill Abbott or Quinn and carry off their bodies."

"Well, if it kept them safe, won't it do the same for us?" Grace looked from one face to the next, looking for reassurance.

"One would think so," responded Rivers, although he wasn't completely convinced.

Neither was Fields. "Need I point out that whoever lived here is gone now? That might mean that their precautions proved inadequate."

The consensus was clearly for staying, however, and they chose one of the buildings in comparatively good repair in the outer circle, close to the fresh water stream, and moved their supplies inside.

"The one next to us is also in good shape," Grace pointed out. "Maybe it's time for the girls to have their own place away from the boys."

Walters wasn't happy with the idea. "Let's see what happens for a day or two before we think about splitting up. We don't want to have to maintain extra fires at night or keep separate watches."

Rivers was standing a little way apart from the others, staring toward the distant mountain cone. Walters came up beside him and followed his eyes with his own. "Is your cave over there?"

"Yeah. It's not visible from here, but I think it's right below that jagged scar that looks a little like an axe."

"I see it. At least an hour away."

"Or a little more. The ground's not as even down that way. There's a flight of steps leading up to it though you can't even see them from here."

"We'll have to check it out, but our first concern has to be food. We don't have a lot left."

"I know. We saw some kind of small animal here yesterday, something like a ground sloth, but only the one and it bolted when it saw us."

"Afraid of men?" Walters scratched his jaw. All of the men were whiskered now, particularly Walters and Fields. Harding had already worn a short but full beard so he was the least scruffy looking. "Why would they be afraid of men if the island is deserted?"

"Maybe it isn't."

Once they were settled in, Walters, Rivers, and Harding started toward the jungle, leaving Fields with his own weapon to guard their new campsite. They headed almost directly toward the nearest line of trees, angling toward the spot where it narrowed into a projecting point where Rivers suggested they might find it to be less dense. Less dense was a relative term, however, and they soon found themselves facing what appeared at first to be an almost impenetrable wall. Harding finally found a narrow gap similar to the one they had spotted the first day, and Rivers was relieved when it led to what was obviously a game trail.

"That'll make things easier," said Walters.

"Better than that. If there's a game trail, there must be game."

They also saw several strands of the odd vine, although it was much newer growth here than it had been in the ravine, about the thickness of a man's thumb. Rivers used a branch to trigger its offensive system, demonstrating it to the others, and they all gave it a wide berth after seeing the tiny but wicked looking thorn emerge from its hiding place in an almost invisible crevice in the roughed bark.

They were almost overwhelmed by the variety and volume of plant life around them. They even saw a few winged insects, although these were still far less numerous than they should have been. Rivers was delighted when he almost stepped in what was obviously the droppings of some good sized animal, and twice they heard rustling in the bushes, on both of which occasions Walters drew his weapon as they moved close to one another defensively, but they never caught sight of whatever was hidden there.

They crossed a good sized stream that disappeared underground, and just beyond that was a pool perhaps twenty meters across, partially concealed by floating plants and vines dropping from the canopy of branches that arched overhead, some of which were the distinctive bluish shade they knew to avoid. The pool did, however, contain fish, not very big ones but Harding predicted they'd be tasty enough when filleted, one of the few times he volunteered a comment without being asked.

A shadow passed over them a short while later and they all looked up, but whether it was a bird passing above the trees or some arboreal animal leaping from one branch to another it was impossible to determine. They also noticed several small trees bearing oblong yellow fruit. "Do you suppose it's safe to eat?" asked Walters.

Rivers crouched and pointed to the rotting remains of several husks scattered across the ground. "It looks like some kind of animal has been eating them. If they can, we should be able to as well."

"All right, we'll take some back with us. We'll try a small amount and if we're still alive in the morning, we'll have more for breakfast."

Rivers glanced up at the sky, trying to gauge the position of the sun. "We've been gone longer than I thought. Maybe we should head back."

Walters agreed. Harding looked as though he might balk, but thought better of it. With a wistful glance toward the pond, and presumably the fish, he turned and started to follow them back the way they had come.

CHAPTER ELEVEN

Although Walters described their trip into the jungle in dry terms, his obviously raised spirits helped improve the general mood as well. Even Nathan managed a slim smile and unbent enough to be polite throughout the remainder of the day. While Walters and his companions had been gone, the others had amassed a considerable store of fire wood, but once again they were faced with the problem of replenishing it in the long term. This part of the island had little vegetation other than thick, wiry grass, and they had been forced to walk two thirds of the way to the jungle after depleting all that was closer. There appeared to be even less to the east; the slopes of the volcanic cone were loose ash and drifting sand and very little grew there.

"Tomorrow we make ourselves some weapons and go hunting," Rivers announced.

"Are you going to whittle us some rifles, Captain Rivers?" asked Nathan, but less sarcastically than usual.

"No, we'll have to make do with knives, spears, and stone axes, I'm afraid. Fortunately we have lots of stone with sharp edges."

"How about a bow and arrow?" asked Grace.

"Beyond my capabilities, I'm afraid," admitted Rivers.

"Not beyond mine." Several heads turned in surprise, because it was Sharon's voice. She laughed, but was mildly miffed at the skeptical looks on several faces. "Don't look so surprised. I grew up on a farm, remember, and I have brothers. Three of them. They taught me a few things that young women don't normally put on their resumes."

Walters still didn't look as though he believed her, but he nodded. "We'll put your training to the test then."

They spent the afternoon gathering materials and preparing their armory, accumulating a handful of jagged stones suitable as spearheads and other, smaller ones that could serve as arrowheads. Sharon borrowed Rivers' pocket knife and went looking for a sapling suitable for conversion to a bow and straight shafts destined to be arrows. She assured them that she could make do with the surgical twine from the medical kit although she would prefer something stronger and more flexible. Fields made himself a serviceable hand axe and began cutting pieces of vine, not the bluish one, with which to construct snares. There was a general sense of purpose that raised spirits considerably, although the approach of dusk dampened them again.

Sharon and Rivers built up the fire, but both suffered from an attack of shyness and they spoke very little. Whoever was on watch would keep the fire going, moving it just inside the doorway if it rained. They were getting low on matches and although Fields assured them he could start a fire without them if need be, he admitted the process would not be an easy one.

Since this was their first night in a new location, Walters decided that they should stand watch in pairs, and Sharon immediately insisted that she be included in the rotation. She found herself paired with Rivers for the first watch, which pleased her immensely, and she noticed a fleeting look of jealousy that Grace quickly concealed under a mask of indifference. Nathan and Harding were to take second watch, while Fields and Walters would handle the last.

For a change, the night passed without excitement. Rivers thought he heard something moving nearby at one point, but even though he and Sharon strained to see or hear anything, there was no further evidence that they were not alone, and neither of them was foolish enough to investigate more actively. If Nathan or Harding had a similar experience, neither mentioned it the following morning, and the last watch was completely uneventful except that both men saw several shapes flying above the jungle as they passed in front of the moon.

The quiet night fueled their optimism and even Fields was fairly garrulous over breakfast and agreed to take Nathan with him and teach him how to set snares along the stream. He planned to build one at every spot which looked as though it might be a place where animals came to drink. Sharon had found the materials with which to make her bow, but confessed it was going to take longer than she had originally expected. "If you happen to find some cat gut out there, be sure to pick it up for me."

This was addressed to Rivers, who was going to accompany Walters and Harding on another foray into the jungle. They had sampled the odd looking fruit the night before, and no one had reported any untoward effects, so they planned to bring back a larger supply today. But they also wanted to give the nearest parts of the jungle a more thorough examination.

"We've found one animal trail already. If we build a couple of deadfalls, we might catch something interesting." Walters' tone was only slightly ambiguous. He wanted to make certain that no one forgot that two of their party had been killed, and although both attacks had come at night, he wasn't willing to assume the daylight was therefore safe.

Rivers still wanted to visit the cave but he knew that food was a higher priority. They had salvaged a duffle bag from the wreckage of their supplies, although one strap had been torn off, and he slung this over his shoulder. They would fill it with fruit and samples of anything else they encountered that looked as though it might be edible. The other men carried similar but smaller containers; Harding was equipped with a torn dress shirt that Sharon had stitched up as a rough pouch.

Mrs. Galt was determined to give their new home a thorough cleaning, and Grace had volunteered, after a fashion, to help, complaining that her feet were sore and swollen from their trek the previous day. Given the shoes she'd been wearing, she was probably exaggerating only very slightly. Mrs. Galt had already made herself a couple of brooms from freshly cut branches and she was raising a remarkable amount of dust as the various parties left on their respective missions.

The three men reached the sheltered pool without incident. There was some disturbed soil that Rivers thought might be evidence that an animal had been there to drink, but the ground was too hard to show a clear impression. Harding pointed out a scrawny looking bush with curved thorns, suggesting that they would serve as fishhooks, and Walters spotted a patch of the fruit bearing plant they had already found palatable. "At least we won't have to worry about scurvy." They harvested a few of these to take with them for lunch.

At first they thought the game trail ended at the pond, but Rivers finally located its continuation, partially concealed by low hanging fronds from a nearby tree. It was narrow and so completely hidden from the sky that it was like peering into a pool of night, but after a hundred meters of twisting and turning, it opened up and began to climb a gentle rise. They found themselves in a small meadow bordered on one side by trees so large that they couldn't wrap their arms around the trunks. The bark was gnarled and covered with vines and creepers, some of them so ancient that they were as big around as small trees themselves.

Once again they had trouble discovering where the trail led next, but Harding eventually forced his way between two of the towering trees and found a sliver of bare ground. The trail led slowly downhill at first, curving slightly but steadily to their left, toward the high side of the island. After perhaps half an hour, it began to rise and straighten out, weaving around trees and irregularities in the ground, once crossing another stream, this one slow moving and partially covered by unpleasant looking scum. The ground began to rise to their right even faster than ahead of them, and jagged rocks began to jut out of the soil with increasing frequency.

Although they were sheltered from the direct sunlight, the humidity was higher than ever and they were very uncomfortable by the time they stopped for lunch, sitting on a flat plate of rock. The absence of mosquitoes or similar flying insects was a minor blessing; they had seen a few flitting in the shadows as they walked, but on only one occasion had Rivers actually been forced to brush an intruder away from his face. They ate the few rations they had brought with them and satisfied their thirst primarily with fruit, saving their water.

The trail began to bear toward their left again, more sharply than ever, and when it straightened out Walters looked up at the sun for a few seconds and told them that they had turned almost completely around. "We're headed back toward the coast, not far from where we came ashore."

It was Harding who suggested climbing a tree. They had just finished another steep ascent, and this hill was relatively clear of low brush, with a stand of immensely tall trees dominating its crest. Their trunks were largely denuded of branches below the crowning spread, and there were none of the thick vines that clung to the trees they'd been passing all day. Harding pointed out one in particular. "It's just like a ship's mast. I can look around from up there, see what's to be seen."

Walters only hesitated a few seconds. "All right, but be careful."

He went up the trunk with a speed and grace that Rivers could only envy. When he reached the lowest branches he slowed, proceeding more deliberately and occasionally disappearing from sight. It was during one such period that he shouted, with anger or surprise or fear. They could never decide which. There was a violent rustling in the branches and something broke free, something that looked a little like a bird and a little like an oversized dragonfly. It swept down toward them and Walters instinctively took out his pistol and raised it. There was a single pop and a high pitched cry and the plummeting body jerked to one side, struck a glancing blow against a low hanging branch, then slammed into the trunk of another tree and fell heavily into the brush out of sight.

"Ezra? Are you all right?" Walters craned his head back, shouting.

"Yes, I'm here. There's a nest here. A big one. Guess I surprised something."

The something was thrashing violently a few meters away, but suddenly fell silent. Rivers started to move toward it, then stopped, thinking better of it.

"Can you see anything?" shouted Walters.

"I'm looking around. Give me a minute."

Walters shook his head and sighed. "Shall we take a look?" He raised his arm to show Rivers that he still had his weapon ready.

"After you."

It wasn't dead, but one wing was completely torn off and a second was broken. Which left it with two that still functioned. It also had two feet, each ending in a trifurcated claw. It looked more like a dragonfly than a bird, although the wings were feathered as was part of the body. The underside appeared to be scaled. The head was round, vaguely owl-like, set at one end of a slender body that stretched the better part of a meter, but the eyes were much too large and appeared to be prismatic, and instead of a beak it had mandibles, jaws that opened from side to side rather than up and down. They opened and closed a few times, but then the creature gave a long shudder and stopped moving altogether.

"What the hell is that?" Walters kept the pistol pointed squarely at the thing's head.

Rivers just shook his head. "I think that's what we saw hovering above the trees. Other than that, your guess is as good as mine."

"Is it dead, do you think?"

Rivers looked around, picked up a fallen branch, and prodded the body. There was no reaction. "I think so. Do you suppose it's good to eat?"

Walters shuddered. "I'm not that hungry."

Rivers nodded agreement. "Not yet anyway."

Harding came down the tree even faster than he'd gone up. He couldn't tell them very much because the canopy of foliage concealed most of the immediate vicinity. "If we keep going this way, we'll come out of the jungle after a bit. There's bare rock there, a lot of it. Only a few trees, big rocks. Then more jungle and past that, flat rock all the way down to the water."

"It's probably quicker at this point to go forward than back," said Walters. They had passed three side trails but each had been smaller than the one they'd been following, and all three had angled off into denser jungle.

The vegetation began to thin out very soon after that, with more rock showing through the soil. They were also climbing again, sometimes at an angle so steep that they had to use their hands as well as their feet to clamber up brief stretches. They were out of the shade, but the sun was beginning its long fall to night, and although they were confident that they had plenty of time to get back before dark, they didn't feel inclined to linger and their rest periods, though more frequent, were also much shorter.

Rivers had done a lot of walking during the past three years, but his feet were starting to get sore and his two companions were even less comfortable. "I don't mind being on my feet all day," quipped Walters, "but not when the ground is this hard and doesn't rise and fall regularly."

The trail leveled off, then abruptly began to descend, and they had to be careful not to let their momentum build until it got out of control. It also wound back and forth down a mercifully gradual slope, although not far away the rock face dropped off suddenly, a wall of white disfigured by cracks and ridges. There were also several openings that were almost certainly narrow caves, although they could not even guess how deep they might be.

They were approximately one third of the way down when a rock turned under Walters' foot and he lost his balance. He avoided a potentially serious fall by grabbing one of the scraggly trees that somehow managed to find enough soil to support their roots, although he took the skin off the palm of his hand in the process.

"Let's take a break." He sat down with his back against a rounded stone, not waiting for an answer.

"No complaint here." Rivers immediately dropped down facing him, but Harding remained standing.

"Rest your feet, Ezra. We're not in a race."

There was no convenient shade nearby, but one of the small caves was a scar on the rock only a few meters away. The ledge in front of it was narrow, but it looked firm enough. Harding tested it with one foot, pressed both hands against the sheer rock, and began to half walk, half sidle around the curve to the opening.

"Watch yourself, Harding!" called Rivers. "There might be animals living in there."

Harding's head moved in what might have been a nod of acknowledgment, but he didn't say anything, just continued his careful movement until he was able to step down into the mouth of the cave. Walters had been watching intently and he shouted another warning. "Don't take any chances, Ezra! We don't want to have to carry you back to camp! Do you see anything?"

Harding ignored Walters completely, crouched and peered into the darkness. He found a small stone beside his foot and picked it up, then tossed it into the interior. "I think it's empty," he said at last. "But it smells bad, like something crawled in there and died." He tossed a second stone and then a third. "It's pretty deep. I could hear one of the stones rolling a long way before it stopped." He took a step forward as though to enter the cave.

"Ezra! Don't go in there!" Walters got to his feet and Rivers followed suit.

Harding held up one hand, as though to ward them off. "I can see something just inside."

Walters swore under his breath and Rivers didn't blame him. Harding stepped out of their line of sight and it was as though he had disappeared from the face of the earth. Rivers had the sudden feeling that they would never see him again, and for a few seconds he was incapable of action, couldn't even move his feet. Then Harding slowly emerged, apparently unharmed, and Rivers managed to draw another breath.

Harding turned around and held out what he grasped in his hand. It was a human arm, or part of one anyway, still half covered by a white sleeve with dark blue braid. It was what Michael Quinn had been wearing the night he disappeared.

Harding held it out until he was sure they had seen it clearly, then tossed it back inside. Walters opened his mouth to order him back, but it was unnecessary. Harding was already inching his way back to the main trail. He was almost all the way back when they heard something moving inside the cave. Something big.

Fields was quite obviously pleased with himself. He and Nathan had set out an even dozen snares at intervals along the stream bed, and on their way back had discovered that one had been tripped and that a furred animal the size of a small dog was dangling by one foot. Nathan looked away as Fields methodically shattered its skull with a convenient rock.

"That seems to answer one question. There's not much meat on this little fellow, but it'll taste like the finest beef when we make a stew out of him."

Nathan still looked a bit queasy, particularly when Fields handed him the body to carry. "We'll have to wait until we're back to dress the meat. My little pocket knife won't do the trick as well as the utility knife from the lifeboat. No, don't hold it like that!" But it was too late. The animal's bladder let go and Nathan dropped it and jumped back as warm fluid spilled down his side.

"Wash yourself off while I take care of this."

Wet, embarrassed, and thoroughly annoyed, Nathan almost balked when Fields handed him their catch a second time, but there was something about Fields that made him nervous and he decided not to argue. Once they were out of this place, back in civilization, his father would see to it that any indignities he suffered were suitably addressed.

Another snare had been tripped, but whether by an animal which had then escaped or just because it was too sensitive it was impossible to determine. Fields reset it and they continued on until they reached the end of their trap line. "Most animals probably won't come out until it's dark. We'll have to check first thing in the morning."

"Yeah, well, it'll be somebody else's turn tomorrow."

"Why? Do you have a tennis date you forgot to tell us about? Or are you due for a manicure?"

Nathan's temper suddenly flared. "I do my share. You forget that I'm not one of the crew. I'm a passenger, just like you are, and I have my rights."

"We aren't passengers and crew any more, in case you haven't noticed." Fields' voice was cool, unruffled, perhaps even slightly amused. "We're just survivors now, and that means we're all equal. We have equal rights, and equal obligations. Anyone who shirks his responsibilities puts all of us in danger." He smiled. "I've been in dangerous situations before. I don't like them."

Nathan's eyes flashed but he wisely chose to remain silent, turning away and plodding on toward their camp, their catch awkwardly cradled in his arms. Fields sighed, watching for a second before following.

The three women were sitting around the fire and they all looked tired but pleased even before they saw what Nathan was carrying. He was still sulking a bit so it was Fields who had to summarize what they'd done during the course of the day, which he did in his usual terse manner.

"Come inside and see what we've done!" Grace seemed almost childishly excited, and Nathan felt a fresh pang of unhappiness when he noticed that she had addressed herself to Fields rather than him. Mrs. Galt waved to him to follow Fields inside, and once there he had to admit, to himself anyway, that they'd made a considerable difference. The stone floor was clean and the cobwebs had been cleared out of the corners along with whatever debris had been lying about. A fragment of canvas had been stretched over a frame of bent wood to make a small table, and their supplies were now neatly arranged there and in an orderly pile against the rear wall. It was still gloomy because the narrow windows didn't let in much light, but considerably more welcoming than it had been when they set out for the day. There were even a few flowers scattered about.

"Very nice, ladies. I feel like I've walked into the Ritz Carlton."

"The Ritz. I like that, Mr. Fields." Mrs. Galt fairly beamed. "We've started on the side chambers as well, but we really need to bring in small branches and leaves and make ourselves mattresses. I can't speak for anyone else, but these bones are getting a little too old to sleep comfortably on bare rock."

Harding leaped to firmer ground and scrambled away from the cliff face. Walters and Rivers crouched and watched from their own inadequate cover. At first there was just a hint of movement, one shadow inside another, but then a definite shape began to emerge, a blunt, armored head weaving slowly from side to side. It hesitated for long seconds, as though testing the air, then thrust itself forward.

Rivers knew instinctively that this was their mysterious night time killer. It had an extended snout and very powerful jaws, although when it opened its mouth it revealed serrated bone rather than individual teeth. The face was rough and jagged, as though someone had carved it from a block of wood using an axe, leaving all the rough edges and sharp angles in place. There were no visible ears although gnarled knobs on the sides of its head must have filled that function. The eyes were almost impossibly large and, although he could not be certain from such a distance, Rivers was almost certain that they were faceted like those of an insect. Its body was dark, almost black with a faint hint of blue, its body covered with overlapping scales.

The head was followed by two forelegs and a thick neck that seemed disproportionately long. Each leg ended in a splayed, clawed foot with which it gripped the lip of the cave as it looked for the source of the disturbance. Its limbs were better articulated than Rivers expected, because it shifted position, raising one leg to grasp the cave above it and ease its body further forward. As it did so, a second pair of legs became visible, then still a third as its four meter long body slid out into the daylight, stretched awkwardly from the cliff face to the level land adjoining. One leg was so close to Harding that he could have reached out and touched it from where he crouched, undetected, around the curve of the cliff wall.

Walters eased the pistol out of his pocket but it couldn't possibly be effective against a monster like this one. The armored head swung slowly back and forth, still searching, and none of the men dared move. Then its eyes began to blink rapidly, apparently ill suited for the bright daylight. It is possible that they could have slipped away undetected, but it proved unnecessary to test that theory. As slowly as it had emerged, the giant reptile shrank back into its lair, flicking a trifurcated tongue just before its head vanished from view.

They remained frozen for another few minutes, half frozen with terror. Harding broke the spell first, moving away from the cliff in a circuitous route that would eventually bring him to where his companions waited. Walters put away his weapon with a hand that shook visibly and he and Rivers exchanged meaningful looks but no words. When Harding reached them, they started immediately for the trail, and for the next few minutes their steps were as light and enthusiastic as they'd been when they'd first set out.

The trail turned away from the cliffs and descended steadily though more gradually into the jungle. There was no doubt in their minds that they had just seen Michael Quinn's killer. "Either that same creature or one just like it undoubtedly took the reverend as well," said Walters, breaking a long silence.

"I don't get it," complained Rivers. "Lizards and things like that, I thought they liked the sunlight. This thing apparently holes up by day and hunts at night."

"Turtles are active at night. And salamanders." Walters' voice was still not completely steady.

"Are you trying to tell me that's some kind of oversized salamander?"

Walters didn't even attempt to answer.

The trail became much wider, so wide in fact that the three men could walk side by side, which suggested that it might be the same route the predator used to descend to level ground. That possibility also quickened their steps. The sun was noticeably lower in the sky now, and the irony that they might now be the game on the game trail was not lost on them.

They emerged from the jungle less than an hour later and quickly oriented themselves. Their ruined lifeboat was almost directly in front of them, though concealed from view, so they angled to their left. By unspoken agreement they reverted to alternating a rapid walk with a jog, and none of them suggested a rest break. Walters stumbled once and nearly took a bad fall, but he recovered and continued without saying a word. They slowed down only when they could see the rings of buildings ahead of them with a thin column of smoke rising above them, and knew that they would reach cover before the light was gone.

It was Sharon who caused the next commotion at the camp. She had just returned carrying a small bag of jagged stones which she thought might become serviceable arrowheads when she saw Nathan standing beside the slumped form of their first successful hunt. He greeted her with some warmth and seemed inordinately proud of his prize, although it was actually Fields who had designed and rigged the snares. Sharon had hunted with her brothers and knew it wouldn't provide much of a meal for eight people, but it would be the first fresh meat they'd had in almost a week, and the prospect cheered her.

"We need to dress it as soon as possible," she said. "I'll gut it right now. Bring it over here."

The utility knife was both sturdy and sharp. She had been using it to whittle the shafts for her arrows after the pocketknife proved inadequate and had left it on the flat rock that she'd been using as a work table. Nathan waited while she cleared a space, then dropped his burden unceremoniously in front of her. When she picked up the knife, he turned away. "You won't mind if I don't watch, will you?"

Sharon rolled the small body over onto its back, preparing to disembowel it and then cut away the edible portions when she paused, eyes narrowing, and set the blade down, leaning forward to look more closely.

"Nathan, did you or Mr. Fields notice anything odd about our little friend here?"

"Not that I recall." He continued to walk away.

"I think you'd better get the others."

Something in her voice alarmed him. "What's the matter?" He stopped walking but made no effort to turn and look.

"Just get them. I want everyone to see this."

CHAPTER TWELVE

When the three men finally returned, they were bombarded by questions from every side. Their prolonged absence and the closeness of nightfall had generated considerable apprehension. "We're in no position to mount a search and rescue mission," said Fields testily.

Walters recounted their adventures, occasionally supplemented by Rivers. His description of what he called the "cave dragon" created a small sensation. He was circumspect about what else Harding had discovered in the cave, saying only that they had found "human remains" which almost certainly were those of Quinn. When they were done, Rivers glanced around the fire. "What about the rest of you? Anything new to report?"

Sharon and Fields exchanged glances, and she nodded for him to tell their story.. "We caught something in one of our snares, an animal of some kind, probably the same thing we saw yesterday. It's not very big but there's enough to feed us for one meal, if we decide to eat it."

"If?" Rivers glanced from one face to the next. "What's wrong with it?"

"Here. Let me show you." Sharon was sitting next to a flat stone atop which something sat covered with a handkerchief. She removed the cover to reveal the partially butchered body. "I was just about to carve it up when I noticed these." She pointed to two swellings about halfway between the two sets of legs.

"What are they? Teats?"

"No," she shook her head. "It's a male. I cut one of them open. See here? Those white things are bones, and see here where they differentiate at the bottom. I think they're feet, not completely developed, but still feet."

"Are you trying to tell us this thing was growing a third set of legs?" Walters lurched to his feet and walked over to examine the animal more closely. "How is that possible?"

But Sharon was shaking her head. "No, I don't think they were growing any more. This is a mature animal. It has already reached its full adult form. I think these are either vestigial, you know, an old characteristic that is gradually going away, or more likely a new one, some transitional phase that didn't quite take."

"Six legs," said Rivers thoughtfully. "We've seen an awful lot of things on this island that have six limbs. Those insects and the bird we ran into all had four wings and two legs. And that dragon thing up on the cliffs."

"Don't forget our friend Franz," added Fields, which led to a short detour while he explained his naming of the statue.

"You're not going to tell us that the people who lived here had an extra set of arms, are you?" It was the first time Nathan had spoken.

"No, Mr. Porter, I'm not suggesting that. But if some of the local wildlife changed, maybe they thought it was a message from the gods and created a new icon for themselves. One more relevant to their current situation."

Walters made an impatient sound. "Do you have anything else to show us, Miss Porter?"

Sharon shook her head. "No, not really. The rest of its body seems perfectly normal, at least to look at. But I'm not sure if we should eat it, under the circumstances."

Walters never hesitated. "Maybe we should and maybe we shouldn't, but unless we find a reliable food source soon, we're all going to die anyway. I don't know about the rest of you, but I'm ready to risk it. Those who feel otherwise are welcome to eat the packaged rations instead."

If anyone had been tempted to refrain, the smell of cooking meat a short while later overwhelmed their reluctance.

This night also proved uneventful, at least until just before dawn when a sudden downpour caught Rivers and Harding by surprise, soaking them thoroughly and drowning the fire so quickly that they just managed to get a few burning sticks and some hot coals inside before it was completely extinguished. The rain only lasted a few minutes, and by the time the sun came out, the last of the dark clouds were already disappearing toward the horizon. They re-established the fire with the help of Mrs. Galt and Sharon, and when Walters was up and about they discussed building some sort of enclosure to protect it in the future.

Fields set out with Nathan to check the traps. They found four of them tripped, but only one still occupied. There was blood and remnants of a small body at the other three, suggesting that something or someone else had emptied the traps before they arrived, and Fields found one clear print in a soft patch of earth that suggested the cave dragons ranged this far as well, unless there were more of them with closer lairs. They reset the snares and Nathan carried their single prize back – a duplicate of their first catch - without complaining this time.

Rivers had taken Sharon with him to harvest more of the fruit. They picked only enough to last them for two days, and Sharon found a berry bearing plant and took a sample of that as well. The two parties arrived back at the Ritz almost simultaneously, and the mid-day meal was the best they'd had since leaving the *Sturtevant*, providing a needed boost to their morale.

They were just finishing when Rivers suggested that this might be a good time to investigate the cave in the volcano. Walters agreed after a brief hesitation, and glanced toward Fields, who shook his head. "I twisted my ankle coming back this morning. No long walks for me today, I'm afraid. Take young Porter with you."

But Nathan balked, insisting that he didn't feel well, and Walters had already decided that he and Harding were going back to the beach to salvage some of the wooden boards from the lifeboat and anything else they might have missed the first time. Rivers wasn't about to suggest that he go alone and was about to drop the idea when Sharon looked up from the arrow she'd been fletching. "I'll go with you, Mr. Rivers."

There was an awkward silence because Walters and Rivers both wanted to veto the idea, but both also knew that Sharon would be offended if they objected. Fields, on the other hand, appeared to be amused by the situation and he reached inside his jacket and took out his pistol. "If you're going out exploring, Miss Bartleby, then perhaps you should take this with you."

Instead of answering, she bent down and picked up her newly made bow in one hand, one of her crude arrows in the other. Without saying a word, she notched the arrow and raised the bow, aiming at a cluster of three small trees that grew behind one of the houses in the next row in. There was a low pitched thrum and the arrow flew forward and came to rest driven solidly into the rightmost of the three trees. "I don't think that will be necessary, Mr. Fields."

There was laughter, some of it uneasy, but no further objections were raised and Sharon and Rivers set out a short while later.

"Nice shot with that arrow, by the way," said Rivers.

"Yeah, well, I was aiming for the middle tree, but don't tell on me, okay?"

They made small talk for the first few minutes but soon fell into a companionable silence, saving their breath and attention for the business of walking through the increasingly broken and uneven landscape. The two men had skirted this area during their earlier trip and Rivers hadn't realized just how pockmarked and barren the land was in the area directly in front of the volcano. Most of the vegetation was low to the ground and scraggly, and as they grew closer, they were forced to detour around eroded pits and jagged boulders with increasing frequency. Although their view of the area around the carved steps had been unobstructed before, they frequently lost sight of it now as they walked twisting paths through fields of tortured rock, or climbed down to walk the floor of shallow ravines rather than risk the treacherously undercut rims.

When they turned a corner and found themselves staring directly at the stone staircase, it took them by surprise.

There was no chance that it could be a natural formation. The steps were roughly cut and uneven across the tops, but they were almost identical in height and depth. They were broadest at the base, which was perhaps fifty meters wide, narrowing as they rose. Rivers whistled; there were a lot more steps than he had expected.

Sharon must have had the same thought. "There must be a couple of hundred of them. I wonder where they lead."

"That's what we're here to find out."

The ascent was more wearing than they'd expected. They were forced to stop half way up, sitting side by side sipping water. At this point, they were high enough to see all the way back to the Ritz and beyond, until the dark swath of the jungle intervened.

Sharon broke the silence. "I wanted to include a visit to a small Pacific island on my trip, but I thought I was going to have to make do with Hawaii."

"Believe me, the experience is over rated. I spent some time on Truk and a month on a little island off the Philippine coast. Heat and bugs and inadequate toilet facilities."

"Not many bugs here."

"No, but the accommodations and cuisine leave a lot to be desired."

They continued their ascent at a slower pace but still had to pause once more before they were done. The cave entrance was visible long before they reached the top step, but it was outwardly featureless, just a dark hole in the side of the mountain. Even when they stood directly in front of it, few details were visible.

"What is that, Jerry? Some kind of wall? It doesn't look natural."

Rivers had brought two torches and used a match to light them. Sharon stepped forward first and his jaw tightened as he hastened to catch up with her. "Let me go first."

It was indeed a wall, built of stone and extending three quarters of the way across the throat of the cave. Two rows of small openings had been built into the structure, one at eye level, the other around their knees, each large enough to stick an arm through but no larger.

"That's odd," said Sharon, but Rivers thought he knew their purpose.

When they moved around the open end of the wall, they found a second one of exactly the same design, except that the first had been anchored to the wall at their right, while this was snug up against the left wall with the right side open. "What is this?" asked Sharon.

"I think I know. Come on." He led the way around the second wall and, as expected, found a third, this time situated like the first.

"Is this some kind of a maze? Are we trespassing on sacred ground or something?"

Rivers shook his head. "No, this is a fortress. Look, see how the holes are lined up? If you wanted to defend this place, you could run poles through the holes to block the entrances. It wouldn't stop a determined enemy, but it would slow them down. If it were me, I'd leave every third position empty, and when an intruder penetrated far enough, I'd have spearmen thrust at them through the wall. They'd be perfectly safe until the enemy made it to the corner, and then they could just retreat to the next wall and start all over again."

"Wow! How many of them do you suppose there are?"

"Let's find out."

There were six walls, then an open space that narrowed dramatically and angled downward so steeply that they had to be careful of their footing. Fifty paces took them down into a hollow beyond which three much narrower openings led deeper into the mountain.

"Now what?"

"Well first of all, we don't separate and we don't get lost. Let's take the right hand passage for a while and see where it takes us. But if we come to any other forks, we stop and rethink the situation."

Their path curved very gradually to the right for the first two hundred paces, then began to curl back toward the left. The only indications that humans had passed this way before were in a few spots where the walls or floor showed evidence that they had been widened or smoothed by artificial means. Rivers had only one spare torch and he was about to call a halt when Sharon touched his arm.

"Wait a minute. Take my torch and go back a little way."

"I'm not going to leave you here alone."

"I'm not going anywhere. Just take the torches back around the curve. Trust me."

Reluctantly, he did as she asked, retreating until he could no longer see her. He stopped and called her name anxiously.

"I'm fine. I haven't moved. Just wait a second while my eyes adjust."

"What is it? Do you see something?"

"Yes, I think I do. It's very faint but there's light up ahead of us."

He rejoined her and tried to see the light, but with the torches flickering near at hand, it was impossible to distinguish any change in illumination. They continued forward cautiously and after another hundred paces the subdued glow was clearly visible. Fifty paces after that, Sharon's torch began to gutter and smoke and Rivers stamped it out. "We should go back now."

"Oh come on! You know you don't want to go back until we see where the light is coming from."

"No, I don't, but it might not be safe." Even in the uncertain light, he could read the expression on her face. "All right, we go on. But have that bow of yours ready, all right? And if I tell you to run, you do exactly that."

"Yes, sir, Captain!" She saluted him, then slipped the bow off her shoulder.

The lifeboat was in even worse shape than it had been before. Something clearly had come back to wreak more damage, perhaps searching for another meal. Walters and Harding separated out a number of lengths of board to carry back with them, eventually salvaging enough to require at least three or four trips. He planned to build a door to block the entrance to the Ritz, and possibly even shutters for the windows. Mrs. Galt had suggested fashioning crude frames which they could fill with leaves and other soft debris to form makeshift mattresses. They also kept an eye out for other supplies which they might have missed earlier, but the best they came up with was a torn section of the now ruined sail that was snagged on a rock.

It was Harding who discovered the footprint. They were searching through the low brush just above the high tide line, hoping to find some debris that might have been washed up and been trapped somewhere rather than swept back out to sea. Walters had already found a seaman's cap and a small ball of twine, and Harding had picked up a flashlight, although its battery was completely dead. Walters was on the verge of calling a halt to the search – they still had to carry everything back to the Ritz – when Harding stopped short, his head tilted downward. There was something about his posture that told Walters something was wrong, and he was already closing the gap when he spoke, keeping his voice low.

"What is it, Ezra?"

Harding glanced up but held his peace, letting the evidence speak for itself. In a little puddle of sea water that had been trapped in a hollow there was the distinct outline of a foot. It was a human foot, without question, but surprisingly large.

"One of us must have stepped here," said Walters, but he knew right away that wasn't the explanation. It was remotely possible that one of the men might have taken off his shoes for a moment or two while they'd been searching the morning after Quinn's death, but the tide had covered this entire part of the land at least twice since then. There was no way that the footprint could have survived that long, and no one from their party had been in this area since.

"We're not alone here, Mr. Walters." Harding put into words what they both already knew.

"A survivor from the other boat. It must be."

"Maybe so, maybe not. Why would they be hiding from us if it was them?"

Walters shook his head. "I don't know. But there's been no sign of anyone still living here. The village is deserted and has been for a long time. Where would they be?"

Harding didn't answer, but both men's eyes strayed to the distant jungle. Was it possible? They had explored only a very small portion. There could be entire communities hidden just out of sight in the densely overgrown areas.

Walters had been feeling more optimistic for the past few hours, but now his old uneasiness came back stronger than ever. "Let's load ourselves up and get back."

Rivers knew that they were being watched even before there was any overt evidence. The tunnel had just opened up in front of them, revealing a much wider cavern with stalactites hanging from the ceiling and stalagmites jutting up from the floor. There was a thin curtain of water running down the far wall and gathering in a rippling pool that extended back beyond their line of sight. They could see quite clearly, even without their torches, because the cavern was illuminated from the far side, where at least three wide passages broke the far wall. He couldn't be certain of their orientation after the twisting passage that had brought them here, but he sensed that they were still well inside the volcano. There also seemed to be additional light filtering in from somewhere over their heads, although they couldn't detect the source, possibly a rent in the roof.

They stopped only a few steps into the cavern, partly because they were so stunned by the comparatively bright light, partly because there was no obvious trail from this point onward. The ground beneath them was rock in some places, hard packed soil in a few places, and fine sand in others. There were a few clusters of mushrooms, and thick gray moss hung like curtains in several spots. The only sound was the falling water, which echoed oddly, and their own footsteps.

"It's beautiful in a way, isn't it?" Sharon was craning her head to look up at the overhanging roof.

"Don't let that fool you. Caves are always dangerous, even when they don't look like it." It was just as he finished speaking that he began to sense that they were no longer alone. His head snapped around and he did a slow traverse of the visible portions of the cavern. Sharon noticed his sudden tension and her eyes widened, but she didn't say anything. She did, however, slip the bow off her shoulder and ready an arrow.

"Someone's here," Rivers whispered. "I heard them move."

Sharon didn't argue. She turned slowly, her eyes narrowing as she also tried to see what didn't want to be seen. They were only about a dozen paces from the tunnel through which they'd entered. "Should we go back?" Her whisper was even fainter than his had been.

"I think that might be wise."

They began to retreat, backing slowly toward the tunnel, but when they were about half way there, the ground erupted on either side. Two figures burst up out of a sandy spot to their left and a matching pair to their right, each draped with a rough cloth that had covered their heads and shoulders as they squatted in concealed pits. Sharon brought her bow up but it was knocked from her hand. Rivers saw a face coming toward him, a human face, and he lashed out with his fist. The impact jarred him to the shoulder but the attacker flew backward and fell sprawling with a surprised look on his face.

He spun around in time to see Sharon struggling with two men, each of whom had hold of one of her arms. Twisting his body, he slammed a shoulder into the nearest one's side, breaking his grip and sending him staggering back. Sharon immediately twisted around and aimed a kick at the other, but Rivers didn't see the outcome because he was turning back toward his own second assailant. He cocked his fist and swung as another face loomed into view, but at the last possible second, he realized that it was a woman and he checked his blow.

She was less fastidious. Her short wooden club came up fast and caught him across the bridge of the nose. He fell backward, paralyzed by the pain, and hit the ground hard enough to take his breath away. Still conscious, he tried to raise his upper body, but the man he'd struck initially leaped at him, landing with both knees, bruising his ribs and robbing him of breath. Then something struck him across the forehead and everything went very dark.

When he came to, he was in darkness again. At first he thought it was complete, but when he raised one arm in front of his face, he saw a hint of movement. Blinking, he made a tentative effort to sit up, but stopped and waited for his head to stop spinning. A voice came out of the darkness.

"Jerry? Are you all right?"

"Sharon! What happened?" He propped himself up on his elbows before he was forced to rest again. His head hurt and his ears were ringing so loudly that his voice sounded funny. "Where are we?"

"We're in a small cave. There's a door of some kind. I think it was woven from branches and very big leaves, like from a palm tree. It's only tied shut, I think, but I can hear someone moving outside, probably a guard. Or guards."

"Did you get a good look at them? The ones who attacked us?"

She came closer, kneeling beside him, and put a hand on his arm. "How's your head? I thought they might have killed you. You're bleeding from the scalp."

"I'll live. Hurts like hell though." He reached up and found something hard and crusty on one side of his forehead. It was much too large to be dried blood.

"There's something on my head."

"One of them did that before they put us in here. I think it's some kind of poultice. I'd leave it alone if I were you. It seems to have stopped the worst of the bleeding."

He reached into his pocket, took out the matches, and sat up. "I'm going to give us some light here but it'll only last for a few seconds, so look around fast. We need to know everything we can."

A moment later he struck a match and held it up, peering around at their surroundings. There wasn't much to see. They were in a small chamber, probably natural, not much bigger than a closet. The walls were solid rock on three sides, and the thickly woven door that Sharon had already described blocked the fourth. There was absolutely nothing else to see.

The match sputtered and went out.

"Okay, what did you see before they threw us in here? The guy who hit me looked Polynesian."

"They all did, except for one of the women. She looked at least partly European and she was blonde. I think they must be the original inhabitants of the island, or their descendants."

"They abandoned their town to live underground? Why would they do that?"

"Maybe to get away from whatever it was that killed Mr. Quinn and the reverend."

"The cave dragons? Maybe. But why not build a stockade instead? Or some kind of trap to catch them and kill them? I'd try a lot of different things before I abandoned my home to live in a hole in the ground."

"Maybe they did."

"Okay, what else? How many of them were there?"

"Four at first, the ones who had buried themselves in the pits along the path. But there were more of them hiding out of sight in the cavern. There must have been, I don't know, maybe a dozen. Mostly men but at least three women."

"What kind of weapons did they have?"

She hesitated. "Clubs mostly, and a couple of knives, and I think one of them was carrying a sword."

"Maybe just a long bladed knife."

"No, I'm quite sure it was a sword." She hesitated again. "It had a fancy hilt with jewels in it."

"Okay, maybe some pirate landed here years ago.   Did you see anything else that might help us?"

"Not really. Their clothing was woven, not animal skins, and some of it looked fairly new. They're not just savages."

"In my experience, technological know how is no guarantee against savagery. But they didn't kill us out of hand, and that's a mark in their favor."

"What do you suppose they want with us?"

"Well, that's the question, isn't it?" He drew in his legs and sat completely upright, waited for his dizziness to subside again. "Technically, I suppose we're trespassers. Let's just hope they're lenient with first offenders."

By the time they had finished their third trip back to the Ritz, Walters decided to call it a day even though there were still some serviceable boards they hadn't retrieved. It wasn't quite dusk yet and they could probably have managed one more trip safely, but he was exhausted and even Harding looked as though he'd overtaxed himself, although he never complained. He was also beginning to worry about Rivers and the Bartleby girl, who had promised to be back well before the light began to fade. Not only were they not back, but they had to be at least a half hour away as there was no sign of them even when he stood atop the Ritz.

Mrs. Galt was clearly concerned as well, although she kept her thoughts to herself. Even Fields climbed up onto the roof to watch for a while, though he said nothing. It was Nathan who first spoke of their absence. "If they aren't back soon, I assume we're going to eat without them."

Even Grace seemed mildly shocked by her brother's callousness. "Nathan, you can be a real jerk sometimes, you know."

Oblivious to the impression he was making, Nathan snapped back at his sister. "They've probably taking a break for a little love making. That's the only reason you care where they are."

Walters took a step in their direction, expecting to have to break up a fight, but Grace surprised him. She met her brother's eyes until he glanced away. "You're such a child sometimes, Nathan." Without waiting for him to respond, she got up and disappeared inside the Ritz.

Nathan glanced at Walters with an expression that implied he was tolerating a willful child, but Walters just turned away, thankful that he needn't get involved any further. Mrs. Galt caught his eye and beckoned him over. "Do you think we should go look for them?" She kept her voice low enough that no one else could hear.

Walters sighed. "No, I'm afraid not. We just can't afford to spread ourselves any thinner, particularly now that it's nearly dark. I'm sorry, Mrs. Galt, but I'm afraid they're on their own, at least for the time being."

Sharon and Rivers had no way to accurately measure the passage of time, but they were quite sure that darkness must have fallen before they heard or saw anything further of their captors. The door was thrown open so suddenly that even the pale light from the outer chamber made them raise their hands protectively. Five people stood in the doorway, two of them obviously their guards, one of whom carried a stone tipped spear and the other a well worn but serviceable cutlass. The other three seemed to be unarmed, a man and two women. As Sharon and Rivers scrambled to their feet, one of the men set down a ceramic bowl filled with fruit and what appeared to be a kind of bread or biscuit. He pushed it into their chamber with his foot, watching them warily but without any sign of fear. The second man set down a dark colored pouch beside it, then stepped back. The pouch sloshed suggestively. All three were clearly Polynesian. The men wore short pants and their upper bodies were swathed in a pastel colored cloth that they'd apparently wrapped around their shoulders and chest. The woman was similarly attired above the waist, although more colorfully, but substituted a skirt that fell to the middle of her calf and was slit up to mid-thigh.

The woman spoke then, a melodic succession of syllables that meant absolutely nothing to either of the captives. When she paused, Rivers prepared to respond, then turned to Sharon. "You try to answer her. She's doing all the talking and it may be that the women are in charge here."

Sharon tried to keep her voice calm and her expression friendly. "Hello. I don't speak your language, obviously, but we really want to be friends. My name is Sharon," she tapped her chest and repeated her name. "And this is Jerry." She pointed to her companion and repeated his name also. "Will you tell me your name?" When she gestured toward the woman, there was a flicker of recognition, but no response.

"She understands what you want but she's reluctant to tell you," whispered Rivers.

"Some cultures believe that knowing a person's name gives you power over them."

The woman spoke again, a long string of syllables that conveyed no more meaning than before although her tone was self evident. She was irritated by their presence, but puzzled as well. One of the men said something to her and she nodded, and it was his turn to address them, but with no better results.

"I really wish I knew what you were saying. We want to be your friends."

The man who hadn't spoken blinked and frowned, then stepped forward and asked some sort of question. Sharon shook her head. "I'm sorry, I really am, but I have no idea what you're trying to say to me."

He was obviously listening very intently and when she paused he nodded to himself, then turned to his companions and spoke hurriedly and in a hushed voice. Neither of them answered but when he was done they gave their prisoners a long, searching look, then turned away. The door closed behind them with a dull thud, but one of the guards adjusted a slat so that more light entered their cell.

"Well, that could have gone better," said Rivers.

"At least they didn't kill us out of hand." Sharon collected the gifts they'd received, the pouch contained water and the bread was quite palatable. Both spent the next few minutes filling their stomachs. They were just setting aside what remained of their food when the door opened again, once more without warning.

It was the same threesome as before, but with them now was a second woman, not much more than a girl actually. She could not have been older than sixteen, and she was a decided contrast to her companions. The newcomer had markedly European features, although she had shells woven into her long, brown hair and her clothing, which resembled a sarong, was almost brashly colorful.

She was frowning at them, as though they were an annoying problem taking her away from more interesting things. Her eyes moved from one to the other, then fastened on Sharon. "These say you talk book words. Say them to me." She spoke with a peculiar accent and as though it was a badly learned second language, but it was definitely English.

CHAPTER THIRTEEN

Sharon's excitement caused her to speak quickly and not too clearly, and the girl's face betrayed complete bewilderment. Realizing her error, she forced herself to calm down and start again. "We speak the same words you do." That seemed to penetrate. "My name is Sharon. This is Jerry. You are...?"

This time the message got across. She nodded her head and introduced herself. "My name is Emma." Sharon and Rivers exchanged looks.

"Go on," he urged her softly. "You're doing fine."

"What do I do? How much should I tell them?"

"Tell them the truth, but keep it simple. And don't mention the others unless she brings it up." Emma gave him a quick, mildly hostile look, clearly having understood at least part of what he'd said.

It took a while to explain how they had come to the island. Emma was familiar with the concept of boats, but apparently had trouble with the concept that people could actually cross the ocean in one. Sharon managed to convey the idea that they had been crossing the water and that the storm had forced them to come ashore. When she was done, the girl turned to her companions and spoke at length in their language, doubtless retelling the tale and adding an additional layer of misunderstanding. The other three occasionally turned and looked toward the captives, and even less frequently asked short questions. They didn't appear any friendlier at the end than they had at the beginning. But they didn't seem more hostile either.

"When will you and the others go?" Emma's accent was still thick, but it was getting progressively easier to understand her.

The question was blunt enough. They obviously knew that the couple were not alone Sharon looked at Rivers for guidance, but he just shrugged. "We don't know. Our boat is broken. Emma, our friends don't know where we are and they will be worried about us."

"Your friends are in the place where no one lives. They kill the lost animals and eat them. They will be lost also."

"That must be the village she's talking about." Rivers considered that for a moment. "They obviously know what we've been up to. Don't try to keep any secrets."

"No secrets," Emma repeated, making it an order. "You must speak all."

Sharon did the best she could. Sometimes she had to rephrase things, often she had to oversimplify. When she was done, Emma turned to Rivers and demanded that he speak to her, and she asked him many of the same questions, as though wanting to check on Sharon's veracity. Rivers had always been good at picking up foreign languages, and he approached her version of English in much the same fashion. She had a very limited vocabulary and occasionally used words he was unfamiliar with; occasionally they were mispronunciations of a familiar word, more commonly words drawn from the local language.

When Emma seemed to have run out of questions, he asked her one. "How do you speak the same as us? Are there others like you here?"

"Some," she answered unenthusiastically. "We speak the words of our fathers and mothers and their fathers and mothers. We remember the book words and honor them."

"They must be descended from the survivors of another wreck," suggested Sharon. "I wonder how many of them there are."

Emma had been in the midst of another conference, which now seemed to have ended. They had all been sitting on the floor for the last hour or so, and now the entourage stood up as one. Sharon and Rivers hastened to imitate them.

"Things will be carried here for you. You will stay here. We will talk more later."

Sharon took a step forward. "Please! Can't you let us go? We need to speak with our friends, tell them we are safe."

Emma's face was solemn. "It is night. No one goes in the night. Night belongs to the Nempi."

"The Nempi?" Sharon frowned. "Who are the Nempi?" Rivers thought of the cave dragon and wondered if the "who" should be "what".

But Emma did not seem inclined to explain. "More talk after sleep." And she turned her back and followed the others out. The guards immediately closed the door.

The mood at the Ritz was distinctly downbeat. Even Nathan kept his peace after querulously complaining about how inconsiderate it was for the others to get lost without thinking about the consequences for the rest of the group. Grace took him aside and spoke to him heatedly after that, and he had the good sense to look at least slightly abashed. Fields was clearly concerned, but agreed completely with Walters that they couldn't risk sending anyone out to look for them.

"We'd just compound the problem by getting lost ourselves. Or worse."

Only Harding seemed unaffected, since he never varied from his gloomy silence.

The watch situation was suddenly more complex. The possibility that the missing pair had encountered active trouble rather than simply having gotten lost was worrisome enough that Walters would have preferred to continue with two guards per shift, but now that they were reduced to a total of six, two of whom he considered marginally reliable at best, this no longer seemed practical. A secretive conversation with Fields revealed that both men had the same reservations, so they decided to make do with a single guard, Harding first, followed by Walters, and then by Fields. Mrs. Galt would be insulted at being overlooked and would probably sit up with Harding just to demonstrate her endurance, but that couldn't be helped. Walters hoped to convince her that he wanted her as a reserve but knew she wouldn't be fooled.

Walters double checked their store of firewood even though he already knew they had enough to last at least through the night, and he and Fields made a wide circuit of the Ritz at dusk, primarily to work off nervous tension rather than to actually accomplish anything. They had increased the size of the fire so that it would serve as a beacon if Sharon and Rivers were still wandering about in the darkness, although he was sure they would have the sense to find cover once they knew they could not return safely before night. If one of them was injured, the other might remain until morning, and then come back to get help. That seemed the least unpleasant scenario. They could hardly have gotten lost given the open nature of the landscape, unless they had gone into the caves and become disoriented there. Rivers seemed too sensible for that, and so did Sharon, but there was always the possibility.

It was going to be a long night.

It was a long night for Rivers and Sharon as well, although they were saved the necessity of sleeping on the cold stone floor when two men they hadn't seen previously delivered bedding to their cell. The two mattresses were actually woven cloth unevenly stuffed with something that yielded reasonably comfortably, and it was certainly much better than they had expected. They each received a woven blanket, which they welcomed because the temperature here was much cooler than above ground.

Rivers was a light sleeper and he heard muffled conversations from time to time from outside the door, probably between the two guards, and always in a language he could not have understood even if he'd heard it clearly. On at least one occasion, he was certain he'd heard the guards being replaced with new ones, but since that didn't alter their situation any, he just rolled over and went back to sleep.

He was wakened by his internal clock, because the light level hadn't changed since they'd been taken prisoner. Sharon began to stir a few minutes later and once she was sitting up, he retrieved the small portion of fruit left over from the previous day and they shared it between them.

"They'll have to let us out of here pretty soon or it's going to start getting messy," she said when they were done.

As if that had been a signal, the doorway opened. Emma was there with another, older woman, and two men, only one of whom looked familiar. "Come with us now," said Emma.

They were heavily escorted, two armed guards in front and another two behind, as they traveled along a short length of narrow tunnel, then much farther along a passageway so wide that the whole party could have walked abreast if they had wanted to. Portions were dimly lit from apparently natural sources, others had lamps that were clearly fueled by some kind of oil, although the odor was unfamiliar. The ground dropped ahead of them steadily, sometimes steeply, before opening out into another cavern, much larger than the first. There were a dozen or so people scattered about, most of whom gave them curious looks as they passed, although none approached or spoke.

A natural archway loomed ahead, and the light was much brighter beyond it. The cavern opened up in all directions as they turned the next corner, and the roof vanished as they stepped out under the open sky.

Steep natural rock walls rose to dizzying heights on every side and Rivers felt momentarily disoriented until he realized where they were. "We're inside the volcano," he said softly to Sharon, who nodded her agreement.

After another few steps he realized that this was only partly true. The cone, or what remained of it, towered above them on their left, but it was heavily fractured and the top showed deep notches where portions of the perimeter had collapsed, leaving gaps wide enough to fly a small plane through. To their right lay a tumbled mass or broken rock extending beyond their line of sight, the remains of that portion of the volcano which had collapsed entirely. There was no visible sign of a lava flow; it was as though some entirely different cataclysm had torn an extended arc out of the side of the mountain and left the remains strewn about. At the very limit of their vision, they could see ocean to the east.

Their path led up and over a rise in the ground and what they saw from that vantage point was even more breathtaking than the ruined volcano. Spread out in front of them was a patchwork of tilled fields, what appeared to be a well tended orchard, several small pools of open water, and a fenced area behind which at least several score animals grazed quietly. They looked a lot like short horned antelope but their bodies were thick and round, like dairy cows. There were small buildings here and there, some with thatched roofs and walls, but most built of stone. The largest concentration was just beyond the orchard, what appeared to be a community center, and even from this distance they could see that the houses were arranged in concentric circles and bore the same style of construction as the ones they had already seen.

There were people working in the fields, and others walking from one place to another. A small knot of children was playing some elaborate game involving long sticks. It all looked so peaceful that Rivers had to remind himself that they were still being held prisoner.

Their guides/captors urged them forward.

The night was not nearly as peaceful for the others. Harding stood his watch stolidly, and was so unresponsive to Mrs. Galt's efforts to engage him in conversation that she finally surrendered to the inevitable and went off to sleep. He sat a while longer, added fresh wood to the fire, then started a slow walk around the limits of the lighted area, carrying a torch in one hand. Walters had considered giving him the pistol while he was on watch, but decided against it. There was still something in the seaman's demeanor that made him uneasy.

There had been a heavy rain late in the afternoon, but it had ended almost as soon as it began and the air was dry and almost pleasantly cool for a change, although faint spears of lightning lit up the distance as the small storm slowly moved away. Harding's right shoulder and hip had been bothering him for the past year, probably the onset of arthritis, and it was sometimes difficult for him to find a comfortable position, particularly if he had been sitting for a long time. Walking about usually helped, but he often sat stubbornly and suffered, assuming that God would not have visited the discomfort upon him if he had not been meant to suffer it.

He had almost completed his circuit when he heard something that brought him up short. It hadn't been much, just the scraping of a pebble across rough ground, but it was enough to draw his attention. He turned and faced outward, raising the torch slightly higher, leaning forward and squinting to better pierce the darkness. A hint of movement caught his attention and a distant flash of lightning struck just in time to reveal its outline.

For a second or two, Harding relaxed, because it was unmistakably a human head and shoulders that he had seen, and he assumed that it must be Rivers or the girl, finally making their way back. That momentary hesitation almost cost him his life because the intruder was not alone, and strong arms wrapped around Harding from behind, pinning his right arm so tightly that he dropped the torch.

He shouted, in rage rather than fear, and twisted his body, trying to tear himself loose. His feet got tangled and he lost his balance, but managed to throw himself backward so that he came down on top of his attacker rather than beneath him. Bellowing with rage, he drove an elbow back and had the satisfaction of feeling it connect solidly, but the arms holding him tightened rather than loosened. Although he heard voices responding to his shout, he wasn't about to wait for assistance. He jerked his head backward, hoping to break a nose, but managed to inflict only a glancing blow, and now his assailant seemed to have wrapped his feet around Harding's body as well as his arms.

With considerable difficulty, Harding managed to pull his right arm free and he felt around for his belt sheath. They rolled and he cried out as his fingers were pinched between their bodies and the ground, but then they rolled back and he touched the hilt of his knife. He pulled it free and made a wild stab at his attacker, had the brief satisfaction of knowing he had struck truly, although he inflicted no more than a shallow cut before they rolled again, and this time the pain in his fingers made him lose his grip.

Walters came running with Fields only a step behind. Both men had their weapons out and Fields grabbed a burning brand from the fire as he passed. They could see two figures struggling in the shadows, but they were rolling in a patch of taller grass and neither man had a clear view. Walters fired a single round into the air, and the results were far more dramatic than he expected. There was a hoarse, guttural cry and Harding found himself suddenly free, his assailant rushing off so quickly that he never got a clear look at him. More significantly, the other two men heard rustling all around them, as though they had been completely encircled until the sound of the pistol frightened the enemy into retreat.

Walters closed the gap and helped an obviously shaken Harding to his feet. "Are you all right, man? Are you hurt?"

Harding bent down to retrieve his knife and replace it in its sheath, then looked himself over as though amazed to find no serious injury and shook his head. "Nothing to complain of." His voice shook.

Fields joined them, his eyes betraying his uneasiness. "We should retreat to the fire before they get their nerve back."

Harding seemed incapable of movement until Walters touched his arm, then shook his head to indicate he was all right. They walked back quickly and found the others waiting for them.

"What happened?" asked Nathan anxiously.

"Something jumped Harding when he got too far from the fire, but he's all right. We scared it off."

"It wasn't one of them dragon things." Harding's voice was uncharacteristically subdued, and they all turned to him. He seemed quite calm now, unnaturally so. "It wasn't any creature of this earth. It was a demon from hell that grabbed me. I felt its claws on my flesh and its hot breath against my face and when I tried to break free of its arms I knew the truth." His eyes moved defiantly from face to face, daring anyone to contradict him. "When I was wrestling with it, I knew it wasn't any mortal being I fought. Because it had too many arms."

They were escorted to one of the buildings on the outer circle of the cluster, but only Emma and the older woman, who had thus far remained silent, accompanied them inside. Their first glance confirmed what they had already surmised, that they were not the first outsiders to arrive on this unnamed and uncharted island. On either side of the entrance stood stacks of apparently randomly assorted items, some in boxes, others carefully set in place, although in no obvious order. Metal tools were mixed with odds and ends of jewelry, an ornate hand mirror, a pair of antique pistols, a snuff box, several wooden chests, a mortar and pestle, a pair of scissors, several panes of glass, some of them cracked, what looked like a pair of brass bedposts, and others items, both practical and decorative.

In the center of the room was a table, which looked equally out of place. It was circular, finely finished, and sturdily built. Four matching chairs had been placed around it, and a white haired man, obviously not descended from Polynesian stock, sat in one of them. "Please to sit," he said solemnly. He had the same accent as Emma.

They both took chairs and the silent woman slipped into the last one, while Emma stepped back, hovering silently. "I am called John. Martha is my daughter." He nodded to the silent woman, who nodded almost undetectably, her displeasure evident. "Emma is the daughter of Martha."

Rivers and Sharon introduced themselves again, suppressing the urge to ask the dozens of questions that occurred to them.

"You come from Home." There was no doubt that he meant the last word as the name of a specific place.

Rivers tried to remember to keep the explanation simple. "We were lost and came here by accident. Our boat was destroyed during the night."

John looked puzzled and asked Emma something, not in English, and she responded in the same fashion. John nodded his understanding. "You are not alone. There are more."

"No," said Sharon. "I mean, yes, we have friends waiting for us."

"The Nempi know of them. They will not live."

Rivers leaned forward. "We have fire. The Nempi will not hurt our friends."

John sat back, looking puzzled. "The Nempi do not fear the fire. They are wise in that way and use it as we do."

Rivers and Sharon exchanged looks. Something was wrong here. "But the Nempi are just animals!" said Sharon. "Aren't they?"

It took a few exchanges to straighten things out. The Nempi were not in fact the cave dragons. Even Martha laughed lightly when she realized the nature of their confusion. John explained that the creature which had killed Quinn, and possibly the reverend, were called golas and there were only a few of them. The Nempi, whatever they were, were far more numerous. John was evasive about them, as though there was some kind of taboo involved, and shifted the subject whenever it came too close. All that Sharon and Rivers were able to determine was that they lived outside the mountain and that they were dangerous.

They didn't have much better luck learning where John and his people had come from, but it was less because of evasiveness than from simple ignorance. John knew little himself, except that his father's father's father several times removed had come to the island with many of his own kind. John insisted that they had flown down inside the cone of the volcano, but that was obviously impossible. The island's inhabitants had taken them in and the subsequent generations had become increasingly assimilated. John's wife had been an islander, although there was little sign of her heritage in her daughter or granddaughter.

"You still talk English though," said Sharon.

John looked puzzled. "We talk book words to honor our father's father's father. But we are few." He looked sad. "Emma has no brother. No sister. There is no one else to learn the book words. Soon no one talks so."

Martha stood up and left after about half an hour, but Emma remained standing despite the empty chair. John talked to them patiently and seemed to be evasive only when the subject of the Nempi came up, although his vocabulary on some subjects was so limited that they weren't satisfied that they completely understood what he was saying. His description of life among what he called the People cheered them considerably. The community was governed by a council of elders, some of whom were apparently chosen by popular vote, others by virtue of their age and perceived wisdom. They rarely ventured out of the mountain and adjoining labyrinth of caves and tunnels, partly because of the mysterious

Nempi, partly because they were self sufficient thanks to their fairly sophisticated knowledge of agriculture and animal husbandry. They also harvested fish from the ocean, although it appeared that they did so by casting from shore. They used boats on the large freshwater pond but apparently nowhere else.

Sharon noticed that the distinctive fruit they'd been eating did not seem to grow inside the volcano, but John frowned when she described it. "Nempi food is not good. Bad for the children." He refused to elaborate, or perhaps lacked the words to explain.

Rivers tentatively broached the subject of their own status. John's dour expression cleared. "You are like us. You stay where it is safe, grow food, build house, have children."

"What about our friends?" asked Sharon.

"They are same. Must come here though. Nempi will kill if they stay."

"Will you send someone for them?"

John looked uneasy. "You must go to them. Bring them here. All will be safe here."

Martha returned with two of the islanders, both male. They carried woven baskets filled with fruit, more of the rough textured but tasty bread, and long pieces of roasted meat twisted around skewers. Martha herself carried a flask and she served them drinks – a rather tart fruit juice – in finely wrought, metal wine goblets she retrieved from one of the wooden chests.

Rivers examined his thoughtfully. "This came from France," he said. "And I think it was hand made."

While they were eating, the conversation became more casual. Sharon stood up to stretch her legs and took a moment to look at some of the artifacts. Emma joined her and began pointing out things she thought might be particularly interesting, but they tended to be the gaudier items like the mirror and jewels. Sharon was looking for something more practical. "Don't you have any records from the original landing?" Emma looked at her blankly and she simplified it. "Are there papers? Pictures of book words?"

Emma's eyes lit up. "We have books! We have many books! Come see!" And she led Sharon to a large wooden chest in one corner, lifting the lid with both hands because it was so heavy. There was a whiff of mustiness and a puff of dust, but inside the chest was a kind of treasure. There were books, quite a few of them, with an ornate Bible on top. There was also a very thick stack of thin sheets of some kind of parchment, each one covered with very fine writing.

Harding was clearly offended by the skeptical looks that greeted his announcement, and he refused to respond to any further questions, just stalked off to his sleeping chamber inside the Ritz. The others remained puzzled, disturbed, and incredulous.

"Well, whatever attacked him ran off promptly when we showed up," said Walters, but even he felt only partially reassured.

They doubled up the watch. Nathan didn't even complain about being paired with Walters, and Grace volunteered to sit up with Fields. "If something happens, no one goes to investigate until the rest of us are awake," cautioned Walters. "Harding was lucky. Those things can kill quickly and silently. Reverend Abbott barely had time to cry out when they got him."

Fields wasn't convinced that they were dealing with the same danger, but he didn't argue the point. He counted the rounds in his pistol and then counted them again. Not even a full load, and the two boxes of cartridges he'd taken from the *Sturtevant* had been in his bag at the lifeboat and had not been among the salvaged goods. As a rule he never indulged in regrets, but he really would have felt safer with one of those boxes in his pocket.

No one looked in on Harding, who hadn't gone to sleep after all. He sat rigidly on the ground with his legs crossed, staring into the darkness, his lips moving silently, repeating the same few words, over and over again. A prayer.

Dawn came at last, and with no further incident, although Fields thought he felt eyes watching him all through his watch. Grace was sulky and snappish when she discovered he was not about to respond to her flirtations, although her mood shifted again just before dawn, perhaps improved by the faint glow on the horizon. Without makeup, and with her hair in near disarray, Grace was not nearly as stunning as she had been when she'd been aboard the *Sturtevant*, but Fields thought that on balance she was probably more attractive as she was at present. She had even shown some signs of having an actual personality hidden somewhere behind her petulant facade. Fields was no stranger to women, but in his line of work he had always been careful to keep business and pleasure separate, and right now he was in the business of survival. In fact, he admitted to himself, he was always in the business of survival.

As soon as it was light enough to see, he climbed to the roof and walked around its perimeter. It was possible that whatever had attacked Harding was still nearby, hidden behind one of the other structures, or in one of the scattered clumps of scraggly trees and spiky bushes. But he didn't think so. It no longer felt as though eyes were following his every movement.

Walters emerged a minute later, rubbing his eyes. Fields waved to him to indicate everything appeared to be okay and Walters waved back an acknowledgment, then started toward the new latrine they had dug the previous day. Grace stood up and went inside, then returned with Mrs. Galt, who wore her inevitable cheery smile. Fields was always alert when he wakened, but rarely cheerful. He envied her that ability.

They had finished the last of their meat the night before, and unless his traps had caught fresh victims during the night, they'd be living on fruit and the rapidly dwindling rations for the rest of the day. Sharon had sampled the berries she'd found and they hadn't made her sick, but they were so bitter she declared them of use only if they faced actual starvation. He'd seen only a handful of very small fish in the stream, but there was a good sized pool of water that they hadn't looked at yet, and it might be big enough to support a larger variety.

He climbed down, chatted briefly with Mrs. Galt, then decided to go for a short walk. The only jungles Fields felt comfortable in were made of steel and stone and asphalt, but it didn't take much skill to find the blood trail. It had dried to a dark brown stain, but there was a discernible line of droplets leading from the Ritz out into the scrub growth and beyond. He followed it for several paces and confirmed that it was headed directly toward the distant jungle.

There were no footprints though, at least none visible to an untrained eye. The surface of the ground was just too hard. He looked at the jungle speculatively, and one hand slid inside his jacket to confirm that his weapon was still there.

Sharon reached down and picked up the *Bible*, opened the cover. It was inscribed to John Marion Wallingford and dated 1790. She set it aside and reached for the next, which turned out to be the journal of John Marion Wallingford. The first entry was dated

January 30, 1792. "Jerry, there's a journal here and some other papers. Maybe they'll tell us something."

Emma touched her arm. "You know the book words? You can bring them to life?"

Sharon was momentarily puzzled. "Oh, you're asking me if I can read these? Yes. Yes, I can read. Can't you?"

Emma shook her head but it was her grandfather who answered. "We have lost the magic of the book words. We can say them but we cannot see them in the marks."

"Can't anyone here read?"

He shook his head. "My mother knew a little. She said them to us when I was a child. But they were hard and not important and the times were bad. My mother was the last to know the magic of the book words." He brightened. "You could teach us."

Sharon nodded absentmindedly, already turning back to the books. There were several more journals, all meticulously filled with writing, by at least two hands, but alternatively not successively. When she reached the bottom of the chest, she turned to the sheets of parchment, which were stiff with age but not as brittle as she had feared. It looked to be the same mix of handwriting there. The top sheet was dated 1799.

"We should read these, Jerry."

"Right." But he said it absentmindedly. Another consideration was more pressing. "John, we must tell our friends about this place."

"They must come here or they will die."

Although he wasn't completely prepared to trust their new hosts, Rivers had to admit that this hidden village was almost certainly safer than where the others were camped. Entry, at least from that side of the island, was apparently limited to the cave entrance and tunnels, and they were obviously watched by guards prepared to prevent any dangerous predator from entering. "We could go get them. Bring them back here."

John looked serious. "I speak to others first. They must choose whether you stay or go." His face brightened. "I think they will say you may stay. I will tell them you will teach us to know the book words again."

He stood up and Rivers rose as well, but John shook his head. "No. Wait here. I will be back soon."

CHAPTER FOURTEEN

"Soon" is one of those relative terms that lose their utility when the parties involved don't share the same definition. It was mid-morning when John left them, and they had just been brought another meal - this time consisting of hot meat and vegetables rolled in thin, crusty bread – when he returned. He was smiling as he entered, but there was a hint of anxiety as well.

John asked if they had been treated well and urged them to eat, but Rivers wanted to know where they stood. He was so obviously determined that John made no further effort to dissemble. "The elders have agreed. Your friends will come to us. If they come, they will be our friends also. If they stay, the Nempi will kill all."

"Great! If we leave now, we can break camp and get back before it gets dark."

John began to look actively uncomfortable. "One must go. One must stay. Some of the elders are afraid. They think you maybe not what you say you are, that you give your eyes to our enemies."

"You think we're spies?"

John looked perplexed, obviously didn't recognize the term. "I do not believe this. Only some elders fear it. We must be safe. One of our people goes with you to see that you do not help the Nempi. You bring back friends. We all live here and the Nempi stay in Nempi land."

"It's all right, Jerry. I don't mind staying." She had been reading the earliest of the journals and it was still open in her lap. "I want to get started on these. Wallingford and his wife kept very detailed notes and some of this is fascinating. They chartered a ship called *Windlover* to take them all over the Pacific collecting curios. They must have had all sorts of things with them when they were shipwrecked here." She leafed back through the book. "Some kind of disease broke out on board just before they reached the island. That was December, 1793. The captain and several of the crew members died."

"Is that why they never left?"

She shook her head. "I don't know. I haven't gotten that far yet. But a lot of them were sick and they were very weak even after the fever broke. Wallingford was something of an amateur naturalist and he was fascinated with what he found there. There's a sketch of something that looks like one of those crab things, and some odd looking insects and a bird with four wings."

John spoke up. "You must go soon. You must return before the night."

Rivers still seemed uncertain, but Sharon felt no alarm. "Go ahead and get the others. I'll be fine here. If they had wanted to hurt us, they could have done so long before now."

"Unless they are using us to get the others within reach." He kept his voice low so that only Sharon could hear him.

"You don't really believe that."

"No, I suppose not. All right, but you be careful. There may be things going on here that we haven't been told about.

"Don't worry. They're not going to sacrifice me to their pagan god, if they even have one. And I haven't seen any signs of a giant ape looking for a bride. Get the others and come back as soon as you can."

John and Emma guided him to the mouth of the tunnel. There were people about, some of whom glanced at Rivers curiously but without any evident sign of fear. John seemed surprised to find no one waiting for them. "Jezra was to be here. He will show you the way to your people."

Emma seemed ill at ease. "Jezra is not coming. I will go in his place."

John's expression went from puzzlement to anger. His tone was stern as he let out a stream of words in a language Rivers didn't recognize. Emma waited patiently for it to end before answering in English. "Jezra does not know the book words."

John continued as before, but some of his fury had ebbed. Emma seemed exasperated and answered in the same tongue and at considerable length while Rivers stood helplessly to one side. Although her grandfather was still visibly upset when their exchange concluded, he nodded, first at her, then at Rivers. "Be watchful. Come back quickly."

Emma, looking quite pleased with herself, took three steps toward the tunnel, then paused and waved for Rivers to follow. He did.

They spoke very little as they walked, Emma in the lead, but they must have taken a different route because they bypassed the cavern where the ambush had been sprung, and emerged at the point where the tunnel split from a different artery. From there it was only a few minutes to open sky, and when they reached it Emma stopped, looking out over the landscape. "I stand here many times before," she said slowly. "Never have I walked in Nempi land until today." She turned to Rivers. "Now you must lead and I will follow."

She was almost certainly playing up to him. Although her claim that she had never been beyond that point might well be true, she knew that they were living in one of the abandoned buildings and the circle of structures was quite visible from their present, elevated vantage point. Rivers felt amused rather than flattered, but he also felt a sense of urgency. If he was to return, convince the others to relocate, get them packed up and back here before nightfall, they would have to move briskly.

He set a fairly rapid pace, once they had descended the steps, but they had to slow down considerably whenever they reached a section where the footing was less certain. Emma was not barefoot, but her rough cloth footwear could not have provided much cushioning. The broken land seemed even more formidable now, although it was probably his anxiety coloring his perceptions. Emma had no trouble keeping up with him, and it was in fact Rivers who first called for a brief rest stop.

"Sharon. She is your mate?"

Rivers laughed. "No, we're just friends."

"Then your mate is with the others?"

"No, I don't have a mate."

Emma thought that over. "Good," she said at last, but then frowned. "Why have your elders not given you a mate?"

"It doesn't work that way. We choose our own mates."

"Your women also choose?"

"Yes, they do."

There was a longer pause. "I like your way."

They resumed the march a short while later, occasionally sipping water from the pouches slung under their arms, provided by Emma just before they left. She had also insisted on carrying a bundle of dried meat and fruits, even though Rivers had told her that it wouldn't be needed.

Grace was the first to spot the two figures in the distance. Mrs. Galt had managed to patch some of the ruined clothing that they'd salvaged and Grace finally could change into a new blouse and a more practical skirt. She had washed what she'd been wearing and was spreading it on the roof of the Ritz to dry in the sun and when she turned toward the volcano, she spotted them as they topped a rise. "They're coming!" she called down to the others. "I can see them!"

Fields and Walters both climbed up to join her, shading their eyes. "I believe you're right, Miss Porter."

But Grace had been watching while they were climbing up and she shook her head. "No, I'm wrong. I mean, that looks like it might be Captain Rivers, all right, but the second person, that's not Sharon."

Walters looked again, squinting. "Are you sure? That certainly looks like her to me."

"No, she's taller, and she doesn't move that way. I wonder why she isn't with him?"

But Walters was more interested in knowing who was coming in her stead.

It wasn't long before they found out. Walters, Harding, and Grace went out to meet them while Fields remained behind with the others, just in case this was a feint designed to draw them out. They relaxed only after they'd closed the distance and Rivers gave them a brief but accurate description of what had happened, though he kept any lingering suspicions to himself. Walters felt somewhat awkward dealing with Emma, who responded to questions but had volunteered nothing. She seemed to have lost some of her self confidence, either because she found herself among strangers, or because she was in Nempi territory and the day was advancing quickly. Grace gave her a quick once over and dismissed her, obviously not worried about the new competition. It was Harding who watched her the most closely, and with an intensity that might have worried the others if they had noticed it.

The reaction to the news that Rivers thought they should all immediately move inside the mountain was not enthusiastic, and even Mrs. Galt had several objections. Fields and Walters both agreed that it was probably safer there than where they were, but Mrs. Galt and the Porter siblings were less willing to uproot themselves again so quickly and without having so much as having seen their proposed new home. Harding surprised everyone by expressing his own opinion, in his usual terse fashion. "It's not safe here. There are demons about."

Mrs. Galt soon succumbed to persuasion, and Grace flitted back and forth, as though trying to decide what role would be best for her image, cooperative team member or thoughtful doubter. That left Nathan as the only steadfast negative, and the others had been playing increasingly less attention to his opinions. He was overruled and the packing operation began.

It didn't take long because they didn't have that much worth taking. "Leave the rest. If we need it for some reason, we can come back for it later." Walters felt much more comfortable now that there was a distinct goal in sight.

Emma remained silent throughout the packing process except on two occasions.
The first came when she first caught sight of the statue in the center of village. Her eyes widened and she took an involuntary step backward. Rivers asked what was wrong and she raised a shaking hand to point at the four armed figure. "Nempi!" He asked her what she meant but she just shook her head and would say no more on the subject.

The second occasion was just before they broke camp. Mrs. Galt had filled a makeshift bag with freshly picked fruit and carried it outside. Emma's eyes widened when she saw it, and she shook her head furiously. "No! That is Nempi food! Nempi food stays on Nempi land. Nothing of the Nempi is allowed."

The others exchanged puzzled looks and Mrs. Galt took out one piece of the fruit. "We've been eating it for two days. There's nothing wrong with it. Here, have a piece."

But Emma shrunk back from the proffered fruit, shaking her head even more furiously. "Nempi food is bad! No one should eat of it."

So the fruit was left behind to rot in the sun while the seven survivors and one teenaged girl started the long march back to the caverns.

It took longer to get back than Rivers had expected, and it was dusk when they finally saw the steps directly ahead of them. Emma had been looking back the way they had come every minute or two and was obviously and increasingly nervous. Her mood was contagious and they took no further rest stops despite one prolonged spell of complaints from Nathan, until they had reached the cave entrance itself. As they did so, three men and two women stepped out of the shadows. Emma spoke to them in their own language and they quickly relieved the others of some of their burden.

The land of the Nempi, whoever they were, was behind them.

They spent their first night inside the mountain as a group, bedded down in a large, single roomed structure that was probably some kind of meeting hall. Sharon was already ensconced there, with a pile of journals beside her, reading by the light of an oil lamp. Emma went off to report to her grandfather shortly after they arrived, and while two of those who helped them settle in were also theoretically able to speak English, they were not nearly as fluent as Emma and her grandfather, and Rivers wondered how much longer the language would survive. Emma might teach her children someday, but what inducement would they have to learn it? Of course, if the present party was stranded here permanently – a situation he refused to consider except as a theoretical exercise – then it might linger on for a few more generations.

The natives seemed to be friendly, but wary, which in fact mirrored the newcomers' attitude toward them. Except for Nathan, of course, who was openly hostile, and Harding, who seemed as indifferent as he always did, although his eyes occasionally followed one or another of the local women. Walters made a tentative effort to discuss their options once they were alone, but everyone was so tired from the latest trek that he gave it up until morning. Their sleep was undisturbed, but they posted a watch anyway, just in case.

When Rivers woke up the following morning, he was chagrined to learn that he'd out slept most of the others. Only the Porter siblings and Fields were still abed, and Fields had taken the second watch. Sharon was sitting in a cane backed chair with one of the journals in her lap and she pointed toward a table in one corner, upon which sat fresh fruit – similar but not identical to the one they had found in such large numbers earlier – and an assortment of breads and pastries. "Try the long, skinny ones. They're very good."

They were filled with a mildly spicy meat paste and they were, as she had said, very good.

"Where are the others?"

"Out and about. Emma and some others came by and offered to give them the grand tour. We've been given use of this," she waved to indicate the building around them, "but only until we can build ourselves places of our own. They're willing to help but only if we work along with them."

Rivers tried one of the fruits. It was sweeter than the ones they'd found in the jungle. "Discover anything interesting in those journals?"

"Oh yes. Quite a bit in fact. The Wallingfords kept very detailed records, at least about the things that interested them. While the rest were recovering from whatever sickness stranded them here, they were out and about observing the local plants and animals. The natives were very friendly, and very eager to learn. Actually, in many cases they were recovering lost knowledge."

"How's that?"

"This place used to be much bigger, Jerry. There were an entire city out there, and several thousand people. They had a fishing fleet, although they never learned to navigate and couldn't go beyond sight of land, simple metal working, a written language, codified laws, and a surprisingly sophisticated medical system. They knew how diseases were spread, at least functionally, and they even performed simple surgery."

"What happened to the city? We didn't see any sign of it." But he thought he already knew the answer, or at least part of it.

Sharon set the journal aside and stood up so that she could pace, a habit she found helped her to organize her thoughts. "Wallingford didn't understand how it happened, but the city sank under the ocean. The natives told him that it happened so many generations ago that they had lost count, and that it happened in a single day, and when he seemed skeptical they took him out and showed him the ruins. They're underwater, the entire city is gone, along with a few smaller communities."

Rivers remembered the carved stone he had noticed when they were coming ashore, just barely submerged. The tip of a tower of some sort? "An earthquake maybe. Or some kind of collapse in the seabed. Or maybe that was when the volcano exploded."

She shook her head. "Not if the native stories are true. According to Wallingford, they told him that steam used to rise through the ground inside the cone, but when he described an eruption or a lava flow, he drew a blank. If it was ever active, it must have been before the natives were here, or so long ago that even the memories are lost. And when the disaster hit, whatever caused it, the volcano cooled down and it's been like that ever since."

"All right, so part of the island sank. Why haven't they tried to rebuild the village where we stayed, or the land surrounding the jungle? Their resources here are limited."

"I haven't gotten far enough yet, if the answer is in here at all. Part of it might be because the disaster came so quickly that most of the skills they needed were lost. It wiped out most of the population, and there were shortages of food and other problems for years afterward. There are only a couple of hundred of them left. But it's even more complicated than that. It appears that the island may still be sinking. Wallingford describes how they were forced to abandon some of the fields on the eastern border because the ocean broke through the dike they'd built.

"All the more reason to expand westward."

"Maybe. But that's Nempi territory. They didn't tell Wallingford much. The whole subject is some kind of taboo. He thought they might be another group of survivors who split off from the rest."

The party was not altogether again until the mid-day meal, which they ate in the open air sitting on the grass in a well cultivated garden while they were more or less inspected by a group of about a dozen older islanders. John introduced them all around, but the names all seemed very similar and it was very hard to remember who was who. Two of the elders spoke some English, but not enough to be useful. One of them clearly had at least one European among his recent ancestors, but the rest looked predominantly Polynesian. John translated back and forth, and Rivers was amused to hear many of the same platitudes here that were spoken in the social elite of his father's associates. People really are the same all over, more or less.

It was explained to them that the People welcomed them and would support the newcomers until they could earn their own way. They would be expected to abide by the local customs, which did not appear to be particularly restrictive, would be given land to build on and help to fashion homes for themselves. In return for what they ate, they would gather fruit, work in the fields, fish, or help tend livestock. The islanders had no system of hard currency, however, one could accumulate credit by working extra hours for the community, which would be recorded and exchanged by mutual agreement. The local shoemaker, for example, almost never worked outside his home. He traded custom made footwear for work credits. If any of the newcomers proved to have viable skills, they were welcome to take advantage of the same arrangement.

When everyone was fed and the council members had dispersed, the eight outsiders had their own separate meeting in which they shared the observations they'd made during the day. Neither of the Porters accepted the possibility that they might have to make a permanent place among these people, and surprisingly Fields sided with them, even though Walters grudgingly revealed his own doubts that they would ever be located. "Even if they do find us, it could be several years from now. We're just going to have to adapt to the situation as it is, not as we want it to be."

The argument remained unresolved and Rivers finally changed the subject by suggesting that Sharon provide a summary of what she'd learned from the journals. She repeated most of what she'd told Rivers earlier, but added one new piece to the puzzle, the explanation of why the Wallingfords never left.

"There was some kind of landslide or earthquake a few months after they arrived. The natives thought the island was going to sink completely this time, but that wasn't the case. Wallingford goes into less detail than usual, but he says that their ship - *The Windlover* – was rendered useless to them by falling rock. I don't know whether it was sunk in the harbor or what but he never refers to it again and it's quite obvious they had resigned themselves to staying here for the rest of their lives."

That brought another round of uneasy protests that died out of its own accord.

"Does it say anything about these Nempi, whoever they are?" asked Fields.

"Only in passing. The Nempi are as close to a taboo subject as these people have, apparently. Wallingford believed that they were criminals or deviates of some sort who were driven out of the city into the jungle at some time before or right after the cataclysm that destroyed the city. They're connected to something called the Seed of the Gods, but at least as far as I've read, no one would tell him what that was either. And remember, there was no common language between the two groups when they arrived here, so part of the problem might simply be a misunderstanding rather than an evasion."

"What about this rule they have about not bringing in food from outside?"

Sharon shrugged. "Nothing yet. But I've only read through the first two years, there are four more years of journals, and another five or six on parchment."

"Well, I think you've just appointed yourself the group's historian," said Walters. "How are the rest of us going to earn our keep?" That evolved into an occasionally heated conversation because neither of the Porters felt they were suited for manual labor. Grace finally admitted that she wouldn't mind picking fruit or something similar, "so long as it isn't too dirty", and Fields shamed Nathan into agreeing that he ought to do something to earn his keep, perhaps fishing. Rivers smiled to himself, assuming that Nathan pictured himself sitting under a tree with a pole rather than trawling with a woven net..

Mrs. Galt was appointed housekeeper, but she also wanted to interact more directly with the natives, either by teaching them English or preferably by learning their language. "And I've picked up more than a few medical skills in my time. When your husband builds bridges in out of the way places, you learn to fend for yourself."

The day passed, and then the next, and when they started building the framework for a pair of thatched houses on the second day, more than a dozen of the islanders joined them. The first hut was up and roofed by nightfall, and the second was completed in a few hours the following morning. The women moved into the first and smaller of the two and the men were in their slightly larger accommodations by mid-afternoon.

They had already picked up a few words of the local speech, enough to convey simple ideas, and two of the local men, Natal and Bomir, seemed particularly friendly. Walters saw Harding watching one of the women one day as she walked past wearing the common abbreviated sash and slipper arrangement that left her breasts uncovered, and added another worry to his already long list. Emma came by frequently, although she admitted that she'd been chastened by her grandfather for spending too much time away from her chores.

Sharon finished the journals and turned to the parchment sheets, but she had already learned a great deal. "The Nempi were in fact part of this community, and they were exiled before the island began to sink. If I'm not mistaken, that little community where we stayed, and the temple, all belonged to the Nempi. The parting seems to have been a peaceful one, at least at first, but they remained strictly segregated. Wallingford says they didn't even trade with one another, even though some families were split up by the exile."

"What caused the schism then?" asked Mrs. Galt. "As far as I can see, they don't have much of a formal religion. They believe that God or the gods are everywhere but unknowable and that they rarely if ever intercede in human affairs. Not much room there for heresy."

Sharon shook her head. "Wallingford didn't know, at least not as far as I've read. He says it had something to do with the Nempi eating forbidden food, food tainted by the Seed of the Gods, whatever that is. He tried to be strictly objective, but you can feel the frustration in his writing. And his wife didn't make any effort to conceal how she felt."

She had also gleaned a good bit of detail about the people among whom they would be living, at least for the foreseeable future, but most of it had no immediate application. "I think the most important thing we can do now is learn enough of their language to get by when John and Emma aren't around to translate."

Mrs. Galt had actually picked up a fair amount of the language because she was attempting to teach English to a half dozen village children. "It's a novelty to them at the moment, and I think three or four will quit as soon as something better comes up, but the other two seem genuinely interested. I'm surprised John and Emma haven't been able to interest them."

"Maybe it's the chance to be with the strangers rather than the language lesions that's attracting them," suggested Walters.

On the morning of the third day, Sharon came looking for Rivers. He was helping repair the fencing around the largest pasture, holding the crossbars in place while Natal expertly redid the lashings to the posts. Emma had come by earlier to watch, and Rivers had been secretly pleased when Natal told her to go off and do something useful. She'd been following him around a lot lately, and she was a complication he'd rather be spared.

Sharon watched silently until they finished the section they were mending. Natal clapped Rivers on the back as a sign that he had done a good job, then flopped down on the grass to lie flat on his back with his hands crossed on his chest, enjoying the warm sunlight. Rivers sipped some water, offered it to Sharon, who declined.

"Last night I read something very interesting. The natives eventually told the Wallingfords a lot more about the Seed of the Gods. He didn't know how much of it was true and how much was legend, but it sounds pretty strange."

"All right." He pointed toward a grassy patch in the shade. "Let's find a comfortable spot and you can tell me about it."

They sat down quite close together, closer than was really necessary. "Apparently, something fell from the sky one night, something big enough or hard enough that it destroyed one of their buildings when it hit. The Wallingfords thought at first that it might be connected to the destruction of the city but apparently this all happened many years before that. Their father's father's father and all that."

"Might have been a meteorite. A seed of light from the sky. It would probably have made quite an impression."

She shrugged. "The Wallingfords never speculated after they got the sequence of events figured out. Anyway, the meteorite or whatever isn't the Seed of the Gods. But it might have brought them."

He frowned. "How's that again?"

"There were people in the building when it collapsed. When they cleared away the wreckage, they recovered the bodies. They also found seeds everywhere, seeds of some plant they hadn't seen before. Apparently no one thought much of it at the time, but later on they found this new plant growing in the ruins." She leaned over and touched his arm. "The plant was a bluish green vine."

"The one that bit you?"

"Or one of its ancestors. Anyway, they cultivated the plant because it grew quickly and their livestock ate the leaves and later the fruit. Some of the people ate it also but not all of them."

"We haven't noticed any fruit growing on it."

She shook her head. "Wrong season. It blossoms and bears fruit for only a very short period of time. The thorns don't show up until the vines were several years old. That caught them by surprise but they didn't stop growing it, according to what they told the Wallingfords, although they did have to take precautions."

"No mention of our crabby friends?"

"No." She shook her head. "Unless that comes up later. I've still got some of the parchment to read but I stopped last night when I reached Wallingford's last entry."

"His last entry?"

"He got sick and died. His wife must have written everything from that point on."

Rivers glanced around. "I haven't seen any of the vines since we've been here."

"No, and you won't. These people make regular searches for any sign of it. Sometimes seeds get blown in by the wind and take root. They destroy it whenever they find it, just as they've done for generations. Lots of generations. They were already doing it before the city was destroyed, but long ago were forced to give up any idea of clearing it out of the jungle. It was too well established by then. There was a wall all around the city, separating this part of the island from the rest. But when the city sank, the only survivors were those who had been outside. They moved in here and abandoned the rest, and apparently that's when they started guarding the tunnels."

"It makes sense. This is a natural fortress, at least on the side facing inland."

"Yes, and they needed one. Because of the Nempi."

Harding didn't mind the work. He had always done more than his share aboard the *Sturtevant*, not out of a sense of duty or to help his mates, but simply because he saw that it needed to be done and it struck him as right that he do it so long as he was capable. If God saw fit to add to his penance, then so be it. When he saw three of the islanders hauling rocks to rebuild a collapsed section of wall, he joined them without being asked. They looked at him oddly at first, but soon began to smile and chatter at him in that peculiar language of theirs. He recognized that they had accepted him, but that affected him no differently than it would if they had turned their faces away and ignored his presence. It was the work that he was interested in, not the company or their approval.

They had nearly finished when two young women showed up carrying gourds filled with what looked like water but tasted like some mild fruit juice. It was surprisingly cool going down and Harding was not so enamored with the work that he wasn't willing to stop for some refreshment.

He was even more interested in the newcomers. They looked enough alike to be sisters, both in their late teens. The older one was swathed in cloth from knees to her throat, but tightly enough to show off a well developed figure. The younger one was less endowed, but she wore only a bright red skirt and was bare from the waist up other than a twist of flowers in her long black hair.

It was a temptation sent by Satan, he knew. He had known this was the devil's island even before he had wrestled with the demon two nights earlier. It had spared his life then and he'd been surprised to find himself alive when it was all over. Surprised and confused. But now he thought he might be figuring it out. He couldn't die until he had compromised his soul completely and irredeemably. That's why he was being tempted now. To damn his soul for all eternity.

But Harding had always assumed that he was bound for Hell eventually. He lowered the gourd and wiped his lips and let his eyes linger on the girl's bare breasts as she talked to one of the men. If he was already damned, why not enjoy whatever remained of his time in this world?

CHAPTER FIFTEEN

"It's hard to believe that there are still people living out there. Those buildings have been empty for generations and there was no sign of anything in the jungle."

"How much of the jungle did you actually see?"

"Not very much," he admitted. "But we'd have noticed something."

"No, you wouldn't. Not if they didn't want you to. The Nempi don't like the daylight. They hunt at night and spend the days in caves or other dark places."

Rivers shook his head. "I'm finding this a little hard to accept, Sharon. You're relying on something written by people long dead who may not have been in their right minds, or who might have been repeating lies they'd been told. Who knows how much of this is legend and how much reality?"

"I think it's the truth." She took a deep breath. "The vine is the cause of it all, Jerry. Animals ate the fruit, and they began to change. It took a long time, generations, but they did change. Some of them had birth defects so bad that they died, but others survived and became dangerous, and once one of them changed, it bred true. I've lived all my life on a farm, Jerry, and I know how heredity works."

"All right! All right. How did they change?"

She took a deep breath. "The ones that lived became larger and more vicious. Sometimes their skin became scaly, almost armored, and their nails were more likely to be clawed. There was a kind of lizard on the island, something like an iguana, and they were particularly drawn to the vine. Eventually all of the old strain was gone. They were replaced by a more aggressive variety and they grew to be larger than a man." She paused. "And like all the other animals affected, they grew a third pair of limbs.

"The cave dragons?"

"Yes, I think so. The natives hunted them almost to extinction but the catastrophe brought that to an end and they creatures survived. They would have been all over the island by now except that the Nempi hunt them and keep their numbers low."

"Just who are the Nempi?"

She ignored his question. "Before they realized the danger, these people's ancestors ate the fruit from the vines, and they ate the animals that grazed on the leaves. It was slower with them but eventually the people began to change as well. They became more aggressive, larger, and their skin changed, toughening." She hesitated. "According to the Wallingfords, they also grew a second pair of arms."

"That's ridiculous!" But even as he spoke, he remembered the odd statue standing inside the circle of empty buildings.

"Just bear with me for a minute. There's more. Once they realized what was happening to them, they tried to wipe out the vine. Obviously they didn't succeed everywhere, but they did destroy all of the plants in their city. They were sophisticated enough to know, or at least suspect, that the taint was carried through succeeding levels of the food chain, so they killed any of their livestock that showed any sign of infection, and then kept what survived penned up in their city. They started patrolling regularly to root out any stray seedlings that might be blown over the wall." She paused. "And then they drove out everyone among their people who had changed. All of them, mostly children I think. They built that settlement where we stayed and moved them all there. There was communication between the two, but those exiled were never allowed back inside the city."

"Then why aren't they still there?"

"I don't know. Maybe I'll find out when I read the last of the journal. But I asked John about them."

"And what did he say?"

"He said that the Nempi don't like the light and went away to the dark places, but that it was bad luck to talk of the Nempi and he wouldn't say any more."

"We all ate some of that fruit." His heart was suddenly beating very fast.

Sharon shook her head. "I don't think we have to worry about that. It took generations before the effects started to show up. A couple of days won't matter."

Rivers was silent for a moment, thinking. "All right, that doesn't change our situation then. These people have accepted us. We can make a place for ourselves here."

It was her turn to hesitate. "You don't think we're going to be rescued, then?"

He shook his head. "No, I don't. Walters still pretends to hope but I think he gave up when the lifeboat was smashed. We're too far away from where we should have been. Even if they make an honest effort to find us, the odds aren't favorable."

She slowly got to her feet. "Well then, I need to get back to my reading." Her voice betrayed only the faintest hint of a tremor. "If we're going to stay here, we need to know as much about what's going on as possible."

Walters and Mrs. Galt were sitting together in the shade of another tree when Emma joined them, as animated as always, and spilling over with new questions. They took turns trying to explain the world they came from, hampered not only by the lack of common referents but by the truncated version of English that had survived on the island. When it became obvious that their worlds were so utterly different that comparisons were difficult, Emma changed the subject to their advent on the island.

"Your boat must have had great wings to fly so far."

Walters laughed. "No, I'm afraid not. We came in a boat like that one." He pointed toward the pond, where two women were fishing from a flat bottomed boat. "Ours was bigger, of course."

She nodded that she understood. "When my people first came, their boat had great wings like those of a mero."

A short diversion convinced Walters that the mero was some kind of bat that lived in the caverns. Mrs. Galt was ready to move on to the next subject, but Walters was a stickler for detail. "You must be thinking of sails, Emma. Some boats have masts, um, tall sticks pointing up like this." He laid one hand flat on his knee and positioned the other with his forefinger pointing straight up. "Then we put big pieces of cloth," he spread his fingers, "like this, to catch the wind. The wind pushes the boat."

Emma's expression was easy to read. She didn't believe him but didn't want to contradict. "Your boat very small. Ours very big. Too big I think for wind to push." Walters was trying to figure out how to explain when she said something else that took him completely by surprise. "Would you like to see it?"

He had to try twice before he could get the words out. "See what, Emma?"

"The boat which brought my people here."

Once the work was done, Harding's co-workers tried to thank him, but were limited by the language barrier. He still didn't quite understand how some of the people could speak a little English while none of the others spoke any, given that they lived together in such close quarters, and assumed that it was partly a pretense, that they were hoping he would give away some secret in an unguarded moment because he didn't believe they could understand him. What secret that might be was beyond Harding's imagination, but he was past the point where logic was a major component of his thoughts. Harding had known all of his life that he was damned, that everyone around him was damned, and he was halfway convinced that this island was itself a suburb of Hell.

And if he was doomed already, then it wouldn't matter if he accumulated a few more sins during his last days.

He left the others, waving neutrally to them to indicate he wanted to be left alone, and turned toward the cluster of homes where the majority of the natives lived. A few individual families had built comparatively isolated places elsewhere in the ruined mountain, but the majority, several hundred, occupied small but neatly kept houses arranged in the familiar concentric rings. The older ones, closer to the center, were built of stone and looked almost identical to the Ritz and its neighbors, but the outer rings were constructed of wooden poles and heavy thatching, some of it quite elaborate. There was still more than enough fallen stone around the inner rim to provide raw material for sturdier construction, but there were probably no longer enough able bodied adults to make such more enduring buildings practical to construct.

Harding had no precise plan, and was smart enough to know that he needed to be patient and alert. Fate had brought him here and he trusted Fate to show him what to do and when to do it.

Mrs. Galt wasn't quite as full of energy as Emma and she lagged behind their guide as they made their way out through the tilled fields, then through a maze of broken stone that was the residue of the most devastated portion of the volcano. The wall here had collapsed on a massive scale, most of it sliding down toward the coast and even into the sea while bits and pieces collapsed in the other directions, leaving piles of rubble that towered over their heads. Walters slowed his own pace to match hers, and occasionally called to Emma when she vanished from sight. Once they were beyond the immediate devastation, however, the going was easier and the view was breathtaking.

The ground sloped down here, rather steeply in fact, and they had to be careful of their footing. Ahead of them they saw the remnants of a stone wall, but the land just beyond dropped off abruptly and was replaced by white crested waves. In the distance they could see the top of what was clearly a stone building of some kind, as well as several trees, all dead. Two men were standing in the shallow water, dragging a heavy net. The ocean had reclaimed this land and would not relinquish it again.

Emma had slowed to wait for them and stood staring out to sea. When they came up beside her, she pointed to the nearest of the drowned buildings. "That was my grandfather's house. I used to play there when I was a child."

Walters just nodded, but Mrs. Galt glanced sharply at the girl. "Emma, do you mean that John used to live there?"

The girl nodded. "This was his farm," she pointed vaguely toward the water. "Now it is lost to us."

"The boat," Walters said, barely disguising his impatience. "You said there was a boat here."

Emma nodded. "It is not far now, but the path is not good. You must be careful."

She spoke truly. The path they followed turned abruptly uphill and angled to their left, toward a forbidding hump of ravaged mountainside. Huge boulders had tumbled down partway before becoming lodged against others, and loose sand buried sharp edges waiting to draw blood. The trail became circuitous, winding back and forth but always rising, and then it leveled off abruptly and they were standing at the entrance to another cave.

Walters looked at it skeptically. "Are you sure this is safe, Emma?"

"Oh yes. We played here as children until grandfather caught us. He was afraid we would not be respectful."

She started in and after a silent, puzzled exchange of looks, her companions followed.

It was so dark that they hesitated, waiting for their eyes to adjust, and Walters was beginning to have second thoughts, or perhaps third ones by the time they rounded a corner and saw brighter light ahead.. Emma had disappeared once again, but they could hear her moving, running now, and quickened their own pace to follow.

They emerged into a magnificent natural chamber with high vaulted ceilings riddled with gaps that let in the sunlight. Water lapped against the rocks lining the path, clearly placed therer intentionally to help secure the walkway, and more water dripped down from above. To their right, they could see light in the distance at the end of a short underground tunnel with a ceiling that was at least fifty feet high at this end, although there appeared to be some sort of obstruction further along that reduced the clearance by at least half.

Emma called to them impatiently and they hurried forward, the route curving around a cluster of fallen rocks and broken stalagmites. As they cleared the barrier, Mrs. Galt came to an abrupt halt and Walters staggered, then whistled appreciatively.

Not far ahead of them a narrow, sandy beach ran along the inner wall of the cavern. Standing in the middle of the beach, just above high tide mark, was an elaborate wooden platform. Mounted on top of the platform was a perfectly preserved sailing ship, with three masts but no sails.

"My God! It's a barque!" Walters was frozen in place, unable to believe his eyes. "Freddie, it's a barque!"

"It looks more like a ship to me," she said breathlessly.

"No! No! I mean, yes, it's a ship. At least a hundred years old, I'd guess by looking at her. Look at those masts. She takes square sails and no tops'l. Except the one at the stern. That takes fore-and-aft sails. I crewed on one once, out of San Francisco, when I was just a kid."

"Do you think you could sail one?" She kept her voice deliberately calm.

Walters shook his head. "It must be a wreck by now, all rotted out."

"Could it be repaired?"

"I don't know." He turned and put a hand on her shoulder. "Shall we go take a look?"

Sharon was tempted to skim through some of the pages but forced herself to read every word. There was no way of knowing what might be important and what was useless. Even worse, she wasn't entirely convinced that the Wallingfords were always accurate. Sometimes they seemed to have missed obvious connections and sometimes it seemed to her likely that they had either misunderstood or that they were being lied to. It was clear that they were valued by the natives for their technical knowledge, but that didn't mean they'd been completely accepted or told the absolute truth.

Although she had not expected to finish in less than a day, Edith Wallingford's frailty expedited her reading. Her eyes had begun to fail during the last two years of her life, along with her health in general. She had made shorter, less frequent entries, and her handwriting was much larger, as though she was having trouble seeing the words as she inscribed them. By the middle of the afternoon, Sharon had set the last page aside.

She had been reading on a stone bench just outside John's house when she finished. John was inside, taking a nap, and she returned the journals quietly so as not to wake him. When she was done, she went for a walk, heading nowhere in particular, processing what she'd just learned, trying to work out the implications. The others would have to be told, of course, and she was worried about what they would make of her findings.

By the time Walters finished his inspection of the ship, he was frankly stunned. It was in a remarkable state of preservation. A few boards had been replaced here and there, but the hull seemed tight and in good shape. The masts were old and the foremast had a suspicious looking fracture line, but he thought it would hold unless it was subjected to a major blow. The interior had been stripped bare, of course, and he was disappointed not to find a ship's log or navigational equipment. A sextant would have been a very welcome sight.

"How is this possible?" he asked.

Emma had been following him, rushing to point out things she thought he might find of interest. "We honor our father's fathers and all who came before. They told us to keep their boat ready in case of need, and so we have done. We pound the tanga leaves until they weep and then spread their tears to keep it safe." She gestured toward the hull. Walters leaned closer and sniffed and thought he detected the faint odor of some natural oil.

"It's the *Windlover*, all right, the Wallingfords' ship."

"I thought Miss Bartleby said it was destroyed."

"Rumors of its demise were apparently exaggerated."

"If we had some sails, or some way of making them," Walters said thoughtfully. "We might be able to get off this island after all."

Mrs. Galt did not look hopeful. "If that was possible, why didn't the Wallingfords leave?"

"Maybe they didn't want to go."

"Maybe." She sounded doubtful. "But I think there was...is a bigger problem."

"What's that?"

"How did the ship get in here?" She waved vaguely to indicate the cavern in general. "And how do we get it out?"

It only took a few minutes to answer her first question. There was a natural channel to the open sea, the tunnel down which they'd looked on their way in.

"That ceiling is awfully low." Mrs. Galt said doubtfully.

"It must have collapsed some time after they arrived. Wasn't there something about a landslide in their journal?" Walters had penetrated as far into the passage as he could without stepping down into the water. "We could unship the masts and get past most of it, but there's another obstruction further along." He started to peel off his shirt.

"What are you doing?"

"Going for a swim. I'll be right back."

"Be careful." She didn't think this was a good idea, but she could tell that Walters would not be dissuaded easily.

He was gone for so long that even Emma became worried, and the two of them called his name several times before he finally shouted back. "I'm all right. Hold on for just a few more minutes."

It was more than a few minutes, but he finally emerged from the tunnel, clearly fatigued. He crawled up onto the rocky ledge beside them, breathing heavily.,

"Well, what did you find?"

"There's plenty of clearance past this little patch. With the masts down, we could sail right under them and out into the open sea. Except for one thing."

"What's that?"

He sighed. There's another blockage, almost a wall of fallen rock and sand like a miniature reef."

"Could we dig a passage through it?"

He shrugged his shoulders. "Given enough time, maybe. But I don't think so. There are some pretty big rocks there as well, too big for us to shift even if we could talk some of the natives into helping us."

"There must be some way."

He smiled, but without enthusiasm. "Maybe. Maybe once I've had a chance to think about it, or maybe one of the others will have an idea. And we'd still have to figure out a way to make some sails."

Emma had been listening quietly but she spoke up now, asking what "sails" were. Walters started to explain, then drew a picture in the sand to illustrate what he meant. As he did so, Emma's eyes brightened. "I see. Sails are wings."

"Well, not exactly," said Walters. He started to search for a way to explain the difference when Emma jumped to her feet. "Would you like to see our wings?"

A spark of hope burst into flame. "Do you really have sails, the sails from that ship?" He gestured toward the *Windlover*.

Emma's answer was to beckon for him to follow her.

Harding had learned to be a patient man. He found a couple of excuses to linger near the house of the bare breasted girl, but left before he could arouse any suspicion, watching it surreptitiously from a considerable distance. She came and went twice while he was watching, once accompanied by the same young woman who'd helped carry water to the workers, once with a young man whose presence made Harding grit his teeth and clench his fists. They didn't appear particularly intimate, though, and when they started out toward the cliff wall that towered above the settlement, Harding followed them at a discrete distance.

When they reached the base of the wall, they separated and began walking slowly back and forth, heads down as though they were looking for something on the ground. Once or twice the man stooped and plucked something, but on both occasions he laughed and tossed whatever it was aside. Their paths diverged and sometimes they lost sight of each other, but they were never beyond hailing distance. Harding concealed himself in a cluster of trees, but was frustrated by his limited view, consoling himself with the fact that they would be unable to return without passing close by. The branches above his head were tightly woven together, but he managed to push his way up and through the lowest tier, and found it much easier to climb from that point onward.

At the highest point which he could safely reach, he spread two branches apart and looked down toward the spot where he'd last seen the couple. The girl was out of sight but he could see her friend, who knelt on a patch of crusty soil just above a rock slide, picking at the soil. He apparently was having better luck than before, because one hand was filled now, and even from this distance Harding recognized the familiar bluish green vine. He had no idea why they would be hunting for such tiny specimens, but now that he thought about it, he hadn't seen any growing anywhere in the vicinity. Perhaps they were looking for seedlings to plant.

The native stood up abruptly and called to the girl. She answered from somewhere out of Harding's line of sight and there was a brief exchange. Then the young man turned and descended to the original trail and started back toward the village.

Harding was not surprised at his sudden good luck. This was all foreordained, as far as he was concerned. His personal road to damnation was clear and well marked.

Emma led them a short distance away from the *Windlover* to a shallow cave they hadn't noticed before. It was obviously a storehouse of some sort, because one wall was lined with wooden casks and boxes stacked as high as their shoulders, while the facing one was occupied by two very large chests made of plain red wood. "These are cedar," said Mrs. Galt, running her hand across the top of the nearest. "These weren't made on the island," she added unnecessarily.

Walters looked around excitedly, noticed a secant and compass covered by dust in one corner, surrounded by a variety of metal fittings and instruments, some unfamiliar to him. There was no sign of any sails and he asked Emma where they were. She pointed toward the cedar chests.

The hinges were well maintained and the lids lifted easily although they were quite heavily. The first was filled to the brim with folded canvas. Walters touched it tentatively with his hand, as though he didn't believe it was really there. Emma had already raised the second lid, and the contents looked to be nearly identical.

"This is amazing!" said Harding. "It's hard to believe this survived for so long."

"Are they in good enough shape to use?" asked Mrs. Galt.

He nodded. "I think so, at least from what I can see. It'll be a challenge to get them all in place without an experienced crew, but I'm sure we can find a way."

"But we'd still have to get pass that barrier."

"Yes, there is that."

Harding waited until the man was completely out of sight before descending from the tree. He could no longer see the girl, but every once in a while there was a faint sound from where she'd disappeared among the rocks. There was no path here, but the easiest way to climb the rock mound was self evident and he started up, feeling a growing excitement with each step.

He advanced cautiously, not wanting to alert her to his presence. When he reached the summit, she was in plain sight. The island girl had advanced along a narrow ledge that ran across the face of the cliff, rising fairly steeply as it disappeared into the distance. She was more than thirty meters away, crouched with her back to him, slowly making her way forward with her eyes fastened on the ground. Presumably she too was looking for shoots of the bluish vine, but her purpose was of no interest to Harding, so long as she kept her back turned.

He had crossed almost two thirds of the distance separating them before the girl heard his footsteps and turned, standing up. When she saw Harding she smiled and waved, but there must have been something about his demeanor or expression that alarmed her because she backed away a few steps and raised a hand, as though to ward him off. He didn't understand what she said to him but he knew the tone. She was frightened.

He kept coming.

There was no way that she could get past him and she was too high to jump down, so she turned and started the other way. Harding quickened his pace but didn't run. The footing was uncertain enough that he preferred to be cautious. He followed her upward, gaining quickly when she reached the end of the flat ledge, even though she continued to climb, using hands and feet now to scrabble over the uneven and increasingly dangerous ground. Harding almost lost his footing once and under ordinary circumstances he might have broken off the pursuit. But he was committed now. His fate was in front of him and he saw it clearly.

He was only a few meters behind her when she abruptly disappeared.

For a few seconds, he thought she might have fallen. There was no sign of her, and he could see the cliff face ahead quite clearly. Puzzled but still not alarmed, he continued forward, and when he reached the point where he'd last seen her, he discovered the truth. There was a jagged gap in the cliff face here, the opening to some sort of cave or passageway. He hoisted himself over the lip and followed.

There was a sharp turn almost immediately and he hesitated, letting his eyes adjust to the suddenly dim light. There were too many shadows to see clearly, and there was no sign of the girl, even though there didn't seem to be any cover large enough for her to hide behind. He considered calling out, but decided against it. They both knew the rules now, and she wouldn't be cajoled out of her caution even if she could have understood what he was saying.

Half way across the inner chamber, he noticed a darker shadow that must be another passageway. He quickened his pace and found himself at the lip of a much narrower, lower tunnel, probably an ancient lava rill. It wasn't high enough for him to stand upright, but if he crouched he could continue. There was never any question in his mind that he might break off the chase.

The passageway went straight for several meters, then jogged to the right and angled upward. He was in almost complete darkness by then, but when he climbed over this new barrier, it seemed to grow lighter, enough so that he could make out his surroundings. It was another cave, narrow where he stood, but opening out in the distance. The terrain under his feet looked as though it had been recently abraded and there were marks on the wall to either side as though something had torn at the rock. It looked as though this was a new passage, recently opened.

He could hear water dripping somewhere.

Ordinarily he would have been more cautious. His prey was a young girl, certainly still in her teens, and not a formidable opponent, but she might well be lurking in the shadows, holding a rock with which to bash out his brains. Harding moved forward brashly, convinced that what was about to happen was ordained by Fate, that he could not affect the outcome in any way. Nor could she. The only question was how long it would take to find her.

The ground dropped away in front of him, revealing an oval shaped cavern filled with pools of standing water. Moisture dripped from the walls, spray from the ocean carried by the wind through several small openings set high above him, which also provided a flickering light. There were odd shadows and the sound of his footsteps echoed weirdly, but he didn't hesitate, jumping down to the lower level and moving forward. There was still no sign of the girl, but he could feel her presence. She was watching him.

There was a good deal of tumbled rock and it took a few minutes before he found her. She was hiding in a shadowy alcove, up to her ankles in brackish water. When he came around the far corner, she gave an involuntary cry and splashed across to the opposite side, trying to climb up onto a ledge that led to one of the openings in the roof above them, but the climb was too steep and eroded and she slipped back down almost immediately. When a second try brought the same result, she abandoned the attempt, turning to face him. She said something in her own language, some kind of threat judging from the tone, but Harding wasn't impressed.

She was half his size, after all.

As he advanced, she retreated, although there wasn't far to go. Another opening loomed behind her, larger than the first, and daylight spilled down more brightly here than elsewhere. She had retreated in a crouch, facing him with her hands up, fingers curled into claws. There was no question that she knew what he intended, and that she was going to fight him. Harding felt a moment's regret. It would be easier if she'd cooperated. He wouldn't have hurt her until the very end, and then only for a moment, just long enough to break her neck. He wasn't a cruel man, after all.

They were almost close enough to touch when it happened, and it happened so quickly that Harding stood upright, blinking. The girl had stopped retreating, was obviously contemplating an attempt to rush past him, when suddenly she was gone. There had been a flurry of shadows and movement, but it was so quick that it hadn't really registered. He stood in the water, trying to replay the previous few seconds in his mind, but unsuccessfully. A small avalanche of pebbles fell from the overhead passage and splashed into the water.

Had she jumped up into the opening? The possibility that she might escape occurred to him for the first time and he started forward, but no sooner had he taken his first step than there was another flurry of movement and shadows and a heavier slide of stones and dirt. And then it was standing in front of him.

Harding smiled as he faced the demon and spread his arms. They'd come for him at last and this time they wouldn't be happy until they'd taken him away. Well, so be it then, he thought, and started to run forward to grapple with fate for the last time.

CHAPTER SIXTEEN

They gathered together for their evening meal, driven inside by a sudden torrential downpour. Walters asked after Harding, but no one knew where he was and no one else was interested. Sharon seemed unusually preoccupied but not inclined to speak. The Porters were too self absorbed to care and Fields had just shrugged. "He'll find his way home eventually." Only Rivers shared his concern and not even Rivers knew why Walters was so worried about the whereabouts of his former crewmate. He didn't much care what happened to Harding, but he was worried about what Harding might do and the effect that might have on their relations with their hosts.

While they were eating, Walters and Mrs. Galt described their discovery of the *Windlover* and the implications of its existence. There were a great many questions, some repetitive, and despite his attempts to emphasize the odds against their escaping in the ageing vessel, it was clear that the others were more optimistic than they had been for several days, although it was a cautious optimism. Only Fields remained inscrutable, keeping his own counsel. Walters had done most of the talking and when he was finished, he asked Mrs. Galt if he'd forgotten anything important.

"About the ship, no, I don't think so. But there's something else we learned today that might have some effect on our decisions. Emma showed us the remains of her grandfather's original home. It's underwater now, down toward the drowned city. She used to play there when she was a child."

She paused and looked around at the others. No one appeared to grasp the implications except possibly Rivers, who suddenly looked very thoughtful. "I asked her a lot of questions on the way back, but some of them she couldn't answer and some of what she did remember might be wrong. Children don't see things quite the same way as adults do."

"So what?" asked Nathan impatiently. "We already knew that the city was underwater. What difference does it make?"

Next to him, his sister's face suddenly changed and her eyes widened. "But the city was destroyed hundreds of years ago, wasn't it?"

Mrs. Galt nodded. "Which means that whatever catastrophe overtook this island hasn't ended, it just slowed down. The island is still sinking, as we know, and it's apparently sinking much faster than we thought." There was an awkward silence while that sank in. "If it continues at its present rate, and I see no reason why it won't, the entire island will disappear eventually."

"How soon is eventually?" asked Fields. "Any idea?"

Mrs. Galt looked uncertain for the first time. "Perhaps not imminently, but based on Emma's description and what I could estimate about the rise over the last decade or so, this whole place will be underwater in a few more years. Most of the settlement is actually slightly below sea level already, but there's higher land in between. I don't suppose any of us will live long enough to see the jungle disappear under the waves," she paused dramatically. "But even that might not take more than another decade."

"Are you certain of this?" asked Walters.

She shook her head. "Not absolutely, no. It's possible that the subsidence has stopped or will stop soon. But the water has claimed more land just this past year. I think these people are going to be in trouble soon, particularly if they refuse to venture out of this place."

"The Nempi might object to that," said Sharon.

Mrs. Galt nodded. "And the Nempi may be in the same position a few years from now. And they have no place to go. They already own the high ground."

The conversation drifted for a few minutes before Rivers roused himself. "Sharon finished reading the journals today. Maybe she has something new to tell us."

Sharon roused herself and smiled lightly. "Actually I do, but it's going to seem pretty anticlimactic after everything else we've heard tonight." She frowned. "I don't think this will be of much practical use, but it does help explain the situation. I know why the village out there is deserted, for one thing."

Grace roused herself from a reverie. "These people, the Nempi, the ones who got changed, they don't like the daylight, right? So they all ran off to live in the jungle where it's dark."

"Not exactly, or at least not at first. When the city sank, it killed off almost the entire population. The normal population anyway. When that happened, it changed the balance of power. The Nempi were still outnumbered, but not by a whole lot. And that scared the survivors." She looked around the room and discovered she had everyone's attention. "Some time shortly afterward the disaster, the surviving normals decided to secure their position. The Nempi were all living out there in the village," she gestured vaguely in the right direction, 'but like Grace said, they mostly stayed inside during the day and slept. So one morning, the normals went out in force and slaughtered them in their beds. They were probably motivated largely by fear, but there must also have been some jealousy as well. The Nempi had suffered no losses in the catastrophe and still had all their material possessions. The normals were left with almost nothing."

"Things didn't go as well as they planned and some of the Nempi escaped. There's no record of how many. The settlement was stripped of everything useful and abandoned but the Nempi never came back. They did, however, attack any of the normals who ventured out of the caves from that point on, particularly during the night but sometimes in the day as well. Eventually the two sides kept to their own territories and the battles stopped. But there's been no intercourse between them since."

"But surely that couldn't last," protested Rivers. "The population pressure would force one side or the other to seek more land sooner or later."

"I don't know about the Nempi," Sharon answered. "But the Wallingfords said that there were almost two thousand people living here when they arrived. There can't be as many as a thousand now."

"About three hundred as far as I can tell," said Fields. "And that might be high."

"So what happened to the others?" asked Grace.

"I don't know." Sharon shook her head. "Edith Wallingford noticed that they had surprisingly few children and thought they might have lost the will to live. Maybe on some level they knew that the island was doomed and they chose to reduce their population progressively as the space available to them contracted. Edith also says that more than half the people had learned enough English to communicate with her. How many are there now? Ten? Twenty? And only Emma and her grandfather are fluent enough to have real conversations."

"So where does that leave us?" asked Grace, but before anyone could answer, they were interrupted.

Ezra Harding staggered in through the door, his shirt and pants glistening with blood. His eyes moved slowly around the room and then he collapsed.

They managed to stop the worst of the bleeding, but Rivers thought privately that this was only because Harding had little of it left to lose. There were superficial cuts and scrapes over almost his entire body, but the serious wounds included a deep cut on his right thigh, a pair of ragged puncture wounds in his lower abdomen, a long gash down the center of his back, and a cheekbone so shattered that they could see some of his teeth. His right shoulder was dislocated and that arm was broken in two places and his left knee was badly swollen. One of the cuts on his face had cost him his right eye and half of his nose. There were almost certainly internal injuries as well, but the visible damage alone was more than they could hope to repair.

Harding was unconscious at first, but when Mrs. Galt began sponging the worst of the blood from his face, he opened his eyes and tried to sit up, obviously in a state of panic. It took both Walters and Rivers to restrain him, although Mrs. Galt calm voice probably did the most good. She tried to get him to tell them what had happened to him, but all he would say was that he had fought with the devil and won and that meant he wasn't going to Hell after all. Eventually he fell asleep, or perhaps simply fainted, his breathing labored.

Walters beckoned Mrs. Galt away from his bedside. "What do you think his chances are?"

She shook her head. "You saw those wounds. It's a miracle he's still alive. What do you think happened?"

"I don't know. I'm worried that he might have gotten into trouble with the natives. Ezra is a strange man, and sometimes he has difficulties dealing with people."

"Women, you mean."

He nodded. She sighed and glanced toward the injured man. "I don't think that's a problem that will trouble him again, Mr. Walters."

"But it might mean trouble for us," he said quietly.

His fears became more immediate a few minutes later when John and several of the natives appeared at their door. John's expression was serious, and his eyes widened when he saw Harding. "What has happened?"

Walters nervously explained as much as they knew. John listened quietly, then spoke to the others in their own language. Their already dour expressions became even darker, and several of them slipped away. "One of our women has not returned from her chores. Her mother and father and brother are very worried."

"Is there anything we can do? Can we help look for her?" Walters hoped that his nervousness was not as apparent as it felt.

"We have looked where she might be. Nothing more can be done until the light comes. But this is bad." He gestured toward Harding and tension filled the room. "This is a Nempi thing. Nempi sometimes steal women."

"But the Nempi can't get through the tunnels, can they?" asked Rivers.

John looked distinctly uncomfortable. "Not through caves, no, but some times they find a way." He spoke to his companions again and they left him alone with them.

"Is there anything you can do for our friend?" asked Mrs. Galt.

John glanced toward the stricken man, then shook his head. "He will die soon. We must worry about those who still live." He looked much older as he turned away, apparently with nothing further to say. But he paused in the doorway. "At first light, we will look for the lost one."

"We will help," answered Walters, but John was already gone.

Harding died during the night, so quietly that Mrs. Galt, who was sitting at his side at the time, didn't realize he was gone until she decided to check his dressings. There was no point in waking the others, but she found herself unable to sleep and spent the rest of the night sitting at the doorway, listening to the faint sound of water pounding the distant shore. It was only her imagination, but it seemed louder, closer than it had the previous day.

Although Harding never told them where he'd been when he'd been attacked, there was no difficulty solving the mystery the following morning. He had left a trail of blood that even an amateur could have followed. The natives were as interested as their new guests, obviously having made the assumption that the attack and the disappearance must be related. To Walters' great relief, John believed that Harding had been injured trying to protect the missing girl, which might even have been the case.

More than fifty people followed the blood while the rest of the community fanned out to eliminate other possibilities, but when the footing became more difficult, only Rivers, Fields, Walters, and Sharon continued forward with a large group of islanders. John was unable to manage the climb but Emma came in his place to serve as translator. When they reached the cave, she was one of the first inside, climbing over the lip of the opening while torches were being prepared. Fields and Walters followed as soon as they could, each man ready to draw his firearm at the least provocation. There was a bloody handprint where a man might have caught hold in order to pull himself out into the open.

"Do you suppose this cuts right through the mountain?" Rivers asked Walters.

It was Emma who answered, insisting that the cave had been checked before and that there was no other outlet. She seemed less certain a few minutes later, when the search party rounded a corner and it became obvious that the torches were unnecessary. Light spilled down from at least two opening far overhead, rents in the mountain wall.

"This is not right," she insisted.

"There must have been a cave-in," suggested Fields. "Part of the roof collapsed."

"Maybe," said Rivers. "But those openings are conveniently man sized."

Rivers was standing with his head tilted back, one hand raised to block some of the glare. "You might be right. The openings are too regular, too smooth around the edges. And they're both the same shape. I think they're artificial."

Fields whistled. "Enemy action."

"So it appears."

The attack came a moment later. Less than a dozen people had penetrated this far into the cave and they were just beginning to search the numerous side passages, crevices, and smaller caves. One of the younger men was climbing over a pile of fallen stone when he suddenly cried out and spun around, both hands clutching his throat. Three figures leaped into sight from behind the rubble, three very large men naked except for breach cloths, each holding knives or axes tipped with sharpened stone. And each of them had four arms ending with six fingered hands.

Most of the natives panicked and started to run for the exit even though they carried knives or clubs. The Nempi were quick to take advantage of the situation, and one of them stabbed a fleeing man in the back while another threw a stone axe that nearly struck Emma in the head. Rivers was standing by himself, and his first instinct was to look for a weapon, but the only thing in sight was a scattering of jagged, fist sized stones. He picked one up and threw it toward the nearest of the attackers, but his aim was so bad that it flew uselessly over the man's head.

Walters had retreated a few steps, so stunned that he had made no effort to draw his weapon, but Fields was faster to react, and his pistol fired, sounding incredibly loud in the confined space. One of the Nempi staggered and fell to one knee, pressing one hand to his chest as blood began to spurt. Through luck or skill, Fields had struck him in the heart. His companions hesitated, stunned by the noise, then watched their companion fall forward without making another sound.

Rivers threw another stone, and this time it bounced off the nearest Nempi's shoulder, sending him staggering back. He turned toward Rivers, who saw that his face seemed perfectly ordinary except that the eyes were significantly larger than in ordinary humans and the skin seemed roughened. Then Fields fired again, less effectively this time, and the third Nempi clutched a wounded arm to his chest and shouted something unintelligible. His voice was like gravel in a metal drum. He and his companion began to retreat the way they'd come.

"What do you think?" shouted Fields. "Should we let them go?"

"Save your ammunition," said Rivers. "We might need it later."

They helped carry rocks up the ledge to fill in the front portion of the cave, even though it seemed to them a fruitless effort. If the Nempi really wanted to come through this way, it would only take them a day or so to clear it out from the other side. But it was as much a symbolic as a real barrier, and they stayed until the job was done.

The fact that they had killed one of the Nempi and driven off two others improved their relations with their hosts rather dramatically. It appeared that no one alive had ever accomplished so much singlehandedly, although John and some of the older ones told stories about a great battle in the tunnel in which four of the invaders were killed and many others wounded. They made no mention of how many defenders had died in the process. Although Walters had his doubts, the natives also believed that Harding had received his fatal wounds while defending the missing girl, who was known to have been searching for seedlings of the bluish vine in the cave area, and who was now presumed dead or more likely abducted by the Nempi.

A guard was to be posted to listen at the cave for any signs of activity while the elders considered alternative courses of action. There were also many questions about Fields' pistol, and John revealed a primitive understanding of how it worked even before Rivers explained it to him.

"Our father's father's father knew this secret but it is lost to us now." The Wallingfords, or some of their company, had obviously been armed.

They buried Harding that evening and Walters said a few words. Everyone attended except Grace, who had not forgiven him even in death, and Nathan, who was sulking again for no discernible reason. They passed an uneasy night, posting an armed guard again, although they were sure that they had nothing to fear from their hosts. But the night passed uneventfully and the first guard sent to watch the cave that morning reported no signs of activity.

Walters tentatively broached the subject of the entombed barque to John, who surprised him by giving him a blank check. "If you can make it fly once more, we will help you if we can. Our father's father's father told us to keep it safe, that it would one day be free."

After lunch, Walters retraced the route to the cavern, accompanied this time by Rivers, Fields, Mrs. Galt, Sharon Bartleby, and the omnipresent Emma, who now seemed to have adopted Fields as her personal protector, much to his chagrin. They found it as before and Walters and Rivers waded in to explore the potential passage to the sea while the others investigated the ship and the contents of the hidden cave in more detail. The rock fall blocking their escape proved to be quite narrow, but the barrier was much too big to be dragged aside, and much too solid to suggest that they might be able to break it up into smaller pieces.

"The ship might not be seaworthy in any case," suggested Rivers.

Walters shook his head, neither agreeing nor disagreeing. "She'd old and she's been out of the water for a long time, but she's better preserved than she has any right to be. I've been to sea in worse. If the sails are all right, she'll do for us."

"If we can get her out of here."

"There is that."

When they returned, Fields and Mrs. Galt had organized the others to help them remove the sails from the chests. "One of them is torn," said Mrs. Galt happily, "but not beyond mending. I think I can deal with that. They're a bit stiff with age but Emma here says they have a kind of oil that they can rub in that makes them more flexible. Apparently they used to bring them out and display them in their village during festivals, but they haven't done so in a long time."

"When I was this high," explained Emma brightly, holding her hand at waist level.

"What are the chances of clearing the passage?" asked Fields.

Rivers and Walters both shook their heads. "It would take a dozen men a dozen years to break up all that stone and cart it away," said Rivers.

"Maybe we could convince the natives to help us. There's more than a dozen of them."

Walters threw the next wet blanket. "All well and good if it was possible, but it isn't. At its narrowest point, we could just manage to get the ship through, but it's so narrow that only a handful of men could work at any given time."

"Maybe we could widen the passage first?"

"Solid rock on both sides. It would take a couple of years even if we could manage it without bringing the roof down on us."

"Well you gentlemen are just full of good news," complained Sharon. "Is there any bright spot in any of this?"

There was a short pause, and Mrs. Galt broke the silence. "What about explosives?"

"If we had any..." Rivers spread his arms suggestively.

"But we do!" She looked very pleased with herself.

"Freddie, what are you talking about?" He looked around and Sharon and Fields were both smiling as well.

"The *Windlover* carried cannon in case of pirates. The cannon themselves are missing, but there are half a dozen barrels of powder and two rolls of fuse back in the cave."

One of the barrels was broken but the others were intact and the powder was dry. Fields took a handful and a small piece of fuse out into the open and they were all delighted by the subsequent small but impressive display of pyrotechnics, although Emma seemed very uneasy. "It is late. We should go back."

They replaced the sails in the chests before they left, and the journey back was remarkably quiet. Each was lost in his or her individual thoughts, and each wrestled to find the right balance between hopefulness and caution.

The next few days passed quickly. Walters made use of their current high standing with the community to enlist aid in refurbishing the *Windlover*. Although there was a large stockpile of food available, there was no point in provisioning the ship until the passage was cleared, if that could be accomplished at all. Rivers and Fields joined him at the site, and they argued about where to place the charges to best assault the barrier with minimal risk to the remaining cave structure. The fact that none of them really knew what they were talking about did not help.

Resolution came from an unexpected source. Walters was cautious and wanted to use small portions of the powder in succession, giving them the chance to clear away the debris from one explosion before dealing with the next. Rivers favored one massive blast initially, with only a small reserve of powder kept for contingencies, believing that the smaller blasts would only inflict superficial damage and leave the backbone of the barrier essentially intact. Fields wavered from one to the other, and frankly admitted that he couldn't make up his own mind.

They were interrupted in their latest round of debates when Mrs. Galt appeared, splashing her way through the shallow water that washed up a steep slope until it hit the sheer wall. She responded diffidently to their greetings, instead waded around to look at the barrier from all angles, even climbing up onto it and walking along its jagged spine. "So this is the only thing keeping us here?"

"We're just trying to figure out where best to lay the charges," explained Walters, followed by a brief account of their conflicting views. She listened patiently until he was done, then shook her head.

"That won't do it. A single charge like that will chew up the surface a little, maybe even break her back, but most of the force of the blast will be upward and outward." She gestured with both arms. "You'll waste most of the effect and probably bring down half the mountain."

Rivers couldn't repress a smile, but she rounded on him quickly. "Lots of little explosions will just take the skin off her. You'd still have to move the meat and bones a little bit at a time. I doubt I'd live long enough to congratulate you when you were done."

Rivers' smile faded. "Are you saying we shouldn't try at all, Freddie?" He sounded miffed.

"No, I am not. Gentlemen, I've been married to a civil engineer for almost forty years. He's dragged me all over the world during that time. No, that's not fair. I made him take me with him all over the world, and I've watched him move obstacles a lot bigger and heavier than this one."

"Then what would you suggest, Mrs. Galt?" asked Fields.

"We divide up the powder into six lots. Any more and we won't get enough of a bang. Then we find or make crevices so that we can get the powder right inside the rock, so that none of the power of the explosion is wasted. Yes, Mr. Walters, we split up the powder, but we measure our fuses and set them off so that they all go off at the same time, or as close as we can make it. After that we clear up the wreckage and, if God is willing, then we go home."

The three men exchanged looks and, almost without speaking a word, agreed to adopt Mrs. Galt's plan.

It took almost a week to get ready. Some of the powder could be placed in relatively dry enclosures and left in the barrels, but Mrs. Galt insisted that some of it must be placed right at the water line. "Below the water would be better, but we don't have fuses here that work when they're wet."

Sharon found a solution in the form of a bamboolike shoot that grew prolifically where it was allowed to prosper. It was hollow and virtually water tight, and the sample she showed them had been liberally swathed in animal fat. "The water will wash it off eventually, of course, but for a short period of time it works as an extra layer of insulation. We run the fuse inside it right down to the explosives." The underwater explosives themselves would be housed in the same gourds the natives used to store fresh water. John provided a natural paste that was water resistant, with which they could seal the join between the mouth of the gourd and the fuse carrier.

As the work progressed, the natives – particularly John and Emma – showed increasing interest and they were never short of help carrying things back and forth, oiling the sails, making minor repairs aboard the *Windlover*, and most importantly, building a launching ramp so that the ship could be returned to the water. Assuming, of course, that there was any point to it.

There seemed to be countless things that needed to be done, but on the twelfth day, Mrs. Galt indicated that she was satisfied with the preparations and that it was time to try to clear the passage. "First thing tomorrow morning," she announced at the evening meal. The conversation, which had been quite lively, fell off quickly after that. They all knew that their fate might well be determined in the next few hours.

CHAPTER SEVENTEEN

More than two hundred of the natives came out to watch, even though they weren't able to see very much. It took considerable persuasion to convince them that it was too dangerous to watch from inside the tunnel, or even from within the larger cave. The charges were placed and the fuses laid, each cut to precise lengths that should cause the detonations to be virtually simultaneous, or at least so it was hoped. Fields and Rivers were to light three each and then retreat as quickly as possible. It was unlikely that the effects of the explosion would reach as far back as the main cave, but Mrs. Galt insisted that it be evacuated as a precaution. Grace protested that if the ship was destroyed, they would be stranded forever, but Sharon quietly pointed out that if they couldn't clear the passage, they might as well use the *Windlover* for firewood. Mrs. Galt wanted to remain at the opening of the passage until the two men returned from their work, but Rivers argued that she would only slow them down from that point on and she was forced to agree.

They made it out of the cave only a few seconds before the blast shook the ground beneath their feet. There was a small landslide nearby and several of the natives cried out in alarm, but it was over quickly. A cloud of dust and smoke erupted from the cave mouth and forced them to retreat a few more steps, but it also subsided and they heard no secondary shocks that might have meant that rocks were still falling inside.

"Well, what do you think?" Rivers was looking directly at Mrs. Galt.

"I think we should wait until the dust has settled and then go in and take a look."

It seemed to take forever for the air to clear, and there was still enough airborne matter to make them cough and sneeze when they finally ventured inside. Fields and Sharon went to check on the *Windlover*, which appeared from a distance to be unscathed. Walters, Rivers, and Mrs. Galt began to wade out into the passage.

At first their hopes seemed dashed, because there was still a dark line crossing the water ahead of them. But once they were closer they found that much of what remained could be carried away without too much difficulty. One large section of rock remained, but it had sheared off cleanly and was well under the water. "If we wait for high tide," said Walters excitedly, "we should be able to ride right over it."

Beyond, the passage widened and the water deepened. There was probably a reef somewhere beyond the rim of the island, because the incoming waves were broken and feeble, but that seemed like a minor problem compared to the ones they had already overcome.

There was good news back in the main cave as well. A chunk of rock had fallen from the roof of the cave and smashed through the deck, but the hull was undamaged and repairs were already under way. Dirt and dust covered every exposed surface and they would need to do another thorough cleaning, but there was no other damage. "Does this mean we can leave here?" asked Grace quietly.

None of the others wanted to jinx the effort by answering affirmatively, but Walters unbent sufficient to assure her that "the chances are looking very good at the moment".

They were all startled the following morning when John came to see them and announced that several of the islanders wished to accompany them on the *Windlover*. "I would like to see the land of my father's father's father before I die. And Emma," he looked wistful. "There is no life for her here. She has always stood apart. Perhaps in your land, this will not be so."

It was more surprising that many of the islanders who had no outside ancestry were equally eager to leave. John was evasive about their reasons, but it was clear that many feared that the recent attacks by the Nempi were more than just a fluke, that the balance of power had shifted and the future was bleak. "These people aren't dumb," added Mrs. Galt. "Some of them know what the rising water implies. Their way of life is coming to an end whether they stay here or not."

Although Walters had reservations about taking these unknown quantities aboard, he surrendered to necessity. They would need more hands than they had to keep the ship functioning, particularly since he was the only professional seaman left, although Rivers and Fields were both moderately familiar with sailing vessels. More importantly, that helped to ensure that they would be adequately provisioned. They could take as much fresh water from the island as they wished, because it was plentiful even inside the volcano, but food was another matter entirely. There were communal fields to which all the islanders held an equal share, but there were also private gardens, and some of those who wished to leave had substantial stockpiles of dried meat, grain, and other provisions.

Six days after the passage was cleared, the *Windlover* touched water again. It was not a completely smooth process, and for a few seconds it looked as though their preparations were inadequate, but then the bow reached the water and with a little effort they overcame inertia and the ship, with its masts now lashed horizontally across the deck, floated in the drowned cavern. Mrs. Galt and the others searched below the deck frantically, but only one very small leak was found, and that was dealt with in short order. Another hurdle had been cleared.

"How do we get down the passageway?" asked Grace, who'd been watching from the sidelines. "If we don't have sails and there's no current, what do we do, get out and push?"

"Almost," explained Walters. "We'll use poles to push off from the rocks. It'll be slow, but we don't want to hurry anyway. It's still a pretty tight fit getting her out and if we're not careful we'll tear a hole in the hull."

They began loading supplies the next day, everything except perishables which would be the last thing brought aboard. Things were running so smoothly that Rivers began to worry that their luck couldn't continue for much longer.

As it turned out, he was right.

There had been no sign of the Nempi since the cave had been sealed. A guard still sat outside the cave around the clock, but no one knew what was happening beyond the blocked entrance. The patrols in the main tunnels continued, and Rivers approved of the defenses there. A handful of reasonably able islanders could hold off an army of Nempi so long as they weren't taken by complete surprise.

But they were.

Full darkness had just fallen and the survivors from the *Sturtevant* were all gathered in their hut, trying to decide on a day of departure. It would be soon, they all agreed, but now that the moment was close, about half the party was reluctant to actually toss the coin that would determine their future. Walters, who was eager to leave, pointed out that they had as much food as they could reasonably expect to carry, and that there was nothing to be gained by delaying. "We should only be a few days from South America, unless the wind turns against us."

Thirty-five of the islanders had asked to go, of whom only John and four children were less than able bodied. They would be crowded, but not unmanageably, and it was not clear that the islanders understood the role of a captain aboard a ship and might not be completely reconciled to following his orders. John assured them that there would be no problem and they took him at his word.

The trouble began, improbably enough, in the main tunnels. There was shouting from all around and when Rivers stepped outside to find out what was happening, he saw several men and a couple of women running toward the cavern and the maze of tunnels beyond. Walters joined him, brandishing his pistol. "Shall we find out what's going on?'

They followed briskly although neither believed it possible that the Nempi could breach the main defenses. Their steps quickened when a man with blood streaming from his forehead and shoulder reeled past them, his eyes wide. Rivers asked what was happening, but the man spoke no English, and might not have responded even if he had. He was clearly in shock.

A woman passed them next, clutching her left arm which was not bleeding but appeared to be broken. She gave them a wild look and babbled something, then ran past them. It only took another minute to reach the crisis point and discover the truth.

One of the cave dragons was in the maze. A half dozen islanders were holding it more or less at bay with long spears, but the poles that had been meant to block the passage lay in splinters. Even as they watched, a clawed foot lashed out and a spear was torn from one man's grasp, leaving a break in the line of defense. The creature scrabbled forward on six legs, then reared up and slashed at another man, who nimbly jumped back.

Walters drew his pistol and approached warily. He doubted that his weapon was powerful enough to pierce this creature's hardened skin, so he would have to place his shot very carefully. When he was close enough, he used both arms to steady his aim, waited until the creature was pausing between lunges, and fired. The bullet must have struck it somewhere in the head because it jerked backward, hissing, but there was no visible damage.

"Damn!" Walters shifted his feet and waited for another opportunity.

Another spear was slapped aside and this time its owner fell back with a broken forearm. As he turned to run, the dragon started forward, in a direct line toward Walters, who calmly stood his ground and fired again.

This time his aim was better. The creature reared back, pawing at its ruined eye, screaming in rage and pain. The remaining spearmen took advantage of the chance to advance, prodding at its comparatively soft underside, but the fight was over. With another roar of outrage, the dragon turned and started away from them, retreating the way it had come. It was only then that Rivers noticed that the beast wore a collar.

Unfortunately, they didn't have much time to celebrate their victory. A young girl caught up to them from behind, one of those few who could speak a little English. She jabbered to the spearmen first, then turned to Walters and Rivers. "Nempi are here! You come!"

They ran.

Mrs. Galt was waiting for them with John at her side. Before either man could ask, she explained what had happened while they were gone. "The Nempi came out through that cave you found. Mr. Fields and Sharon went up to see if they could help drive them back."

"Sharon? What can she do?" Rivers felt a flood of panic.

"She has her bow and arrows. Mr. Fields has his pistol."

"With even fewer rounds than I have," said Walters. "He won't be able to do much to stop them." Even as he spoke, they heard the distant report of a pistol shot.

"We have to go help," said Rivers. "Maybe a few shots will scare them off like it did the other day. They can't know how limited our ammunition is."

"I wish we'd kept some of that gunpowder."

Mrs. Galt frowned. "We needed every bit of it, Mr. Walters."

"I know. Come on, Rivers. Let's go."

They found Fields and Sharon with a large party of islanders at the base of the ledge. Torches were blazing on every side, throwing light halfway up the cave entrance. Above that was only darkness. Fields nodded a terse greeting. "They've fallen back for the moment, but keep your head down. Every once in a while they throw rocks."

"Any idea how many there are?"

Fields moistened his lips with his tongue. "As many as twenty. There were at least a dozen of them coming down the ledge when I got here. I killed one and Sharon nicked another pretty well." She grinned and held up her bow. "They gave up too easily though. I think something's up."

"Is there any other way down from there?"

"Not unless they can fly."

More men and a smaller number of armed women joined them, swelling the ranks of the defenders to more than a hundred. Every few minutes, there was a brief flurry of flying rocks, some of quite substantial size, and they suffered a few bruises and cuts and one apparent concussion. The Nempi never showed their faces.

"I don't like this," complained Rivers. "It makes no sense. If they could have sneaked a good number down the ledge before they were discovered, we'd have a problem. As it is, they're bottled up and can't hurt us. There's no point in continuing an engagement you have no chance of winning. They should withdraw."

"Maybe they haven't read the same military history as you have, Jerry," said Sharon with a strained smile.

"No, it's more than that. They're waiting for something."

It wasn't long before he was proven right.

Surprisingly, it was Nathan who raised the alarm when the main attack started. He had watched Rivers and Walters hurrying away and knew that the manly thing to do would be to follow them, even unarmed, and help in any way that he could. The last few weeks had been a revelation for Nathan, an uncomfortable revelation. He had always believed himself to be as brave as anyone else, but whenever danger had threatened, he had been consumed by a deep rooted fear that was almost like a living thing inside him. Although he was able to conceal his terror from his companions, or at least so he believed, he could no longer hide the truth from himself, and now that he had admitted it, he felt no hesitation in giving in to his fears.

So instead of following them toward the fighting, he turned and walked off into the night, in the exact opposite direction, down toward the drowned city and the rising tide. The sky was filled with clouds and it was darker than usual, but he had made so many trips down to the cavern and the *Windlover* by now that his feet knew the route at least as well as his eyes.

When he saw the figures ahead of him, coming in his direction, he thought at first that they were more of the islanders, rushing to join the fight. He didn't want to be seen running off, so he hastily concealed himself in a thicket of tall brush to wait until they had passed. Several of them came quite close, and even in the darkness he could see that they had too many arms. He cried out involuntarily in fright, realized he had just announced his presence, and rose from his crouch to sprint back the way he had come.

The Nempi quickened their pace and followed.

John may have been advanced in years but his mind functioned as quickly as ever. When Nathan came running toward him, screaming that "they're right behind me", he drew the correct conclusion immediately and began shouting to the others. Emma grabbed his arm but he shook her off, speaking in the islander's language, and sent her to spread the word. Nathan was clutching Mrs. Galt by then, trying to catch his breath, so John leaned toward her. "I think they are behind us as well as in front."

Her head came up and she glanced back the way Nathan had come. "They must have built some kind of boat to get them around the cliffs. We have to tell the others!"

"I have sent Emma. She will tell them."

She did exactly that, and it was a measure of her new set of priorities that she spoke first in English, then in the island language. The natives were caught between conflicting mandates. Their immediate instinct was to rush back to defend their homes, but a few realized that someone had to stay and defend the ledge. While they attempting to work out a compromise, a handful broke off and started back. The three outsiders were among them.

The new wave of Nempi broke over the defenders and swept them aside. There were at least several dozen in the attack, and stragglers kept coming up from behind. A score of the islanders died in the first few seconds without inflicting any damage on their enemies, and their advance slowed but did not stop when the main force of spearmen and a handful carrying ancient swords rushed into the fray. Mrs. Galt stood in the doorway of their hut, brandishing the longest knife she could find, while Grace cowered behind her holding a wooden pole that she probably could not have swung effectively even if she had been out in the open where it was possible.

The islanders tried to form a defensive line, but it crumpled almost immediately, dissolving into individual battles and chases. Mrs. Galt saw at least three of the Nempi fall to the ground, but they were a minority of the casualties. One of them, a woman with six breasts to match her limbs, charged toward Mrs. Galt, but a spearman took her in the side at the last moment and she tumbled to the ground with a scream of mixed rage and pain.

"Where's Nathan?" shouted Grace, but he had disappeared just before the fighting began in earnest.

Two more Nempi appeared out of the shadows, charging directly toward the hut. Mrs. Galt braced herself, was surprised to realize she was screaming defiantly as the nearest raised his arm, brandishing a sword he must have taken from a fallen islander. There was a loud report from her left and the Nempi staggered, lost his balance and fell to his knees, and his companion turned to face this new threat. Another shot sounded and he flew backward, blood spouting from his throat, and never moved after he hit the ground. The wounded one raised the sword again, but his arm wavered, and Rivers ran up to him, easily avoiding the blade, and kicked him under the jaw. He fell as leadenly as his late companion.

"They came from the sea!" shouted Mrs. Galt, as the rest of the party, with John and Emma, came around the corner of the hut.

"There's too many of them," said Rivers. "It's time to go." He turned to John. "Tell everyone you can who wants to go that we're leaving on the *Windlover* as soon as we can get there." John nodded and he and Emma hurried off.

"Do you think they'll be all right?" asked Sharon.

"They're as safe as any of us. We have to get out of here. This war is already over and the Nempi have won, even if neither side knows it yet."

Fields stood in a half crouch, his eyes and head moving constantly. "They might have found the ship."

"If they did, then either we take it back or we die. It's as simple as that."

Fields smiled. "I always did like simple solutions."

The bulk of the Nempi were past them now and the fight was no longer arranged in discernible lines. Clusters of two armed and four armed men and women fought small, individual battles, while a few others ran in search of a safe haven. Walters was to lead the way with his weapon ready, and Fields would guard the rear, although he had only two rounds left. Grace kept insisting that they find Nathan before they left the village, but any kind of organized search was obviously impossible. She was still arguing the point when a thrown spear struck her on the side of the head.

There was a guttural shout and two large forms leaped from the shadows. Fields threw up his arm and the pistol went off, but harmlessly. Rivers sidestepped the figure that rushed at him, delivered a rabbit punch that drove his attacker to his knees, then pivoted and kicked him in the back of the head. The Nempi fell forward moaning. Rivers turned and saw one of the Nempi's arms go up, holding a crude hand axe, and realized that Fields had only seconds to live. He threw himself forward, wrapping one arm around the Nempi's throat, then dragged him backward with a knee planted firmly against the other man's spine. He heard something snap and suddenly he was holding a dead weight.

He staggered to his feet just as Fields stood up. The other man gave him a mock salute. "I owe you one, Captain Rivers."

A few feet away, Mrs. Galt was sitting on the ground with another Nempi crouched over her, but Sharon had jumped onto his back with an arrow in her hand and was driving the sharp point repeatedly into the side of his neck. He let out an enraged growl and shrugged his shoulders, trying to throw her off, and she shifted her grip and drove the arrow down into the man's eye. He screamed and this time did throw her clear, then staggered off holding his head. Several more were charging toward them and Walters turned and fired calmly and methodically. Two Nempi went down and a third staggered and turned away. The remaining three thought better of it, and decided to seek easier prey. Walters straightened up and tossed the now empty pistol into the darkness.

"Where's Grace?" shouted Mrs. Galt, who had regained her feet, though she was clutching her side and in obvious distress.

Rivers looked where Grace had fallen but the ground was bare now. Had she crawled off?

His answer came in the form of a scream, recognizably Grace's voice. He and Fields began to run almost in the same instant.

They saw her almost immediately. She was being carried over the shoulder of one of three Nempi men who were running away from them. The other two also held islander prisoners, both women. Fields slid to a stop and raised his pistol, fired, but if he hit anything it had no effect. "That was my last round."

Rivers started to run again, but hit a slick spot and lost his footing. When he stood back up, his right knee complained, sending shooting pains up his thigh. "Damn it!" He could just barely see Grace's long hair in the flickering light of a burning hut. In another few seconds she would be gone.

There was a flicker of movement and both the Nempi and his burden crashed to the ground. Fields began to run forward, with Rivers hobbling as best he could. There was a struggle ahead of them, apart from where Grace was crawling on hands and knees. Then a scream, a man's scream, and the Nempi surged to his feet, tossing aside the limp body of Nathan Foster. Fields reached the raider before he could prepare himself, slashing him across the throat with the side of his palm. As the Nempi staggered back, choking, Fields hooked one foot around his ankle and thrust both palms against his chest. Two arms waving, two clutching his throat, the Nempi crashed down on his back. Fields leaped into the air and drove his feet into sternum and throat. The body convulsed and shook for a few seconds, then was still.

Grace was disoriented, bleeding from a wound on the side of her head. Rivers helped her to her feet but it was obvious that she couldn't walk without assistance. He tried to slip an arm around her but Fields stepped between them. "You'll do well to stay on your own feet. I'll manage her."

The next hour was a surreal nightmare. They could hear screaming and shouting, usually behind them, sometimes on either side. Numerous fires were burning although they died back when a light rain started. Once or twice one or another member of the party would whisper a warning about figures moving around them, but they were not attacked again and reached the winding trail to the hidden cave without further incident. There they found three of the islanders, one limping badly, obviously headed toward the ship, although none of them spoke any English. The two parties continued as one.

To their great relief, there was no sign that the Nempi had found the cave. A dozen of the islanders were already there waiting for them, and a few more began to drift in after they arrived. They loaded what perishables were available, although they had meant to bring more, then indicated that the passengers should go aboard as well. .

Sharon kept watching for more stragglers, helping one or two who were injured. There was no sign of John or Emma and it began to look as though they were not going to make it, but just as the men started getting in position to use their poles and guide the ship toward the escape route, another small party appeared, eight people, and Emma was there helping her grandfather, who seemed to have sprained an ankle. Once they were aboard, the operation continued and within minutes the *Windlover* had left its new mooring and was drifting slowly toward the tunnel mouth.

Their escape from that point on was anticlimactic. The ship got hung up on the shelf of rock for several minutes and the sound of wood scraping stone was nerve wracking until it ended, but the wind had picked up some and a small surge lifted them clear. They were alert enough to pole themselves forward quickly and from that point on it was just tedious, meticulous, and back braking work. The island men understood readily enough what needed to be done, and they took their turns, though they were always closely monitored. One serious accident could have punctured the hull and ended their journey very quickly.

Walters threw out the anchor just short of the reef, which he did not want to risk in the darkness, and there was another brief scare when the ship started to drift in the wrong direction. Once they had drawn in some of the slack, the situation stabilized and they could finally take the time to deal with their wounds.

Almost everyone aboard had been injured. It was not the most propitious start of a voyage, and the memory of what they had left behind saddened them all, islander and outsider alike. The volcano blocked their view of the settlement, so they were spared the sight of the many fires that burned there all though the night, and they were much too far away to hear the screams. They settled down and waited for the sun to rise.

CHAPTER EIGHTEEN

At first light, Walters found a safe route past the reef and ordered the rest of the sails raised. There was a brisk wind and they filled immediately, billowing outward. The one that had required patching was slightly asymmetrical, but it served its purpose just fine. Their last sight of the island before night fell showed thin columns of black smoke rising from inside the volcanic cone. Fires were still burning there. Many of them. About two thirds of the islanders who had planned to leave were actually aboard, along with several others who fled to the ship when it was obvious that the battle was not going well. Most looked solemn and many of them would not speak. A few were seasick. Only Emma seemed nearly as irrepressible as ever.

As darkness fell, Rivers stood at the stern, staring back the way they had come even though there was no longer anything to see. Fields came up beside him, and the two stood silently for several minutes before Fields reached inside his jacket and pulled out the package he'd been carrying all through their various adventures.

"I've been paid a good deal of money to deliver this, you know. And I've never failed on an assignment. My reputation is very important to me."

Rivers wasn't sure where this was leading. "It's probably just some boring trade agreement."

"No, it's a proposed division of the world into spheres of influence, with some interesting details about Japanese troop strengths and placements. And it suggests that armed conflict is closer than you might expect."

"I thought you didn't read Japanese."

"I said it was a difficult skill to acquire. I didn't say I hadn't taken the trouble to learn it anyway."

Rivers didn't answer, didn't know what to say.

"Your government would probably be very interested in what is contained here." Fields tapped the packet against the stern rail.

"I imagine they would."

"And the Japanese would be very unhappy if it should fall into the wrong hands."

"That seems likely."

Fields tapped it once more, then offered it to Rivers. "As far as I know, it must have gone down with the *Sturtevant*. The disaster happened too fast for me to save it."

Rivers hesitated, then took the offering. It was heavier than he expected.

"I like to pay my debts," said Fields, "in whatever coin seems most appropriate." And then he was gone.

Rivers slipped the packet inside his shirt and smiled into the night.

Their voyage was largely uneventful. Grace was conscious only intermittently for the first two days, and much subdued after that. The death of her brother had affected her much more deeply than anyone would have suspected, and it was impossible to tell if she took any comfort from the knowledge that he had died in the act of saving her. She walked the decks at night a great deal and kept mostly to herself, and oddly enough it was only Walters who was able to coax her into talking at any length. He told Mrs. Galt that from time to time she reminded him of his wife.

They were spotted by a very surprised freighter fourteen days later. The *Windlover* had held up remarkably well, but they were all much relieved to board a powered vessel. Even the islanders seemed to realize that they were finally safe. Walters conferred with Captain Penrose, who had never even heard of the *Sturtevant* and was unaware of any effort to find her.

"But that's not surprising, under the circumstances," he said.

Walters frowned. "What circumstances would those be, Captain?"

"Haven't you heard, man? The Japanese attacked Pearl Harbor ten days ago. The Pacific Fleet has been destroyed."

Rivers re-enlisted and served until the end of the war, after which he married Sharon Bartleby. They spent a few months trying to raise interest in an expedition to find the island again, but the islanders had been dispersed and the brief flurry of interest they had inspired had long since dissipated. Walters had disappeared and without his help, they knew they had no realistic chance of finding it.

John died less than a year after their escape, but Emma had adapted surprisingly well and was working as a waitress when she also disappeared mysteriously.   There were rumors that she'd been seen in France accompanying a tall man whose description sounded a great deal like Fields. Rivers hoped she was happy, wherever she was. They also kept in touch with Mrs. Galt, who was finally reunited with her husband, whose own escape from Asia was more circuitous but less eventful.

Their story ends with one further small incident. While visiting the Galts in San Francisco two years after the war ended, they spent several hours touring the waterfront, browsing through a variety of small shops selling ships in bottles, scrimshaw, treasure maps, and other nautical souvenirs. One of the shops specialized in exotic shell fish and coral. The rear wall was devoted to an impressive display of stuffed animals, mostly lizards and fish. Sharon wasn't ordinarily interested in such things, but as she passed by, something caught her eye and she called to Rivers.

"What is it?"

She didn't say anything, just pointed to a small lizard, not much more than a salamander, mounted on a wooden platform. The lizard had six legs.

Rivers carried it to the front and asked where it had come from.

"Couldn't rightly say, sir. I bought that in a lot from a fisherman's wife last year, but she didn't know where her husband picked it up. I know because I asked her. It's an odd one, isn't it? Some kind of freak of nature, don't you think?"

"I suppose it was," Rivers said quietly. "I'll take it."

www.ingramcontent.com/pod-product-compliance
Lightning Source LLC
Chambersburg PA
CBHW072232170626
46813CB00003B/1179